Shuntoll Road
A Berkshire Hilltown Mystery

Advance Praise for
Shuntoll Road

"Leslie Wheeler's fast-paced new work, *Shuntoll Road*,
takes us to the other Massachusetts, a rural place far from Boston,
where conflicts within intertwined families, resentment of ambitious
developers, and people's dark secrets simmer beneath a tranquil
summer surface. Readers will make new fictional friends as
they puzzle out, along with heroine Kathryn Stinson,
who the good guys and bad guys really are."
—**KATE FLORA**, Edgar– and Anthony–nominated author
of the Thea Kozak and the Joe Burgess series, and true crime

"Leslie Wheeler is a master at drawing convincing characters.
Kathryn Stinson, the protagonist of *Shuntoll Road*, is strong,
competent, and determined to uncover long suppressed secrets
that have dangerous consequences in the present day, all while
coming to grips with a secret of her own. In this powerful follow-up
to *Rattlesnake Hill*, Wheeler once again immerses you in the beauty
of the Berkshires as you are drawn through the pages. I'll be waiting
impatiently for the next installment."
—**ANG POMPANO**, Agatha-nominated author of
When It's Time for Leaving

"Leslie Wheeler keeps you on the edge of your seat—and turning
pages—in this second well-crafted Berkshire Hilltown Mystery. The
hilly landscape of the story includes hidden turns and dangerous
crevices in the geology as well as in the relationships between the
western Massachusetts locals, Bostonian Kathryn Stinson, and other
outsiders. The ending both surprises and satisfies in an engaging
story that makes you wish its sequel was already out."
—**EDITH MAXWELL**, Agatha- and Macavity-nominated author
of the Quaker Midwife Mysteries and award-winning
short crime fiction

For Anne Marie —
Enjoy!

Shuntoll Road
A Berkshire Hilltown Mystery

Leslie Wheeler

Leslie Wheeler

Encircle Publications, LLC
Farmington, Maine U.S.A.

Shuntoll Road Copyright © 2020 Leslie Wheeler

Paperback ISBN-13: 978-1-64599-034-5
E-book ISBN-13: 978-1-64599-035-2
Kindle ISBN-13: 978-1-64599-036-9

Library of Congress Control Number: 2017951090

Editor: Cynthia Brackett-Vincent
Book design: Eddie Vincent
Cover design: Deirdre Wait, High Pines Creative, Inc.
Cover images: pond by Leslie Wheeler; woman © Getty Images
Author photograph: © Focus Photography

Published by: Encircle Publications, LLC
PO Box 187
Farmington, ME 04938

Visit: http://encirclepub.com

Printed in U.S.A.

Dedication

For all the women I have known who have dared to take wild trails.

Acknowledgements

L ike *Rattlesnake Hill, Shuntoll Road* began as another character's story. This character was a librarian in a small Berkshire town not unlike the one where I have a house. She was married to a local man, and they had two children, a boy who was athletic, and a teenage girl who was beautiful and rebellious. The librarian was from New York originally. While she lived in the city, something happened to her that was so terrible she kept it a secret from her husband and everyone else in town. The librarian had a close woman friend who was a New Yorker, too, and whose parents had a weekend house in the Berkshires. A New York real estate developer who knew both women when they were younger also figured in the story. The novel was originally intended to be a standalone, but when I decided to make *Rattlesnake Hill* the first book in a new series of Berkshire Hilltown Mysteries, I realized that the librarian's tale could fit into my main character, Kathryn Stinson's, ongoing story. The result was *Shuntoll Road.*

The process of merging these two women's stories turned out to be more difficult than I had imagined. Once again, I am grateful to the members of my writers' critique group, past and present—Mark Ammons, Katherine Fast, Cheryl Marceau, Frances McNamara and Barbara Ross—for their help as I tried to find my way. I am further grateful to beta reader, Susan Oleksiw, for pointing out rough patches in the narrative, and to Cynthia Brackett-Vincent of Encircle Publications for her editorial suggestions. I also want to thank the following people: Don Bertolli for sharing his book of old maps of Berkshire County and other books dealing with the history of the area, as well as his stories of growing up in another Berkshire town; my long-time friends, Raul Acosta and Selma-Gluck Acosta for accompanying me on a research-related trip to the General Grant National Memorial in Manhattan; and Christopher "Sierra" Willoughby, Lead Interpretive Park Ranger at the General Grant National Memorial, for sharing maps of the National Memorial and the surrounding area of Riverside Park, and for telling me about the "wild trail." This is a trail running through a bird sanctuary, designated as "Forever Wild" that extends from 116th to 129th Street in Riverside Park. While it may not have been in existence in the 1990s when an important action in the book takes place there, the "wild trail" was too perfect for my purposes not to use it.

On the subject of place names, there actually is a "Sodom Road" in my town of New Marlborough that intersects with a road that used to be called "Shunpike Road," but is now called "Old Pike Road." Also, on old town maps, you can find the name "Gomorrah," where there was once a hamlet by that name. However, the descriptions of these places and the stories connected with them are purely fictional.

Finally, I would like to thank the New Marlborough Land Trust for all its good work in preserving and protecting "treasured places" within the township; and the New Marlborough Historical Society for sharing knowledge about the town's rich history through publications and presentations.

Part 1: Reflections in the Water

Chapter 1

In the old days, there were two tiny hamlets most folks avoided, because of the evil ways of the inhabitants. They were called Sodom and Gomorrah after the Biblical cities of ill repute. Gomorrah was in Massachusetts, and Sodom was across the border in Connecticut. The hamlets are long gone, but you can find the name "Gomorrah" on some maps of the area, and a stretch of the original Sodom Road still exists. Sodom Road intersects with Shuntoll Road that passes through the area where Gomorrah used to be. As for how Shuntoll Road got its name, well, that's another story.

−Recollections of Emily Goodale

Kathryn Stinson slowed to take the Lee exit for the Berkshires. After two and a half hours of high-speed driving on the Massachusetts Turnpike, she welcomed the shift to a more leisurely pace of travel and life in general, here in the westernmost corner of the state. As she approached Stockbridge, her cell phone chirped a cheery tune. The name on the dashboard screen made her feel less than cheerful. It was Brandy Russo, the realtor who was trying to sell the house Kathryn rented on Rattlesnake Hill. With a sigh, she took the call.

"Hi, Brandy, what's up?"

"Remember that New York City developer I told you about a while back?"

"I think so." A knot of worry coiled in Kathryn. She recalled mention of a developer who was interested in the property, but had pushed him to the back of her mind while the purchase was a remote possibility.

"Well, have I got news for you," Brandy said. "The closing was yesterday, and he's coming up this weekend to get a better look at his new property."

"You're kidding."

"No, what's the matter?"

"You might have given me advance notice this was about to happen. Then, I wouldn't have planned a two-week stay in New Nottingham."

"Not a problem. He knows you're the tenant there, and he's not going to boot you out right away. In fact, he's one of the most charming men I've ever dealt with. I'm sure you guys can work out some sort of arrangement."

Brandy's assurances notwithstanding, Kathryn was skeptical. She'd have to wait and see for herself how agreeable the new owner was.

She continued into Stockbridge. The sidewalks were clogged with tourists at all times of the year, but especially in the summer. To most people who visited the area, Stockbridge and the neighboring town of Lenox *were* the Berkshires. Visitors came for the chi-chi shops, gourmet restaurants, quaint country inns, and cultural amenities.

But it was the other Berkshires she was headed toward—the Berkshires of lonely towns perched high on hills, of narrow, winding back roads, where wildlife outnumbered humans, and the residents often led hardscrabble lives. Earl Barker was one of them.

She and Earl had met and fallen in love last November when she'd come to the Berkshires to solve an old family mystery. She'd solved that mystery—as best she could—and also a more recent one. But the solution of the more recent mystery had almost cost them their relationship, and they were struggling to rebuild it. Whether they could, or even should, remained an open question. Kathryn hoped an extended stay in the area would give her the answer.

*****

Just short of the New Nottingham village center, Kathryn turned onto a side road that took her past the elementary school. On the far side of the school lay a playing field. Here, the town's youth soccer team was playing its last game of the season. Behind the field, the land sloped upward into a grassy hill that made a natural grandstand. The hillside was jammed with spectators. Kathryn searched the grandstand for Earl and found him, midway up, seated on a camp chair with an empty chair beside him. Her spirits lifted at the grin on his handsome face when he saw her. Lean and muscular, he wore jeans and a faded blue work shirt that matched the color of his eyes. He waved to her and she waved back. Then, when she reached him, he gave her a big hug.

"Sorry I'm late," she said, "but the traffic was bad getting out of Boston."

"I'm just glad you made it, Star," he said in his soft baritone, calling her by the nickname he'd given her and that she loved.

She was glad, too, especially now that he seemed more relaxed and happier than he'd been in months. His face had regained its tan, and the haunted look in his eyes was gone. She was also glad they'd have a full two weeks together instead of only a weekend.

"How's the game? Are we winning?" she asked.

"Yup," Earl said. "Billy scored another goal right before you got here."

"You must be so proud of your son," Kathryn said to their friends, Gwen and Tim Waite, seated on a nearby blanket.

"We are," Gwen Waite spoke for both of them. "And you must be proud of Pete, too," she told Earl. "If our team didn't have such a first-rate coach, we might not have done so well."

"Yeah, let's hear it for Pete. You raised him good, man," Tim said to Earl. Gwen smiled. She and Tim were an attractive couple, both blond and nice-looking. Tim's face had a boyish cast that together with his "gee whiz, oh wow" manner made him seem younger than his years. In contrast, Gwen's face with a tracery of lines around her eyes and a long scar on her left cheek hinted at age and experience, not all of it pleasant. But whatever trouble Gwen might have had in the past, she'd recovered from it long since. She was unfailingly calm and collected. So much so that when Kathryn tried to imagine what it would be like to marry Earl and leave Boston for the Berkshires, she looked to Gwen, a former New Yorker, as an example of someone who'd made the transition successfully. Kathryn even suspected this was the reason she'd been introduced to Gwen in the first place.

She settled into the camp chair, and took a long drink of the ice-cold beer Earl gave her from his cooler. As the liquid coursed through her, the last vestiges of tension from the trip and worry about the developer left her. Leaning back in her chair, she gazed at the field, pretending she was Gwen watching her son achieve victory.

The two teams ran and kicked, kicked and ran in a seemingly endless struggle to score, interrupted only when the referee called foul, or a player tumbled to the ground. Kathryn gave up trying to follow what was happening. Half-closing her eyes, she tilted her head upward. It was a perfect summer afternoon, sunny but not too hot with a brilliant blue sky. White seed-filled tufts of fluff from the nearby poplar trees drifted lazily through the air, like snowflakes in June. She drifted with them, the game and her surroundings left behind until a voice brought her back to earth.

"Hey, Star, where've you been?" Earl said. "Billy just scored his fifth goal."

"That's great." Kathryn tried to inject the right amount of enthusiasm into her voice. She made a mental note to scratch "soccer mom" from the list of ways she hoped to emulate Gwen.

"It's not just great, it's fantastic!" Earl said. "Looks like we're gonna end the season with an unbeaten record." He patted her thigh and gave her a fond look. "You know, with you by my side, watching our team win, it's… well… about as good as it gets."

Kathryn smiled, but the "yes" that was on the tip of her tongue stayed there. Why the hesitation when she'd just been thinking how happy she was to be here with him? Was it because she was afraid this afternoon's happiness couldn't last, that having reached a high point, they faced a downward slide?

When she didn't immediately reply, Tim rushed to fill the silence.

"Right, Gwen?" Gwen also hesitated—long enough to make Kathryn suspect the happily married soccer mom had doubts of her own. She and Gwen found their voices at the same time, Gwen's "uh-huh" tangled up in Kathryn's "yes."

No matter. Tim and Earl's attention had shifted elsewhere. A girl wove her way precariously toward them in three-inch platform sandals. Kathryn recognized the Waites' teenage daughter, Scarlett. With her mane of shoulder-length, raven black corkscrew curls, she was hard to miss. Sunlight glinted on the metal rings that decorated her white face, its pallor accentuated by her dark hair and the blood red of her lipstick.

"You're late. The game's almost over," Tim said with an edge in his usually genial voice. Scarlett shrugged and plopped onto the ground, her short pencil skirt hiking up on her thighs. Tim regarded his daughter with bafflement, as if she were an alien who'd suddenly landed in their midst. The "good as it gets" moment was over.

*****

The pizza parlor in Great Barrington, where Kathryn, Earl, Pete and the Waites went for a celebration dinner, was crowded with families, but fortunately they'd reserved a table in the rear. As she passed the bar, Kathryn couldn't help noticing a man seated there. He faced away from her, large, square, black-framed glasses wrapped around the back of his shaved head. The sight was unnerving. Where she expected to see features, there were none. While Kathryn stood gaping, Scarlett impulsively snatched the glasses from the stranger's head.

He turned around, revealing a face that was striking rather than handsome with dark, hooded eyes, an aquiline nose, and a wide mouth.

Scarlett held out the glasses. "Are these yours?" she asked, though Kathryn assumed they were.

The man nodded.

"Oh, I thought someone stuck them on the back of your head as a goof."

7

The man gave Scarlett a once-over, his gaze lingering on her breasts peeking out from her low-cut top. "No, I put them there." He took back the glasses.

The woman sitting beside him had turned also. Kathryn recognized Maxine Kepler, Gwen's long-time friend from Manhattan. "Hey, Scarlett, Kathryn, what are you guys doing here?" Maxine asked. Anyone meeting her for the first time might have thought she was simply raising her voice to be heard over the noise in the restaurant, but Kathryn knew better: Maxine rarely spoke below a shout.

"About to have a post soccer game dinner." Scarlett pointed toward the rear of the restaurant, where Tim, Gwen, Billy, Earl and Pete were taking seats. "Hey, Mom, it's Maxine." Scarlett signaled Gwen to join them. She did so, Tim and Earl trailing after her.

"This is Niall Corrigan," Maxine introduced him. Kathryn and the others introduced themselves. "Niall's a real estate developer from New York," Maxine said. "He's here to inspect a property he just acquired. Maybe you remember him?" she said to Gwen.

Gwen squinted at Corrigan, frowned and shook her head. "No. Should I?"

"Niall used to hang with us. He was part of the party scene in Manhattan when we were all young and..." Maxine paused and glanced at Tim who was watching her intently. "Well, you know," Maxine finished.

You know—what? Kathryn wondered.

Gwen's face paled. "Oh. Yes. Now I remember." To Kathryn's surprise, Gwen appeared flustered. Scarlett's eyes darted back and forth between her mother, Maxine, and Niall Corrigan, whose face remained a blank. His features registered so little emotion that Kathryn felt as if she were still staring at the back of his shaved head.

He broke the uncomfortable silence. "So, Kathryn, are you the woman who's renting the Farley house?"

Her stomach clenched. "Yes."

"I'm pleased to meet you. As Brandy Russo may have told you, I'm the new owner. But don't worry. I'm confident we can work out an arrangement for you to stay on a while longer. We can discuss this more over the weekend. I'll be in touch."

Kathryn nodded, but she felt anything but reassured. There was something off-putting about Corrigan, and she wondered at Gwen's reaction to him. Her normally unflappable friend had seemed almost… afraid?

Earl flashed Kathryn a puzzled look, but she deflected his unspoken question with a quick shake of her head. She'd tell him about the sale later. After another awkward silence, he gave them an exit line. "Nice seeing you, Maxine, and meeting you, Niall, but we've got two hungry boys waiting at the table."

Chapter 2

Raising herself up on an elbow, Gwen fluffed the pillow, then rolled from her right side to her left. The changes didn't help. The pillow remained a hard lump under her throbbing head, her body, tightly coiled like a spring. She lay awake, listening to the house creak and groan like a querulous old lady.

The house was a relic from the bad old days when the villages of Sodom and Gomorrah thrived as twin dens of iniquity. Tim's great-grandfather, Adsit Waite, had bought it for a song after the previous owners were forced out of town. Over the years, it had suffered the ravages of age and benign neglect. Although Tim's family were builders and he was a carpenter himself, they were too busy working on other people's houses to put much effort into their own. Windows and doors stuck, the roof leaked, and paint peeled in the upstairs bedrooms, including the one where Gwen lay, shielded from falling chips by a canopy. Tim did the minimal amount of repair necessary to keep the house functional, but when asked to do anything more substantial, he invariably replied, "I don't think the old girl would like it."

Thinking of her husband, Gwen twisted her body into an even tighter knot. Tim had left the restaurant before the rest of them to attend a monthly practice of the town's volunteer fire department. She dreaded these meetings because Randy Plungas would be there, railing against the "New Yawkers," as he called them, his anger fueled by the drinking that frequently ended the meetings.

One long-ago visit to Manhattan, when his truck was fire-bombed on what were then the mean streets of the East Village, had turned

Randy into a rabid hater of all New Yorkers, including her. Determined to stop Tim from marrying her, he'd spread an ugly rumor about her. Tim had defended her then, but would he continue to do so if he knew the truth? And now with the appearance of a ghost from her past, Gwen worried the truth would finally come out. Blabbermouth though she was, Maxine was sworn to secrecy, but what about Niall Corrigan? Could she count on him to keep her secret?

It bothered her that Maxine had to remind her who he was. Was the hole in her brain, left by what she referred to as the accident, bigger than she thought? Gwen got out of bed and followed a streak of moonlight that shone through an opening in the curtains to the mahogany wardrobe, her bare feet squeaking on the uneven pine floorboards. She didn't dare turn on a light because of Grandma Waite, or "Crazy Scarlett" as some people called her. The old woman lived across the street, and her eagle eyes were often trained on her grandson's house.

Gwen rummaged among the shoeboxes at the bottom of the wardrobe until she found one that didn't contain shoes. Placing it in a spot where the moonlight was brightest, she surveyed the contents: a hodgepodge of items from when she'd lived in Manhattan in the nineties. She searched scraps of paper, postcards, and newspaper clippings for Niall's name without finding it. Finally, she found him in a snapshot of her and Maxine.

They stood arm in arm with two guys, grinning foolishly at the camera. One of the guys bore a certain resemblance to Niall with hooded eyes and an aquiline nose, although this guy had a mass of curly black hair. Maybe that's why she hadn't recognized Niall: he looked very different with a shaved head, plus the fact that he was twenty years older and had put on weight. Then again, she barely recognized her twenty-five-year-old self: face unlined with no disfiguring scar, and twin hunks of blonde hair sticking up from her head, held by huge butterfly clips. *What* had she been thinking?

Young Niall stood between her and Maxine, an arm around each of them, while the other boy only had an arm around her. Who was he? Someone she'd dated? Yes, but she couldn't remember his name. Niall, she recalled, had been dating Maxine, although according to Maxine, he had the hots for Gwen. "He's only dating me to get close to you," Maxine had complained. Perhaps she was right. In the photo Niall's eyes were trained on her rather than Maxine. Not that it mattered, all these years later.

Gwen was relieved she was able to remember so much. Maybe her memory wasn't as bad as she sometimes thought. And perhaps, after all, it was a good thing Niall had been interested in her then. He might be more discreet now. In the twenty years since she'd been *that girl,* she'd worked hard to build a new identity for herself. She was Tim's wife, Scarlett and Billy's mom, and the town librarian. The locals respected her, Tim adored her, and Kathryn looked up to her as a shining example of a city girl transformed into a satisfied country matron. *If Kathryn only knew.*

No, she could not, *would* not, let Niall destroy the persona she'd painstakingly constructed over time with a chance remark. She had to make him understand how necessary it was for him to be careful what he said about her. But what if she couldn't? A cold terror coursed through Gwen.

Brakes screeched in the driveway. Tim was home. Gwen put the snapshot back into the box and stashed it in the rear of the wardrobe. Then she climbed into bed. The front door slammed shut. Tim blundered up the stairs, singing the song he always sang when he was drunk: "I stumbled in at 2 AM..." He sang a few bars, giggled and whispered "shhh" as if scolding himself. Gwen closed her eyes and lay perfectly still, feigning sleep.

Chapter 3

Niall stepped inside his room at the Kepler house and closed the door behind him. He took in the Spartan furnishings, iron-framed twin bed, plain dresser, and single wooden chair. There were a couple of well-worn rag rugs on the floor, and the log walls were bare of paneling. As anthropologists who spent months in the field, Max's parents were used to roughing it. He, on the other hand, liked his comforts. Come August when Kathryn Stinson's lease ran out, she'd be out on her ear and he'd move into the Farley house.

He plopped down on the bed and closed his eyes. Being with Max was exhausting. He was glad to be alone. He was glad, too, for the relative quiet. He could hear her banging around downstairs, but that was nothing compared to her non-stop talking in an overly loud voice. Still, he'd managed to insert the occasional boulder in the onrush of her words, thereby diverting the current to what he wanted to hear about. And Max, who'd never met a bit of gossip she didn't like, had obliged by giving him the lowdown on the five people they'd run into at the pizza parlor tonight.

Niall laid them out in his mind like Tarot cards. There was Tim, the carpenter, the carpenter's lovely wife, Gwen, and his equally lovely daughter, Scarlett; Earl, the excavator, and the excavator's girlfriend, Kathryn, who was also Niall's tenant. Finally, there was Max herself, old friend and hostess with ties to all five, especially the carpenter's wife and daughter. And now that he had a good idea of their strengths and weaknesses, all that remained was to play them.

He smiled. Let the game begin.

Chapter 4

The next morning, Kathryn pulled into the parking lot at Fairview Hospital in Great Barrington. She sat in the car a few moments, steeling herself for the visit that lay ahead. She'd told herself that during her vacation she should see Emily Goodale at least a few times. Earl had offered to come with her, but he had other things to do this Saturday, and she didn't want him at the hospital anyway.

Might as well get it over with, then I can enjoy the rest of the day. She left the car and went into the hospital.

"Haven't seen you in a while, Ms. Stinson," said the nurse who was leaving Emily's room as Kathryn entered. Kathryn searched the woman's face for signs of reproach. Finding none, she could only assume she'd imagined it, imaginings born of a guilty conscience. "Until now, I've only been here on the occasional weekend." She tried not to sound defensive.

The nurse departed, leaving her alone with Emily. Watching the old woman lying on the hospital bed with her eyes shut, Kathryn recalled an earlier bedside vigil. Then, Emily had lain on her own bed, wearing a green dress instead of a hospital johnny, because she was only taking a nap. Before she fell asleep, she'd turned to Kathryn and said, "I'm so glad you're here." Emily had given Kathryn one of the most beautiful smiles Kathryn had ever seen. Yet if Emily woke up now, there would be no smiles nor grateful words. She pictured Emily breaking free of the many tubes to which she was tethered, and rising up in anger at her, as Emily had at the time of the stroke that had left her in a coma.

The image was so vivid that it was all Kathryn could do to stay in her seat. She stole a glance at her watch. Less than five minutes had passed since she'd arrived. That wasn't long enough to do penance. She ought to remain at least a half hour. She stared at the zigzag of lines on the monitor until she began to feel dizzy. At least she'd managed to put in another five minutes. Ten down and twenty to go. Why hadn't she thought to bring a book? Maybe she ought to get a magazine from the waiting room. She was about to do so when the nurse walked in. "You could read to her, you know," the nurse said. "If patients hear the sound of a familiar voice, it's supposed to help them come out of their coma." The nurse handed her a slim volume of Emily Dickinson poems.

Kathryn stared at the book without opening it. "You really think she'll be able to hear me?"

"Yes," the nurse said. "Why don't you try?"

"I will... in a minute." Kathryn stalled. The thought that Emily might recognize her voice worried her, but she didn't want the nurse to know. Opening the book, she scanned the pages, pretending to search for an appropriate poem. Then, in a low monotone, she mouthed the opening lines of "After great pain, a formal feeling comes." Apparently satisfied, the nurse left the room. Kathryn continued reading in an even lower voice. When she reached the third stanza and the lines: "This is the hour of Lead—/Remembered, if outlived," she stopped completely.

"*Remembered, if outlived*": the words resounded in her brain. If Emily did wake up, Kathryn didn't want Emily to remember the last awful moments before her stroke. She glanced from the book to Emily. Maybe it was her imagination, but the old woman's face appeared to twitch. What if Emily woke up and saw her? Kathryn closed the book and left the room in a hurry. As she passed the nursing station, the nurse looked up, as if to say, "leaving already?" Ignoring her, Kathryn fled.

On her way home, Kathryn stopped at the New Nottingham Public Library, a small, one-story red brick building in the colonial revival style with a gable roof and four pillars in front. She wanted to see Gwen, who was the head librarian. A librarian herself, she had this in common with Gwen, although instead of a public library, she worked at a small private library in Boston, where she was in charge of a particular collection.

Her friend sat at a low table in the children's section, fashioning a creature out of construction paper, tissue paper, pipe cleaners and glitter. Watching her, Kathryn wondered if she'd be as happy doing a craft project like this as she was curating the Lyceum's collection of prints and photographs. She believed in the old adage "a picture is worth a thousand words." The images she dealt with offered windows into the past—windows she never tired of looking through. Pictures not only told stories but raised questions that begged for answers. She prided herself on her ability to find those answers. Over the nearly ten years she'd worked at the Lyceum—she'd lucked into a job there right after college—she'd developed a possessiveness about the collection, and was reluctant to surrender it to another's care, which she'd have to do if she moved to the Berkshires to be with Earl.

"Kathryn?" Gwen said.

"Oh, hi, sorry, I was thinking about something. What's that you're making?"

"A firefly. We're devoting a session of the children's summer reading program to fireflies, so I thought it would be fun for the kids to make their own. What brings you out so bright and early on a Saturday morning?"

"I just came from visiting Emily Goodale in the hospital."

"How is she?"

"The same… except as I was leaving, her face twitched. At least, I think it did, or maybe I imagined it."

"Her face could've twitched," Gwen said. "Comas aren't the deep sleep most people think they are. Coma patients can move, make sounds, and show signs of agitation, but these are reflex actions, not conscious ones."

"How do you know so much about comas?"

Gwen fiddled with the pipe cleaner she'd used to make the firefly's antenna. "I was in one. Afterward, I did some research."

Interesting. Gwen had never mentioned this before, but they'd only known each other a few months, and Gwen was reserved, as was Kathryn. She hardly expected Gwen to reveal everything about herself in one big, breathless dump. Still, she was curious to know more about Gwen's coma. "What caused it?"

Gwen's fingers worked the pipe cleaner so vigorously that it separated from the firefly's body. She continued to twist it while she spoke. "I was in a bad car accident while I was living in New York."

"I'm sorry. If you don't mind me asking, how long did the coma last?"

"A couple weeks." Intent on refastening the pipe cleaner, Gwen didn't look at Kathryn.

Much shorter than Emily's coma, which was going into its sixth month. And Gwen would have been in her twenties, while Emily was in her nineties. Their experiences were hardly comparable. Yet Kathryn couldn't resist a further question: "How much do you remember of the accident?"

"I remember getting into the car, but that's it. The doctors filled me in on the gory details when I woke up."

"That must have been rough."

"Yes." Gwen's face was grim. The firefly came apart in her hands. "Darn. Now I'm going to have to start all over again."

"I'm sorry. That's obviously a painful subject," Kathryn said.

"You had no way of knowing. And it was a long time ago. It's probably just as well I'm don't remember much about it. But other aspects of my years in New York aren't a complete blank. Niall Corrigan, for example. Last night I remembered he used to date Maxine. I just didn't recognize him with the shaved head. And of course, he's twenty years older. Well, guess I'd better get back to work." She gestured at the pieces on the table.

"Want some help?"

"No thanks, I just need to concentrate better."

On her way to the door, Kathryn glanced back over her shoulder. Gwen stared stonily into space, the materials used to make the original firefly untouched.

Chapter 5

K athryn drove slowly up the Farley driveway, taking time to appreciate the summertime beauty. Instead of dead grass and bare trees, everything was a lush green. And what a profusion of flowers! Daffodils in April; lilacs, and red, pink, and white rhododendrons in May; and now purply-red peonies graced the border at the edge of the lawn. Having never seen peonies when she was growing up in Southern California, she'd assumed they were overblown roses, only to be told otherwise. Exotic and extravagant, peonies seemed to revel in their own sheer gorgeousness. Of all the flowers, they were her favorites. She loved them with a passion she wouldn't have thought possible, until she had fallen passionately in love with Earl. She'd cut some peonies for an arrangement indoors before the day ended.

But first things first. Another unexpected source of pleasure needed her attention: the vegetable garden. Earl's sister-in-law, Suzy Barker, had helped her restore the garden in the early spring, as part of her campaign to show Kathryn the upside of country life. Fenced-in with raised beds, the vegetable garden had been the original owner, Diana Farley's, project. But after her death, it had fallen into disrepair. Weeds clogged beds formerly filled with lettuce, tomatoes, green beans, and zucchini. Together with Suzy, Kathryn had pulled out the weeds, turned over the soil, mulched it, and begun the work of re-planting. She'd never grown anything before, and was surprised to discover how much fun this was. She got a kick out of watching tiny green shoots push their way out of the ground.

Before tackling the vegetable garden, Kathryn checked the voicemail on the landline inside. There were two messages. The first was from Corrigan, inquiring about a good time to stop by and have a chat with her. The other was from Maxine, inviting her and Earl to a welcome party for Corrigan at her parents' house that evening. She replied to Corrigan that he could stop by anytime now that she was home, and to Maxine, thanking her for the invite, but saying she'd need to check with Earl first.

*****

Kathryn spent the next two hours clearing two remaining beds in the vegetable garden and struggling with one large rock in particular. When she heard a car pull into the driveway, she yelled to whoever it was to come around to the back rather than abandon her efforts. She went right on working and managed to lever the rock from the ground with a shovel. It rose in the air, landing in a shower of dirt. When she looked up, she saw Niall Corrigan, wearing khaki pants, a yellow polo shirt, and a white baseball hat with two crossed golf clubs and the name of a golf club below them.

"Oh," was all she could think to say.

"I'd offer to help, but I'm not dressed for gardening, whereas you obviously are." He gestured at her dirty jeans. "But wouldn't it be a good idea to wear gloves?"

"I like feeling the soil in my hands."

"Really—why?"

"It makes me feel connected to the earth, to nature."

"Ah." Dark shades hid his eyes, so she couldn't see his reaction. "I can certainly understand why you enjoy coming here," he continued. "Great house. Great pond. Great woods. I'm looking forward to getting a closer look at the property. Until now I've only seen pictures on the realtor's website and the aerial view on Google Earth."

"You bought this place sight unseen?"

"I could tell from the pictures it's perfect for what I have in mind."

"What exactly is that?"

"An upscale development of, say, a half-dozen luxury estate houses, each in a different architectural style. A paved entry road, where the driveway is now, will lead to all the homes, but each will be secluded from the others."

He paused, as if waiting for her to tell him what a terrific plan it was. When she didn't, he said, "Anyway, that's the general idea. I haven't figured out all the details yet, but I expect to in the coming weeks. I'm going to set up an office on the ground floor of the house and work on site. But don't be alarmed. I know you have a six-month lease that runs through July."

Thank heaven she'd had the foresight to insist on a lease from Gordon Farley's mother and stepfather instead of the loose, month-by-month arrangement she'd had when Gordon was alive. Kathryn stuck the shovel into the ground and leaned against it, as if staking her claim.

"And I'll honor that lease," Corrigan said. "I may even give you a break on the rent since I'll be using part of the house. But I see no reason why we can't share the space. I gather from Brandy Russo that with the exception of the next two weeks when you're here on vacation, you usually only come on weekends. I won't be here 24/7 myself. I'll be back and forth between this place and the city, and when I am here, I'll be spending the nights at Maxine's parents' house. How does that sound?"

"Okay, I guess."

If he was bothered by her tepid response to what he probably thought was a generous offer, he gave no sign. "Good," he said briskly. "You and Earl Barker will be coming to the party tonight, I hope."

"I don't know."

Corrigan pursed his lips, then forcing them into a quick smile, he said, "Yes, well, I'll leave you to your gardening."

*****

"What is it, Star? You look like you lost your best friend." When Earl showed up later that day, he found her staring dejectedly at a vase filled with peonies on the screened-in porch.

"I feel like I'm about to." She told him about Corrigan's plans.

"He's going to ruin this place with his development."

"We don't know that yet. He may change his mind when he's presented with some of the negatives."

"Like what?"

"The lack of easy internet access, for one. That's a big issue for second-home owners. For locals as well. And despite what some people would like you to believe, we're not getting it any time soon."

"Maybe not, but I don't see that stopping him. He strikes me as someone who won't let anything get in the way of what he wants."

"Star, we just have to wait and see how this plays out."

"Which reminds me: Maxine invited us to a welcome party for Corrigan."

"What did you tell her?"

"That I had to check with you first."

"You don't want to go?"

"No. You?"

"I think we should."

"Why?"

"I suspect Corrigan's got something up his sleeve, and that's why we were invited. If we go, we'll find out what it is."

Kathryn made a face, but didn't argue.

Chapter 6

"I think you just missed Lakeshore Drive," Kathryn said. Earl made a quick U-turn on the main road and they headed down the drive. It wound past several large and newish looking homes, set back from the road and barely visible through the trees. Perhaps Lakeshore Drive was a model for the kind of upscale development Corrigan planned.

After a few more twists and turns, they arrived at the Kepler home, a rustic two-story log house of an older vintage than the other houses, but with a prime location right on the shore. A wide deck—obviously a newer addition—faced the water, a dock extending from it, with a boat house to one side.

"Hey, guys, welcome! Maxine called from the deck. "Gwen and Tim are down at the dock. Let's join them."

They followed Maxine onto the dock. "Where's Corrigan?" Kathryn asked. Maxine pointed at a white speed boat streaking across the lake, aimed straight at them. Kathryn grabbed Earl's arm and yanked him backward. Gwen and Tim stepped aside, too. At the last minute, the boat swerved sharply to the right, narrowly missing the dock. Corrigan swung the boat around in a half-circle, cut the engine and brought the boat in neatly on the left side of the dock.

What on earth? Was he trying to prove something? Impress someone? While Maxine tied up the boat, Corrigan stepped off, dressed in navy whites like the captain of a much larger ship. "Sorry. Couldn't resist taking that baby out for a run, then having a little fun at the end. Hope I didn't scare the daylights out of anyone."

"Nah, we're fine," Maxine assured him.

Kathryn was strongly tempted to disagree, but since the others remained silent, she held her peace. Neither Earl nor Tim looked pleased, however, and Gwen averted her eyes.

Maxine herded everyone to the deck for appetizers and champagne. When they'd settled into chairs, Corrigan turned to Gwen and Tim and said, "Where's your lovely daughter? I told Max to include her in the invitation."

Gwen started to reply, but Tim cut her off. "She's home baby-sitting her younger brother."

"Pity. I'd hoped to see her again. But another time." He speared a shrimp from the appetizer tray, dipped it in cocktail sauce, and devoured it. "If you don't mind my asking, how did you happen to name her Scarlett? For Scarlett O'Hara?"

Again, Gwen started to reply, and again, Tim cut her off. "My grandmother's name is Scarlett."

"Interesting. If your grandmother's anything like your daughter, I'd enjoy meeting her also. But I'm forgetting my manners. Thank you all for coming to help me celebrate the beginning of an exciting new venture." He rose, popped the cork of the champagne bottle and began pouring bubbly into their glasses. When everyone's glasses were filled, he raised his in a toast, "To Woodland Estates!"

They all joined him in the toast, but only Maxine did so enthusiastically. The rest barely lifted their glasses, and Tim's lift ended with a sudden flip of the wrist that sent the undoubtedly expensive champagne splashing to the ground. Corrigan approached Tim with the champagne bottle. "Tipsy already? I'll give you a refill if you think you can handle it." Without waiting for an answer, he poured more bubbly into Tim's glass.

Tim scowled and muttered something under his breath. He downed the champagne in one quick gulp.

"So Woodland Estates is what you're gonna call the development?" Earl asked in what Kathryn assumed was an attempt to draw attention away from his friend. Tim hadn't seemed drunk earlier. Still, he could have gotten a head start before the party. She'd been around him long enough to know he had a tendency to have one too many, but as far as she knew, booze made him silly rather than mean.

"No, it's just a temporary name until I come up with something better," Corrigan said. "I'm open to suggestions."

"How about Hillcrest, or Lakeside Estates?" Maxine volunteered.

"Those are possibilities," Corrigan said. "Any others?"

Maxine floated a few more names. Tim got himself a beer from a cooler. Gwen gave him a disapproving look, but he ignored it, finished the beer quickly and got another. Midway through his second beer, he said, "How 'bout Assholes' Hollow. Or—"

"That's enough, Tim." Gwen cut him off.

"Yeah, I think we're done with the name game," Maxine said. "Hope everyone's hungry, because I have a feast waiting in the kitchen."

"Can we help?" Kathryn and Gwen asked in unison.

"Not with the cooking, but you can help me carry stuff out. I practically bought out Guido's."

Maxine hadn't been kidding about buying out Guido's, a gourmet market in Great Barrington, where weekenders and summer people liked to shop. There were three roast chickens, three kinds of salad— pasta, potato, and heirloom tomatoes topped with slices of fresh mozzarella and basil leaves—and several loaves of Guido's own fresh-baked whole wheat semolina bread.

Kathryn welcomed the food not only because she was hungry, but because it gave them something to do besides talk. The reprieve didn't last long.

"Speaking of names," Corrigan said, "Why on earth is this beautiful lake called Lake Clyde? You'd think they could've come up with a name that does it justice instead of that clunker."

Earl stiffened, but said nothing. Kathryn broke the silence. "Many years ago, the lake was called Seven-Mile Pond. But when a local man, Clyde Barker, performed a great act of heroism there, it was renamed in his honor."

"What did this hero do?" Corrigan asked.

"He rescued several people from drowning," Earl said.

"Impressive. He was a relative of yours?"

"My great-great uncle."

"Well, well, if I'd known that, I wouldn't have said what I did. My apologies. Really, Max, you should have told me," he said with a mildly reproachful look.

Maxine tapped her head. "I didn't know myself."

"In any case," Corrigan continued, "I'm happy to be in the company of such fine people as I'm sure you all are. I understand you did the excavating on the Farley property—cleared the land, and built the road and pond." He addressed Earl.

"That's right."

"You did a terrific job, as far as it went."

"What do you mean 'as far as it went'?"

"Just that my project is going to be so much bigger—huge, in fact. I'm going to need more and better roads, an enlarged pond, a lot more cleared land, and the swamp needs to be drained and turned into a lovely lake like this one."

Earl cleared his throat. "You know, you can't just go in and drain that swamp. Both the state and the town have strict laws protecting wetlands. You'll need to file a formal application with the conservation commission, there will be a public hearing, and then the commission will either grant you a permit or not."

Corrigan looked nonplussed, but recovered almost immediately. "Of course, I plan on doing everything by the book. And you're the man for the job, Earl. But we can discuss this in more detail another time. I just want you and your friends to know how you'll benefit from the project in terms of the jobs it will provide." Turning to Tim, Corrigan said, "The carpentry will go to you and your dad, given your fine work on this deck and other projects like the Farley house."

Tim gazed into space with glassy, unfocused eyes. The next instant, he tumbled off the bench, where he'd been sitting, with a clatter of glass, crockery, and tableware.

For a moment, they all simply stared at him. Then Gwen went to her husband and tried to rouse him. After several attempts, she gave up. "He's passed out, I'm afraid. I better take him home. If one of you could give me a hand getting him to the truck."

Earl and Corrigan carried Tim to his truck, while Gwen apologized to Maxine for her husband's behavior. Maxine toyed with a strand of hair. "Stuff happens."

Stuff indeed. Kathryn had never seen this aggressive, drunken side of Tim before. She felt embarrassed for Gwen.

After Gwen had driven off with her unconscious husband, Earl started to rejoin Maxine and Kathryn on the deck, but Corrigan drew him aside. Soon they were deep in conversation, and Kathryn grew uneasy. The more time she spent with the developer, the more he reminded her of a snake oil salesman. She felt almost dirty in his presence.

Which was too bad, because it was a lovely evening. The June air was velvety and fragrant with honeysuckle. In the long summer twilight, the view of the lake from the deck was enchanting. Still, she wished she were elsewhere. She wanted to be alone with Earl at the boat ramp on the opposite side of Lake Clyde, its ugliness transformed into a place of beauty, as he described in vivid detail how his ancestor Clyde Barker had rescued from drowning the woman who would become his lover. Instead, she was here with Maxine.

"You and Corrigan must be pretty good friends," she said.

"Not really." Maxine lowered her voice to a normal register instead of her usual shout.

She was a short woman with a curvaceous figure. Kathryn had often wondered if the reason she spoke so loudly was to call attention to herself in situations where she was surrounded by taller people. Perhaps that was also why she wore loud colors—reds, oranges and yellows. Tonight, she wore a bright yellow sundress with black horizontal stripes that made her resemble a bumble bee.

"I mean, we ran with the same crowd when we were younger, but I always thought Niall was more interested in Gwen than me. After Gwen's 'accident'"—Maxine made air quotes around the word—"Niall and I kind of drifted apart. I knew what he was doing from the society pages, because he was a regular fixture on the charity benefit circuit. But it wasn't until we bumped into each other about a year ago that we rekindled our friendship. He asked about Gwen and when I told him she was married with a family and living in the Berkshires, he seemed surprised. He remembered my family had a place in the Berkshires, and said he was interested in looking at real estate there. The rest is history."

"How about Corrigan—has he ever been married?"

"I asked him that very question over drinks a while ago. I was curious if he'd married any of the dishy blondes I'd seen him with in the society pages. He told me no. Either he'd never found the right woman, or maybe he wasn't the marrying kind."

Maxine's expression turned pensive. "You know what they say. The good ones are all taken, and the ones left are either confirmed bachelors or not worth having."

According to Gwen, Maxine had had what Maxine called a starter marriage when she was much younger. It hadn't lasted long, and since then, she'd had various relationships, but none had stuck. Perhaps Maxine hoped Corrigan would decide she was the right woman for him, but Kathryn wasn't about to ask.

"What about you and Earl?" Maxine asked abruptly. "You two gonna get hitched?"

Kathryn bristled. She considered telling Maxine it was none of her business, but let it go. "We'll see."

"Well, don't take too long making up your mind, because if you don't grab him, someone else will."

Kathryn changed the subject. "I didn't know Tim built this deck and did the finish carpentry on the Farley house."

"Yup. Tim's grandfather, Henry Waite, had the reputation of being the best carpenter in the area. We were lucky to get him, the Farleys also. Henry was a real old-fashioned craftsperson, who took great pride in his work. Ran a tight ship, too. He and his son and grandson would show up at 7 AM on the dot, take a half hour at noon for dinner, as Henry called it, then work until quitting time at 4 PM."

Maxine's eyes turned misty. "I loved that old man," she said softly. "But I didn't envy his son or grandson the way he kept them under his thumb. I didn't realize how strict he was until we hired Frank and Tim for a job after Henry had passed. Frank showed up in a flashy sports shirt with a gold chain around his neck, something Henry would have never allowed. He wouldn't have looked kindly on Tim's drinking either. To this day, I don't know how Tim and Gwen managed to get together, given the tight leash Henry kept on him. Tim must have snuck back to the house after work, because I doubt granddad allowed him to exchange anything beyond a hasty 'hi' with her."

"That's when Gwen and Tim met?"

"Yeah, didn't she tell you? After the 'accident'"—again, Maxine enclosed the word with air quotes—"Gwen wanted desperately to get out of the city, and go someplace quiet to recuperate. I offered her my parents' house here. I don't know how quiet it was with all the hammering during the day, but—look, the guys have finally finished yakking."

*****

Kathryn was quiet on the drive home from Maxine's, but once they were back at the Farley house, she said, "Let's go sit on the patio." She and Earl sat in Adirondack chairs overlooking the pond. Like the rest of the landscape, it had assumed a summer green. There was the green of the water, but also the darker green of the surrounding trees that were reflected on the surface. Usually, the sight of the pond had a calming effect on her, not tonight.

"You and Corrigan spoke for quite a while. Are you actually going to work for him?" Kathryn said.

Earl plucked a piece of clover that had come up between the patio stones, and tossed it onto the grass. "Look, Star, I wish I were free to pick and choose from the jobs I'm offered. But as a family man with responsibilities, that's a luxury I can't afford. I've got the mortgage on the white house to pay, a son who'll be going to college in a few years, and two other sons I'd like to be able to help when they need it. Corrigan's promised to pay me top dollar, and who knows when I'll get an opportunity like this again."

His words reminded her of the gulf between them. She was single with a steady job, while he not only had family who looked to him for support, but lived in an area where work was often hard to come by. Still, she couldn't help commenting, "But Corrigan is such a sleaze."

"I worked for Gordon."

"Yes, but look what happened with that." The words were barely out of her mouth when she regretted them.

28

"Gordon *was* difficult." Earl's voice was controlled, but his eyes were hard. "As for the rest of it—making the pond, falling in love with Diana—I don't regret that. Just the way it ended, first with Diana, then with Mill."

"I am so sorry. I didn't mean to hurt you." What was wrong with her? How could she have been so insensitive as to allude even indirectly to his affair with Diana Farley, the previous owner of the house? Their affair had led to Diana's murder at the hands of Earl's ex-wife, Millie. Then Millie died trying to murder Kathryn.

Earl was silent a long moment, no doubt rehashing those tragic events. Finally, he said, "We're both tired, and bound to say things that are best left unsaid. I understand your concern about how Corrigan's proposed development will affect this place. But if I'm the excavator, I may be able to talk him out of at least some of his bad ideas."

"I hope so," Kathryn said, though unconvinced Earl would have much influence.

"Let's go in now." He rose and held out a hand. As they walked to the house, Kathryn stole a backward glance at the pond. A sudden gust of wind raked the surface. In the water's disturbed state, the tree reflections seemed to reach toward her, like drowning swimmers grasping for a lifeline before going under for good.

Chapter 7

The next morning, Kathryn awoke to the tempting aroma of frying bacon, a sign Earl was down in the kitchen, making Sunday breakfast as usual. She stretched and glanced at the clock. It was going on ten. No matter, this was their lazy day. And she'd spent a restless night, worrying about how the land she'd grown to love would be wrecked.

Minutes later, she joined Earl on the screened-in porch for fluffy pancakes with hot juicy blueberries, their tartness complemented by real maple syrup from a local farm, and the meaty taste of bacon, also from a local farm. In the morning stillness, the pond's surface was like a mirror, reflecting crisp, clean images of the trees with their newly minted green leaves. *So beautiful...* But then in her mind's eye, the mirror cracked, tree trunks and branches shattering and flying in all directions. She winced.

"What is it, Star?"

"I was thinking about this place and how it's going to be changed."

"I know, but the changes won't necessarily be bad, just different. The pond itself was a change in the landscape, and look how well it turned out."

"That's because you made it, and Diana—"

"What's she got to do with it?" he demanded with an edge in his voice.

"I apologize for bringing her up again. But she loved the pond and the rest of the property. I think she must've had some sort of vision of how she wanted it kept after she was gone. Did she ever talk to you about plans she might've had?"

Earl frowned at the congealing syrup on his plate. "Diana said a lot of things. Some of them she followed up on, others she didn't. She left this property to Gordon and that's that."

"If she hadn't left it to Gordon, what might she have done with it?"

Earl threw up his hands in exasperation. "All right, if you must know, she mentioned a couple times she was considering giving the woods, the swamp, and the old mill ruins to the New Nottingham Land Trust."

"So, she wanted it preserved in its natural state rather than developed?"

"That's what she said, but it's not what—"

He broke off at a loud rapping on the screen door. They turned to see Corrigan peering in at them. Intent on their conversation, Kathryn hadn't heard him approach. Neither, apparently, had Earl. How long had Corrigan been there, and how much had he heard?

"I hope I'm not interrupting anything," he said, though he obviously was. She almost told him so, but let Earl answer for both of them. "No, c'mon in, we're just finishing our coffee. What's up?"

Corrigan joined them on the porch. "If you can spare an hour or so, I'd like us to look at the property together," he told Earl. "I want your opinion about some of the ideas I have—whether they're feasible or not, and if not, what the alternatives might be. My architect's driving up from New York tomorrow. Before he starts drawing up plans, I want to be sure I'm on the right track."

"That okay with you, Star?" Earl asked.

She wanted to tell him it wasn't okay, that she hated the idea of him going into the woods with Corrigan. But it wasn't fair to prevent him when he needed the work.

"I suppose," she said without looking at him.

"I'll get my boots on then." Earl went into the house.

Corrigan slid into the seat Earl had vacated. "Looks like it's going to be another beautiful day. Max told me June is one of her favorite months to be in the Berkshires. I can see why. Will you be doing more gardening?"

"I don't know. Maybe," Kathryn said.

"You're welcome to join Earl and me on our little tour of the property, if you'd like."

"I guess Brandy Russo didn't tell you." Kathryn looked him full in the face for the first time. "Several months ago, someone nearly killed me in those woods, and I haven't been in there since." It was the truth. Still, she hadn't intended to blurt it out. But now that she had, she was almost glad. Especially if her words had the effect of scaring him off the woods.

"Oh dear, what a horrible thing to have happen," he said with an alarm that was maybe genuine, maybe not. "I hope they caught whoever it was."

"She's dead," Kathryn said.

Corrigan shifted uncomfortably in his seat and glanced over his shoulder to see if Earl was coming. Turning back to her, he said, "I'm sorry about your past troubles, but I hope you and I can be friends. After all, we're going to be seeing a lot of each other in the coming days."

"Yes. Now, if you'll excuse me." She left the porch, brushing past Earl on his way back out.

Chapter 8

From the bedroom window, Kathryn watched Earl and Corrigan walk around the pond. When they reached the far side, they huddled together. Seeing Earl with Corrigan brought home the divide between her and Earl, a divide that was emotional as well as physical, and would only deepen when Earl moved in with his heavy equipment. Until this moment, she hadn't thought much about what he did for a living other than that he improved things like the driveway, and sometimes created things of beauty like the pond. Now, she realized he was a destroyer as well as a creator. And in order to prevent the destruction of the woods, she needed to find a way to stop Corrigan from building his development.

As if her thoughts had somehow reached him, Corrigan looked up. He even waved. Kathryn left the bedroom for Diana Farley's former study on the other side of the house. She booted up her laptop. Usually, the slowness of the connection annoyed her. Today, she took a perverse pleasure in it. According to Earl, the lack of fast and reliable internet service was an obstacle to Corrigan's development. Yet what was a problem for the town, might not loom large for the millionaires Corrigan hoped to attract. They could easily afford the cost of a high-speed internet provider. The realization made her all the more determined to find a monkey wrench to throw into his plans.

But first, she ought to inform herself about the man she was dealing with. She did a Google search of Corrigan's previous developments, and examined them on Google Earth. Most appeared to be clusters of houses with easy access to major highways, which made them ideal for commuters. None was anything like the current project, which looked to be his most ambitious. She wondered a bit at this, but could only assume he knew what he was doing.

Now what? She glanced around the study with its red walls, old-fashioned oak schoolteacher's desk, and book shelves. *Diana, yes.* Earl had just told her Diana had talked about leaving part of the property to the local land trust. She returned to her laptop.

The New Nottingham Land Trust website explained its mission to preserve, protect, and enjoy the land—a goal Diana would surely have approved of. The site named one Charlotte Hinckley as the person to get in touch with for more information, by phone or e-mail. Kathryn did both, and spent anxious minutes waiting for a reply.

When she got none, she wracked her brain for something else to do. Then it hit her: she would search for the second will Emily Goodale believed Diana had drafted to keep her husband Gordon from getting everything, in case something happened to her. But that meant going to the attic, a place she dreaded because of the unpleasant memories it held. Every time she'd gone there in the past, she either hadn't found what she wanted, or had made a disturbing discovery.

Pushing her fears aside, she jerked on the cord and pulled down the ladder. The attic looked much as she remembered: a jumble of boxes, file drawers, and old luggage resting on strips of plywood that created a partial flooring over mounds of pink fiber glass insulation. Mouse dung speckled the plywood, and the entire space smelled musty. Ugh.

She squared her shoulders and attacked a nearby box of papers, then another and another, each time coming up empty. The air was close, and morning heat filled the attic. Eager for a breath of fresh air, she cracked the small window on the side of the house where she was. She'd need to crack the window on the opposite side for cross-ventilation. To reach it, she had to cross a treacherous bridge over the insulation that consisted of a single beam. On a previous attempt, she'd lost her balance and nearly fallen through the bedroom ceiling.

Arms outstretched like a tightrope walker, Kathryn made it across the beam, opened the window, and was soon rewarded by a cooling breeze. Midway on the return trip, a sharp crack outside stopped her. She teetered on the beam, arms tilting from one side to the next like the wings of a plane in distress. She strained to hear another sound, hoping against hope she'd imagined the crack. She heard it again. Someone was firing a gun. Judging from the direction of the noise, it came from the woods.

The woods into which Earl and Corrigan had disappeared. Kathryn dashed across the beam, hurled herself down the ladder and out of the house.

Chapter 9

Kathryn raced down the driveway, then across the field to the break in the woods that marked the beginning of the half-mile road Gordon had put in to get firewood. She pushed through a tangle of brush and climbed over fallen logs until the road opened. Then she followed a path flanked by tall pines. She heard no more shots, but in case the shooter was still in the area, she tried to make as little noise as possible, though every sound she made seemed magnified, including the hammering of her heart.

She had almost reached the end of Gordon's road when she heard a rustling in the brush. She hid behind a tall pine. As the noise came closer, she stole a glance around the tree, and caught a glimpse of something white. Corrigan's golf cap? Craning her neck to get a better view, Kathryn spotted a second man. The two were coming out of the woods on the far side of the gulley, where Gordon's road ended. They were so covered with mud she might not have recognized them but for the cap.

She broke cover and ran toward them. Earl spotted her and rushed forward. She threw herself into his outstretched arms, babbling into his chest. He stroked her hair and murmured soothing words, until she'd calmed down enough to ask, "What happened? How come you're all muddy?"

Earl released her. "We were walking around the swamp when someone started shooting at us."

"Who?"

"I don't know. He was in the woods. Maybe up in a deer blind, judging from the angle of the shots. I'll call Chief Lapsley when we

36

get back to the house."

"If you'd chased down the shooter like I told you to, we wouldn't have to wait for the police," Corrigan groused.

"You actually wanted him to go after the shooter?" Kathryn was appalled.

"Why not? That's what Steve would have done."

"Who's Steve?" Kathryn asked.

"My security guard and a former Marine. Steve would have snuck up behind the gunman and taken him down."

"Earl's not your security guard, and he doesn't carry unless he's hunting," Kathryn said.

"Really? I thought all you good country boys went around armed most of the time. I've heard some of you even sleep with your shotguns."

Kathryn opened her mouth to protest, but Earl intervened. "I made a judgment call at the swamp. I decided it was more important to keep you safe than go after the shooter. That's why I pulled you to the ground and covered you."

"I'm not convinced that was necessary, but—"

"Earl was ready to take a hit for you, and you're complaining!" she cried.

"I'm not complaining. I'm just saying that someone else might have acted differently," Corrigan said.

She wanted to lash back at him, but again Earl cut her off. "We're wasting time arguing. Let's get back to the house so I can call the Chief."

*****

Chief Lapsley showed up in a brown suit with a tie, which meant he'd come from church. He was a big man with round, ruddy cheeks that gave him an almost cherubic look. While on duty, he adopted a stern expression to show people he meant business. He wore that expression now, as Earl gave him a brief account of what had happened, and offered to go back into the woods to show him where the shooting had occurred and help look for traces of the gunman.

"You want to come with us?" the Chief asked Corrigan.

"Hell, no. I could've been the target. I want you to find and arrest whoever it was, and report back to me. I'll be at Maxine Kepler's." Corrigan strode to his car, a yellow Porsche, and drove off.

Kathryn glared after him. *Right. Leave the dangerous work to others.* When Earl and the Chief started across the field toward the entrance into the woods, her anger changed to worry. "Earl?" she called after him.

"It's okay, Star," he said. "The Chief and I will be all right. You go back into the house now."

Kathryn did so, though she was hardly reassured. She stationed herself at the living room window, where she had a view of the field and woods beyond. She watched the men move swiftly across the uneven ground of the field, becoming smaller and smaller until they disappeared into the forest. When she could no longer see them, she strained for signs of them—a flash of color among the trees, the shake of a branch pushed aside. When a crow flew from the woods, she wondered if they had disturbed it. She lost track of how long she'd stood there, watching and waiting, when the ringing phone interrupted her vigil.

"Hello?"

"Hi, it's Gwen… Are you okay?

"Yes—no."

"What is it?" The concern in Gwen's voice unleashed a torrent of words from Kathryn. She told her friend about the shooting in the woods. "That's terrible!" Gwen said. "No wonder you're upset." "Would it help if I came over and kept you company while you're waiting for Earl and the Chief to return?"

Kathryn hesitated. She was about to tell Gwen she'd manage fine on her own, but then realized she could really use some hand-holding. "I'd appreciate that."

Chapter 10

"**D**o you think Niall *was* the target?" Gwen asked, as she and Kathryn stood by the living room window.

"I don't know. He seemed to think he might have been. But I don't see how that could be. He's only been in town a short while."

"True, but news travels fast here, and if Niall was the target, I have an idea who the shooter could've been."

Kathryn looked at Gwen, astonished. "Who?"

"Randy Plungas."

"Who's he?"

"A local house painter. You've probably seen him around. He wears paint-splattered overalls most of the time."

"Oh, *that* guy." Kathryn recalled a short, brawny man with bowed legs and a thatch of red hair. When he planted his feet wide apart and thrust his chest out, as she'd seen him do on more than one occasion, he reminded her of a bantam rooster. "What would he have against Niall?" she asked.

"He hates all 'New Yawkers,' as he calls them. He thinks they'll take over the town if we don't stop them. Tim's on the volunteer fire department with him. That's where Randy could've heard about Niall."

"Okay, but how did Randy know Earl and Niall were going into the woods today? We didn't know ourselves until Niall showed up here this morning."

"Maybe Randy was patrolling the woods when he spotted them, and figured out Niall was the developer he'd heard about."

This was getting more bizarre by the moment. "Patrolling the woods? Why would he do that?"

"I don't know this for a fact, but rumor has it, Randy's got a small arsenal hidden in there someplace, and he doesn't want anyone to find it."

Far from calming her, what Gwen told her about Randy Plungas stoked Kathryn's fears. He reminded her of Earl's crazy youngest brother, Garth, who'd also roamed the forest with a loaded gun. She'd run afoul of Garth soon after her arrival in New Nottingham last fall. He was dead now, but Plungas seemed to have taken his place as the new menace in the woods.

Her dismay must have been evident. "I shouldn't have brought up Randy," Gwen said. "I'm just guessing he was the shooter. But if it turns out he was, don't worry. You're not a New Yorker, so he's unlikely to go after you."

Maybe not, but in Kathryn's experience here, violence led to violence, and even if Randy didn't attack her or Earl directly, they could still be caught in the cross-fire, as Earl almost had today.

The phone rang. This time, it was Tim, and he sounded angry. "Is Gwen there?" Kathryn told him she was. "Then tell her I need to talk to her *now*!"

"What was that all about?" Kathryn asked when Gwen returned to the living room. "Oh, just some silly business involving Grandma Waite and the kids."

Although Gwen tried to make light of the matter, Kathryn could see she was upset. "Want to talk about it?"

"It's nothing really, but… Grandma Waite lives across the street from us. She keeps a close watch on everything that happens at our place. Today she saw a fancy sports car park in front of the house and a strange man got out. He went to the door, Scarlett opened it, then she and her brother got into the car with him and drove away. Grandma Waite called our house. When no one answered, she called the police. No one answered there either. So, she went to the house, found Tim still asleep upstairs, and roused him with the news that his daughter and son had been kidnapped."

"Oh, my goodness."

"I tried to explain that Maxine had most likely invited the kids

40

over for a swim, and sent Niall to pick them up," Gwen said. "But Tim wouldn't listen. 'What if your friend Niall didn't take them to Maxine's at all?' he said. 'What if he really did kidnap them?' He went on like that for a while, until finally I got him to calm down. I promised I'd go over to Maxine's and check on the kids. Then when they finished their swim, I'd bring them home."

"That sounds reasonable. What's with Tim overreacting like that?"

Gwen bit a nail. "I don't think he likes or trusts Niall. I blame Randy with all his anti- 'New Yawker' rants. Tim has issues with Scarlett, too. They got along fine when she was younger, but as soon as she hit her teenage years, they started locking horns. She's headstrong and rebellious, and Tim's a very straight-arrow sort of guy. He doesn't approve of her behavior, especially her choice of boyfriends. She dated this older guy who was bad news. Tim came down really hard on her about it."

Gwen's life was more complicated than Kathryn had imagined. Her friend had to deal with a nosy, possibly crazy grandmother, a difficult daughter, and a husband who drank too much and let himself be influenced by trouble-makers like Randy Plungas.

Gwen stood. "Guess I'd better go ransom my kids," she said with a wry smile.

Kathryn glanced back at the forest. It was quiet and still. If something bad was going to happen, surely it would have happened by now. Perhaps *she'd* overreacted to the danger Earl and the Chief were in. Gwen had been supportive when she was upset. Now, her friend could use some support.

"I'll come with you."

Chapter 11

Angry voices reached Kathryn and Gwen as they parked at Maxine's. Gwen groaned. "Sounds like my kids. Squabbling. Again."

Maxine met them halfway to the dock. "Hi, you're just in time to referee an argument between Scarlett and Billy."

They followed her to the dock. Scarlett and Billy stood on either side of Corrigan, glaring at each other. Scarlett wore a black bikini that showed off her curves; Billy, trunks that were dripping wet. Corrigan had exchanged his mud-covered clothes for a fresh polo shirt over trunks with a tropical design. Kathryn examined his face for signs of his recent ordeal, but found none. Perhaps she was being unfair, but she couldn't help feeling a twinge of annoyance that he should be here at the lake enjoying himself while Earl and the Chief scoured the woods for the shooter.

"Hey, guys," Gwen said to her kids, "what's going on?"

"Billy's been hogging the water skis all afternoon," Scarlett said. "It's my turn."

"She could've had a turn any time, if she'd asked," Billy shot back. "But she was too wrapped up in her stupid phone. She only wants it now to be mean."

Scarlett gave him the finger.

Billy shook a fist at her.

"That's enough, both of you," Gwen said. "If Scarlett hasn't had a turn, she should have it," she told Billy.

Corrigan got the skis and handed them to Scarlett. She looked at them uncertainly. "Have you ever been on water skis before?"

Corrigan asked.

"The one time she tried, she couldn't get up," Billy volunteered.

"All the more reason to give her a chance now," Corrigan said. "You used to water ski," he said to Gwen. "Why don't you give her some pointers?"

"Okay," Gwen said.

"You drive the boat this time, Max," Corrigan said. "I'll stay on the dock and help Gwen get Scarlett ready. When I give the signal, I want you to hit the throttle and give that baby all she's got."

Maxine climbed into the boat and taxied a short distance from the dock while Gwen helped Scarlett into a life jacket, and adjusted the skis onto her feet. When Maxine tossed the tow rope from the boat, Corrigan caught and gave it to Scarlett. Gwen and Corrigan knelt on either side of her, giving her last-minute instructions. Then Corrigan yelled, "Now!"

The boat took off, and Scarlett catapulted head first into the water. She surfaced, gasping and distressed. Corrigan and Gwen hauled her back onto the dock. She shook out her wet curls. "I can't do this."

"I told you so," Billy crowed. "My turn." He reached for the skis, but Corrigan stopped him. "No. Your sister's going to get up on skis, if it takes us the rest of the afternoon."

"But—" Billy started to protest, only to be silenced by a look from Corrigan. "He's right," Gwen said. "Scarlett's entitled to more chances."

On her second try, Scarlett managed to travel a short distance in a squatting position, but when she tried to stand, she toppled over. Again, Gwen and Corrigan hauled her back onto the dock, and again Scarlett was ready to give up. Corrigan wouldn't let her. "You're almost there. Maybe if you started from the shore, it would be easier."

"Can I talk to you a minute, Mom?" Billy said. While Gwen was occupied with Billy, Corrigan led Scarlett to the beach and got into the water with her. He held her from behind to keep her properly positioned until he gave the signal for the boat to go. Kathryn had water skied herself, so she knew this was a perfectly normal thing to do. Still, it bothered her to see Corrigan holding Scarlett's bikini-clad figure, his arms wrapped around her arms, his body against her back. When he bent his head to whisper into Scarlett's ear, Kathryn's unease grew. She glanced at Gwen to see if she had a similar reaction. But Gwen was still focused on Billy.

The image of Corrigan and Scarlett together dissolved into a blur of motion as he gave the signal, and the boat shot through the water, pulling Scarlett after it. She leaned so far forward that for a moment it looked as she'd take another tumble. Then, miraculously, she straightened, and let the boat ferry her around the lake, a beaming goddess on a carpet of foam.

When Scarlett had made a less than graceful landing, she kicked off her skis and hurried over to Corrigan who was waiting on the beach. "I knew you could do it." He raised his hand for a high-five. Instead, Scarlett flung her arms around him in an embrace that seemed at first to surprise him, but that soon became reciprocal.

Alarm bells went off inside Kathryn. She hoped the girl's impetuousness didn't get her into trouble. She glanced at Gwen and caught a glint of worry, which vanished as Corrigan released Scarlett and they joined the others on the dock.

"Turns out your daughter has the makings of a first-class water skier," Corrigan said. "Like mother, like daughter."

"*You* were that good, Mom?" Scarlett asked incredulously.

"Not really," Gwen said.

"How about taking a run now?" Corrigan asked. His voice was low—almost seductive. She met his gaze for a moment, then looked away. "I didn't bring a bathing suit."

"Another time, then," Corrigan said in the same silky voice.

"If nobody else wants to go, I do," Billy chimed in.

Corrigan looked at the boy, then at the lake where wavelets had formed. "The wind's come up. It's too rough."

"You were going to take Mom out," Billy said.

"So I was, but with the wind and now…" Corrigan fanned a hand behind his ear, apparently listening for something. An engine rumbled in the distance, becoming louder and louder until it ceased altogether. The door of a vehicle slammed shut, and a man in jeans and a black tee shirt strode toward them.

"Who's that?" Billy demanded.

"Steve Reikart, my security guard," Corrigan said.

Chapter 12

"**Y**ou're the security guard?" Maxine said. She'd obviously expected a different sort of person, and was surprised and pleased by what she saw.

Reikart's grin suggested he was well aware of the effect he had on her. "Yes, ma'am," he replied with the trace of a southern accent. He was of medium height with the compact, muscular build of someone who worked out regularly. He was also attractive with sandy hair cut close to his head, blue eyes, and a boyish cast to his features.

"Welcome," Maxine said.

"Thank you, ma'am."

"Max, please."

"I appreciate your hospitality, Max, while I'm getting…" Reikart paused and glanced at Corrigan. "Settled in."

Settled in? Kathryn didn't like the sound of that. It implied that Reikart would be around a while, perhaps sharing the office Corrigan planned to set up in the Farley house. He hadn't mentioned anything about a security guard then, so maybe he'd decided to summon Reikart after the shooting.

A series of sharp barks issued from the parking area. "What's that—a dog?" Scarlett sounded alarmed.

"Yup, she's mine." Reikart surveyed Scarlett from head to toe before his gaze returned to Maxine. "She can stay in my truck, if you'd rather not have her in the house."

"That won't be necessary. I just *love* animals," Maxine said. "She can't be happy cooped up in your truck. Why don't you let her out so she can run around?"

Reikart went back to the parking area, and returned with a huge black Doberman straining on its leash. "This is Solstice, Solly for short."

Scarlett gave a little gasp and took several steps backwards until she was half-hidden behind Corrigan. Kathryn eyed the dog warily, and Gwen and Billy were on their guard as well. Maxine knelt and held out her arms. "Hey, Solly, come to Mama!"

Reikart unsnapped the leash, and the dog bounded toward Maxine, hitting her with such force that she went down like a bowling pin. She lay on her side, laughing as the dog licked her.

"Solly's a real sweetheart when she wants to be," Reikart said.

At the sound of another vehicle pulling into the parking area, the dog stopped slathering Maxine with kisses, and stood at attention, ears pulled back, teeth bared, a low growl issuing from her throat. When Chief Lapsley appeared, the dog looked ready to lunge. "No, Solstice. Down!" Reikart commanded. The dog bowed her head and collapsed onto the ground. Reikart snapped her leash back on.

Keeping a safe distance from the Doberman, the Chief went over to Corrigan.

"I'd like to talk to you for a few minutes."

"Let's go over there." Corrigan pointed toward the boat house. "Tie up the dog and come with us," he told Reikart. "I want you to hear what Chief Lapsley has to say."

Kathryn would have liked to hear what he had to say, too. But the men retreated to the far side of the boat house, and kept their voices down.

Gwen looked at her watch. "We better head home before your dad starts wondering what happened to us. Thanks for taking the kids waterskiing," she called to Maxine, who was petting and talking to Solly in her special doggie voice.

"Any time," Maxine said.

*****

Earl sat on the patio at the Farley house, drinking a beer, when

Kathryn returned. He'd showered and changed out of his muddy clothes from the morning.

She sat down beside him. "How did the search go? Did you find anything?"

Earl shook his head. "Some tracks around the deer blind, but that's about it."

She told him about her visit with Gwen, and how Gwen thought Randy Plungas might be the shooter.

"We thought he was a possibility, too, but when we went to his cabin, it was locked and his truck was gone."

"Where's his cabin?"

"On the far side of the woods from here." Earl nodded in that direction.

"Corrigan clearly thinks he was the target," Kathryn said. "His security guard showed up at Maxine's this afternoon with a Doberman."

Earl ran a finger around the rim of his beer can. "I figured he might call in one of his men."

"His goons, you mean."

Earl said nothing.

Frustrated, Kathryn said, "What is it with you? We're looking at trouble here. Maybe big trouble. And you don't seem to care."

"I care all right, but what do you expect me to do? Corrigan has a right to protect himself if he feels threatened. It's not like he's breaking any laws bringing in a security guard."

"No, but the more guys with guns around, the more likely it is that someone will get hurt."

"Star, we'll just have to cross that bridge when *and if* we come to it. I'm hoping we won't. Now, why don't you have a beer and try to relax while I throw some sausages on the grill?"

*****

The next day was Monday and a work day for Earl. He retired early. Kathryn stayed up to read in the living room. But she had too much on her mind to concentrate. Tossing her book aside, she went into the kitchen to get a glass of water. On her way back to the living room, she noticed light pooling under the basement door. Earl must have forgotten to turn it off when he'd taken his dirty clothes down to put in the washing machine. In the basement she found his jeans and shirt lying on top of the machine. She picked them up and began checking his pockets for loose change, which he often forgot to remove. There was no change. Instead, she found a scrap of loose denim in a jean pocket. The scrap's edges were ragged, as if it had caught on something. Examining it in the light, Kathryn noticed a spot of white paint.

Gwen's words came back to her: "You've probably seen him around. He wears paint-splattered overalls most of the time."

Chapter 13

*W*as Randy Plungas the shooter, after all? If so, why was a scrap of what might be his clothing still in Earl's pocket? Those were the questions running through Kathryn's mind when she went to sleep that night. They were also the questions she woke up with the next morning. If Earl hadn't already left for work, she would have asked him. Now, she'd have to wait until they saw each other later today.

The roar of an engine on the road caught her attention. She got out of bed and crossed the hall to the room that had been Gordon's studio in time to see a large truck with a single-unit trailer in tow lumber up the driveway. It squeezed into the parking area. The next thing she knew, a loud pounding sounded at the front door.

Throwing on clothes, Kathryn went to the door. A burly man with a clipboard greeted her. "Mrs. Corrigan?"

"No, what's this about?

The man looked at his clipboard, then back at her. "Got an order from a Mr. Corrigan for a trailer to be delivered here. This is 173 Rattlesnake Hill Road, isn't it?"

"Yes, but I don't know anything about a trailer delivery."

"Maybe he forgot to tell you. Can I speak with him?"

"He's not here," Kathryn snapped.

The man took a step back. "Look, ma'am, I'm just trying to do my job. If Mr. Corrigan's not here, where I can reach him? I need to find out where I'm supposed to leave the trailer. The dispatcher told me to be sure and follow Mr. Corrigan's instructions, but there aren't any instructions on this order. She must've forgot to write 'em down."

Kathryn relented. In a milder tone, she said, "If you'll hold on a minute, I'll get him on the phone for you."

In the kitchen, she dialed Maxine's number. "Hey, Kathryn, how's it going?" Maxine said in a voice that carried throughout the house.

"There's a man here with a trailer he says Corrigan ordered. He needs to know where to leave it."

"Oh, wow, I'll put Niall on."

Moments later, Corrigan came onto the line. "Kathryn, I am so, so sorry! I meant to tell you about the delivery, and be there to meet the driver. But Maxine made such a scrumptious breakfast for Steve and me I totally forgot. We'll be right over."

A full forty minutes later, Corrigan and Steve Reikart showed up in separate vehicles. Taking pity on the driver, Kathryn had invited him in for coffee, a gesture that eased the tension between them, but not between him and Corrigan, for keeping him waiting. As he had with Kathryn, Corrigan apologized profusely to the driver. Kathryn suspected it was the sizeable amount Corrigan paid the driver "for his trouble" that made the driver willing to spend an additional forty minutes getting the trailer positioned exactly where Corrigan wanted it, to one side of the opening in the woods where Gordon's road began. This turned out to be a complicated affair, requiring some tricky maneuvering on the driver's part. He almost took out a utility pole, and managed to flatten a tire on his truck when he hit a big rock in the field on his way back to the driveway.

Kathryn watched all this happen, until the ringing phone called her indoors

"Hello?"

"This is Charlotte Hinkley from the New Marlborough Land Trust returning your call."

Chapter 14

Kathryn spotted a tall, trim woman with an athletic build and a cap of short, silver hair standing by the bar at the Brew N' Burger in Great Barrington. At a signal from the bartender, who knew Kathryn from previous visits, the woman strode over, introduced herself as Charlotte Hinckley, and held out her hand. Her handshake was firm and friendly. Kathryn liked her immediately.

They found a table in the back. While waiting for their orders, Charlotte apologized for not inviting Kathryn to her house. "When I decided to have the kitchen redone, I had no idea it would be so disruptive."

"Things are pretty disruptive on my end, too. And it's only going to get worse." Kathryn said.

"At the Farley house, you mean?"

Kathryn told Charlotte about the chaotic morning delivery of the trailer, where the developer's security guard and his watch dog would stay, while the developer set up an office on the first floor of the house.

Charlotte's expression was filled with regret. "I'm sorry to hear that. I don't know if you know this, but the land trust had hopes of acquiring part of that property—the woods, the swamp, and the old mill ruins."

Kathryn's pulse quickened. "Did Diana Farley talk to you about leaving it to the land trust?".

"We had several discussions about it. Diana said she was thinking of adding a codicil to her will to that effect. But she never got around to it. After her death, everything went to her husband Gordon. When

52

we approached him with an offer on the parcel, he dismissed it. We got a similar response when we approached Gordon's mother and stepfather after Gordon died. They said it was all or nothing, and named a price that was well beyond what we could afford. I think they were hoping a developer would snatch it up for big bucks, and that's what's happened."

Kathryn didn't try to hide her disappointment. "It's such a shame. Beautiful land like that should be left in its natural state for everyone to enjoy, not turned into an enclave for the very wealthy."

"You speak like a true environmentalist. Have you always been a supporter of conservation?"

"Hardly." Kathryn laughed. "I grew up in Southern California, which is about the most artificially created landscape you can imagine. It would be desert if we hadn't stolen water from the Colorado River. Then, I moved to the Boston area, which wouldn't be the city it is without a lot of landfill. I didn't give much thought to my surroundings until I came here and fell in love with the landscape."

"I'm glad that did it for you," Charlotte said.

The waiter brought their lunches and they ate in silence for a few minutes. "What about you?" Kathryn asked. "Have you always lived here? Is that why you're involved with the land trust?"

"My grandparents had a cottage in New Nottingham, and I spent summers here. But most of my adult life has been spent in Madagascar. I'm a naturalist and studied lemurs, which are only found there. But after years of living and working in the rainforest, and nearly dying of the plague, I decided to return to a more healthful climate."

"I see you believe in eating healthy, too. Both of you," a male voice said.

Corrigan stood before them, together with a slender man of medium height with wild hair and rimless glasses.

Charlotte frowned. "I beg your pardon?"

"Sorry if I'm interrupting anything, but when I saw Ms. Stinson, I thought I'd come over and say hello. I'm Niall Corrigan, the developer who just bought the Farley property." He extended a hand.

"Charlotte Hinckley." She took his hand tentatively and withdrew hers quickly.

"This is my architect, David Beller," Corrigan continued. "He came up from New York today to look at the property with me." Beller acknowledged the introduction with a nod.

"Hinckley, eh?" Corrigan said. "That name sounds familiar. You wouldn't happen to be involved with the New Nottingham Land Trust, would you?"

"I am the executive director."

"Yes, I think Brandy Russo, the realtor, mentioned that the land trust made an offer on part of the property, and your name came up."

Charlotte speared a lettuce leaf with her fork, as if to signal the conversation was over.

But Corrigan wasn't finished. "You and I should have a little chat sometime."

Charlotte put her fork down. "Why?"

"Here's the thing. I'm aware that some people around here aren't happy about my proposed development. So, I'm hoping to find a way to make it more palatable."

"What do you have in mind?" Charlotte asked.

"I don't know yet. My clients are wealthy people who value their privacy. I have to respect that. Still, we might be able to do something with the ruins of that old mill. Most of it will have to be torn down for safety reasons. But perhaps we could move one of the pillars to the entrance of the development and put up an explanatory plaque that people driving past on Rattlesnake Hill Road could see. Anyway, I'm open to suggestions."

"Of course." Charlotte's voice held a hint of sarcasm. She picked up her fork again.

"Nice meeting you," Corrigan said. "Enjoy your salads, ladies," he called over his shoulder as he and Beller headed for the door. On the way, he stopped briefly to talk to one of the waitresses. To Kathryn's surprise, it was Scarlett Waite.

"He's even worse than I imagined from your description," Charlotte said after Corrigan and Beller were out of earshot. "Thinking he can placate people with a few stones and a plaque—he's got some nerve. I wish…" She scowled at her plate, as if it were a stand-in for Corrigan.

"I know," Kathryn agreed. "But as for that codicil you mentioned, Emily Goodale thought Diana drew up such a document, only she called it a second will. I can't guarantee a codicil, or another will, exists, but if one does, I'm going to do my best to find it in the house. If and when I do, we'll need a good lawyer."

Charlotte's eyes lit up. "I know just the person. In the meantime, there may be other actions we can take."

"Like what?" Kathryn asked eagerly.

"From what you've told me and what I observed just now, Corrigan likes to do things on the quick, and doesn't always take the necessary steps. The trailer that was delivered to the property today—do you know if he got a permit for it?"

"I have no idea. I didn't know he needed one."

"He does. I'm going to stop by the town hall on my way home, and see if he's even bothered to apply for one."

Kathryn smiled. "Perfect."

Charlotte returned Kathryn's smile with a conspiratorial one. "Then there's the matter of wetland regulations."

"My friend, Earl Barker, mentioned that. He said there were strict laws governing wetlands."

"That's correct. It's almost impossible to turn a swamp into a lake in this state, especially if wildlife like moose use the swamp. And, as I recall, destroying vernal pools is also prohibited. While I'm at the town hall, I'm going to brush up on the regulations, and check to see if there's a history of vernal pools on the land. Finally, if you need help searching for the codicil or second will, let me know. I'm good at that sort of thing."

"Will do," Kathryn promised.

Now that she had an important ally against Corrigan, Kathryn considered returning to the house and resuming the search for the will, but she'd promised herself that while in Great Barrington, she'd pay Emily another visit. In the midst of her worries about Corrigan's development, she hadn't forgotten the old woman who lay in a coma for which she felt responsible. She wanted to do something to make amends. And she'd figured out a way to bring familiar voices to Emily without speaking or reading to Emily herself.

Chapter 15

On her way to Emily's hospital room, Kathryn ran into the same nurse from Saturday. "I've brought a cassette tape to play for Mrs. Goodale this afternoon." She showed the nurse the tape and a small cassette player. "It's one of several tapes that were made of her recollections of the old days in New Nottingham. I'm hoping she might respond to the sound of her own voice and that of the woman who interviewed her, who was a close friend."

"Sounds good," the nurse said.

Emily's room was quiet except for the low hum of the machines that kept her alive. But that changed dramatically when Kathryn started the tape. She might have been eavesdropping on a conversation between two people who sat nearby.

"You want to know about the old families, you should visit the New Nottingham Cemetery," Emily said in her scratched record voice. *"It's like a who's who of the village, because the descendants of most of the people buried there still live in town."*

"Including the Waites?" Diana asked in her surprisingly high, girlish voice—surprising because from everything Kathryn had heard about Diana Farley, she'd been a strong-willed woman with a confrontational manner. *"They seem like they must be an old family, since three generations of them did the finish carpentry on my house."*

"They're old timers, all right. And you were darn lucky to get 'em. Henry Waite's considered the finest carpenter in the county. He's enjoyed great success in his professional life, though I can't say the same of his personal life."

"What happened?"

56

"He fell under the spell of a wicked woman and married her—a decision I believe he lived to regret, though he'd be the last person to admit it."

"What's the story with his wife?"

"Remember how I told you about those two tiny hamlets of Sodom and Gomorrah that existed in the old days?"

"Yes."

"Well, the folks who lived there were so evil that eventually the upstanding residents of New Nottingham forced them out. No one knows where they went, but when Scarlett Lovell showed up in town many years later, some people suspected she was a descendant of an infamous madam who ran a brothel on Sodom Road in the early days. She denied it, but she was vague about her origins, never would say who her parents were, where she'd grown up or where she'd lived before coming to New Nottingham. And most of the men in town were so besotted by her beauty they didn't give a hoot, anyway. Even caught my husband, who was usually a sensible sort, making eyes at her once."

"What was so wicked about her?"

"She was easily offended, and once she'd turned against you, you were her enemy for life."

"What happened to people she considered her enemies?"

"There were accidents, even deaths. Now, some of those events probably would have happened anyway, but there were enough unusual occurrences to make some believe she'd put curses on the people involved."

"What do you think?"

"I can't say for sure. All I know is that Scarlett Lovell Waite, or 'Crazy Scarlett' as people call her behind her back, was and still is a mean and angry woman. I've often wondered if she came back to get revenge against a town that expelled her people long ago."

"How did her husband handle such a difficult wife?"

"In the beginning, Henry was so smitten with her he didn't notice her flaws. When he finally did, he tried to smooth things over between her and others, but it was no use. Eventually, he stopped trying and focused on his work and the care of their children, who

57

needed a steadying influence in their lives."

"Poor Henry. Did he ever consider divorce?"

"No, he was of the school that once you made your bed, you had to lie in it."

"Pity."

Indeed. Kathryn's own grandmother had been difficult, but she'd escaped by moving across the country. She didn't envy Gwen having to endure Tim's grandmother's interference in their lives on a daily basis. Which made her wonder why Gwen had named her daughter after "Crazy Scarlett." Perhaps they'd been on better terms then.

Emily went on to tell the story of another old family, but since it didn't involve anyone she knew, Kathryn only half listened. She kept her eyes trained on the old woman, in case Emily showed signs that she heard the voices. But after twenty minutes passed with no response, Kathryn stopped the tape and left.

Chapter 16

Kathryn noticed Gwen getting out of her car at the library, as she drove through town. She pulled over and called to her friend, "Hi, I didn't expect to see you here. I thought the library was closed on Mondays."

Gwen came over to her. "It is, but I'm behind in my work, so I decided to come in for a couple of hours."

"Is everything okay otherwise?" Kathryn asked.

"I guess." Gwen frowned at the ground, then at the library door, where a teenage boy stood waiting. "I need to let my helper in, then let's go around to the back, where we can talk."

Kathryn went with Gwen to the entrance, where Gwen introduced her to the teenager, whose name was Robert, and unlocked the door. He was chubby with longish red hair. Dressed in a trench coat with an empty coffee mug in his pocket, he resembled a youthful Colombo. "I'm going out back for a few minutes," Gwen told him. "Please check the return bin for books and unload them." She handed him a key chain with keys of different sizes.

"Sure thing, Mrs. Waite."

"Must be nice to have a helper," Kathryn observed, as she and Gwen walked around the library to the rear.

"I tried to get Scarlett involved, but she refused," Gwen said. "Told me it would be too borr-ing."

"She prefers waitressing?"

"How do you know?"

"I saw her today at the Brew N' Burger."

"Ah," Gwen said. "Unlike Scarlett, Robert enjoys coming to the library. And not only for the books. For him, it's a refuge from a tough situation at home. Robert and his father don't get along. And considering his dad is Randy Plungas, I'm not surprised."

At the mention of Plungas, Kathryn wondered again about the piece of paint-splattered denim she'd found in Earl's pocket. But she decided not to say anything to Gwen until she had more information. She followed her friend to a wooden gazebo behind the library that overlooked a stream and offered a quiet place for reading, contemplation, or conversation.

"If I seemed unsure about whether everything's okay, it's because Grandma Waite's still giving me a hard time about Niall and the kids," Gwen said. "Right after I brought them home yesterday, she called to say, 'Just because you got your children back from that man, doesn't mean he won't try again with Scarlett. He's evil through and through.'"

"That *is* strong. She's never met him, has she?"

"No. But that's never stopped her from declaring people evil. She's a strange woman."

"That's the impression I got from Emily Goodale." Kathryn told Gwen about playing the tapes of Emily's recollections while visiting her at the hospital. "What she said about Grandma Waite being such a difficult person made me wonder why you named Scarlett after her."

"It was a big mistake, and one I've lived to regret. But at the time, Grandma Waite was the only person in town who welcomed me with open arms. The rest had serious doubts, and some even warned Tim he was in for trouble if he married me."

"Why were they so against you?"

"People here don't take kindly to strangers. Especially those from big cities. Tim defended me, but aside from him, Grandma Waite was my sole ally. She invited me over for tea several times while Tim and I were dating. I was grateful to her, even though I didn't feel entirely comfortable around her. Part of it had to do with how harshly she spoke about other people. Another part was the tea itself. She told me it was her own special brew, made from various plants she collected, but it tasted terrible. And the biscuits, also homemade, were hard as stones."

"Sounds awful."

Gwen laughed and nodded. "It was. But the weirdest of all was the tea when she persuaded me to name my daughter Scarlett."

"What happened?"

Gwen glanced at her watch. "I guess I have time for one more story. At that tea, she told me she'd had a dream that made her very happy. Tim and I were married, and I was pregnant with our first child. I said that if the baby was a girl, I'd name her Scarlett.

"I pointed out that Tim and I weren't married, and who knew if we'd have children, but she wouldn't listen. Told me to be a good girl and finish my tea. After I did, I began to feel drowsy. The last thing I remember before I drifted off was this strange light in her eyes.

"When I woke up, she said that while I was asleep, she'd looked deeply into my heart and learned my darkest secrets. In exchange for her silence, I'd promised to name my first born, a girl, after her, and signed a document to that effect, which she showed me."

"So, she blackmailed you."

"Right, only she claimed the document was simply my acknowledgment of something that was going to happen anyway, because her dream was a prophesy."

"What a piece of—" Kathryn broke off at the noise of a commotion in the library.

Chapter 17

Kathryn at her heels, Gwen flung open the library door. Randy Plungas was trying to drag Robert from the premises, leaving behind a trail of overturned furniture and fallen books. Plungas's face was red with rage, Robert's pale and frightened.

"What's going on?" Gwen demanded in her best stern librarian voice.

"I'm takin' him outta here!" Plungas fired back.

"But Robert has a job at the library," Gwen protested.

"He's done with this pansy-ass place. I'm sick and tired of him holing up here, when he oughta be helping me paint houses."

"It's Robert's choice to work at the library. He's not only a valuable helper to me, but he's developing skills that will be useful to him later."

"I know what's best for my son and it ain't this." Plungas jerked Robert's arm so hard the boy nearly lost his balance.

Kathryn slipped quickly behind the front desk, ready to call the police.

"Now, Randy, there's no need to—" Gwen began.

"You think you're so high an' mighty," Plungas cut in, "but I know you for the whore you are!"

Kathryn was stunned. Gwen's eyes opened wide, but otherwise, she maintained her composure. Robert sank his teeth into his father's forearm.

Plungas let out a yelp and punched Robert in the face. Kathryn called Chief Lapsley.

The Chief must have been close by. When he walked into the

library moments later, Gwen stood between Plungas and Robert, whose nose bled profusely. Kathryn gripped a heavy paperweight which she intended to use if Plungas moved to attack Gwen.

"What happened here?" the Chief demanded.

"Just came to fetch my boy an' he bit me!" Plungas held up his forearm for the Chief to see.

"Why'd you bite your dad?" the Chief asked Robert.

"He was trying to make me leave the library against my will," Robert said. "When Mrs. Waite tried to reason with him, he called her a bad name."

"That so?" the Chief asked Plungas.

Plungas struck what Kathryn thought of as his bantam rooster pose—chest thrust forward and feet planted wide apart—while glaring at Robert. "Boy's lyin'."

"No, he's not," Kathryn blurted.

Plungas glared at her.

"Gonna ask you again, Randy," the Chief said. "Did you do what Robert said? And here's another question for you. How come Robert's nose is bleeding? Did you hit him?"

Silence.

"I'm gonna take that as a 'yes' to both questions. Come with me, Randy."

"What about my arm?"

"I'll see that it gets taken care of. Come with me."

Plungas held his ground.

"Either you come willingly, or I'm gonna cuff you," the Chief threatened.

Plungas didn't move.

"Go with the Chief." Earl stood in the doorway. His even tone belied the hardness in his eyes. The snake-about-to-strike look, his mother called it.

Plungas looked at Earl and appeared to think things over. He walked sullenly to the door, followed by the Chief. As Plungas passed through, he exchanged glances with Earl. Kathryn caught a flicker of fear in Plungas's eyes. Fear and a question. But whether he got an answer, she had no idea. She started toward Earl, but stopped when he raised a hand and mouthed "later."

When Kathryn went out to get ice for Robert's bloody nose across the street at the general store, all three men were gone. She stayed at the library to help clean up the mess and to help Gwen tend to Robert, who was badly shaken. Although Gwen managed to keep her cool, Kathryn could tell she was shaken also. Plungas struck her as a loose cannon, likely to fly off the handle again, despite the measure of control Earl seemed to have over him. She'd been shocked when Plungas called Gwen a whore, but she could hardly ask Gwen about it in front of Robert.

Her mind in turmoil, Kathryn headed back to the Farley house. The sight of the trailer with the Doberman tied to a nearby post didn't improve her mood, especially when the dog barked at her and went on barking until she disappeared into the house. There, Corrigan and his architect pored over a mass of papers and plot maps, spread unceremoniously over the mahogany table in the dining room.

"You're back." Corrigan regarded her from behind his glasses, perched halfway down his Roman nose. "I hope you had a nice lunch. While you were out, the town clerk called to tell me I need a permit for the trailer I brought onto the property. I guess someone who saw the trailer going to this address must have reported it." He paused and looked at her, as if he expected her to admit she was that person. When she didn't, he said, "It's a bit of a nuisance, but easily taken care of. I sent Steve down to the clerk's office for the application, and now I have it." He smiled and waved a sheet at her.

"Good," Kathryn said with a faux cheerfulness that matched his. She turned to go, but Corrigan called her back. "Oh, and Kathryn, I forgot to mention I'll be using the internet and the phone a lot. Because of this damn dial-up system, combined with the lack of a cell phone signal, you won't be able to make a call or get on the internet while I'm here. You don't mind, do you?" Before she could answer, he said, "I knew you wouldn't. After all, when I'm over at Maxine's or down in the city, you can use the phone and internet to your heart's content."

"Of course," she replied with just enough phony politeness to let him know she was on to his game.

Thank heaven, he's finally leaving. From the window in the red room that had been Diana Farley's study, Kathryn watched Corrigan's Porsche disappear down the driveway. She'd spent the last hour stewing over the fact that his presence in the house prevented her from continuing her search of the attic. She'd considered going up there, while he was either on the phone or using the internet, and had even checked the phone for a busy signal several times. But each time the fear of discovery stopped her. If he heard her rummaging around, he'd want to know what she was doing, rooting among the previous owners' possessions.

In case Corrigan returned suddenly and unexpectedly, Kathryn waited a full fifteen minutes after his departure before climbing the ladder into the attic. Where to begin? The last time, she'd started with the boxes and file drawers closest to the ladder, but couldn't recall exactly which ones she'd searched. How stupid of her. As a curator, she knew the importance of being methodical, yet she'd approached the task in a careless manner. That was about to change.

In the study, she raided the stash of office supplies in her laptop case. Armed with marker pens, a notebook, and a pad of Post-its, she climbed back into the attic. The contents of the first box she checked were familiar to her from yesterday's work. But just to be on the safe side, she went through it again, made a note of what it contained, and left a Post-it to show she'd dealt with it.

Kathryn proceeded in this fashion through the boxes she'd checked the previous day, before moving on to ones that were unfamiliar. Now that she had a system, she felt confident that she would find the codicil or second will if, in fact, it existed and was here. The knowledge that Diana had mentioned to two people her desire to leave part of the property to the land trust gave her more reason to believe it did. Still, the task was daunting. The attic was a huge space, extending over the attached two-car garage, as well as the house. And it was crammed with stuff.

A faint ringing sound made her pause. The phone? She put down the papers she'd been sifting through to listen. Yes. Whoever it was would have to leave a message. But maybe not. A glance at her watch showed her it was six-thirty. Oops. She was supposed to have dinner with Earl and his son Pete at the family house tonight. Now, she was a half hour late. She'd just made what promised to be an awkward evening worse.

Chapter 18

Kathryn made a quick call to Earl to apologize for being late and let him know she was on her way. As she drove down the driveway toward the trailer, the Doberman started barking again. When she was almost abreast of the dog and trailer, another car turned into the driveway. Maxine parked her Toyota on the grass near the trailer and walked over to the dog. She must have spoken in a calming manner, because the barking stopped. Kathryn drove the short distance to where Maxine stood, now holding a large, foil-wrapped dish she'd retrieved from her car.

Rolling down her window, Kathryn said, "What's that—dinner for the dog?"

"Un-uh, though I did bring some treats for Solly. This lasagna is for her owner. These sweet country boys have big appetites, you know."

"Sweet country boys? Really?" Both women laughed. Kathryn wouldn't be at all surprised if Maxine was setting her cap for the security guard. As she drove up the hill to where two *real* country boys awaited her, she almost envied Maxine. Maxine was poised at the beginning of a relationship, where everything was fresh and new, while she was in the midst of one beset with difficulties and complications.

Kathryn steeled herself for the evening in the family house. It was, after all, the home Earl had built for his ex-wife Millie. While she was alive, it had been very much her domain. Now, six months after Millie's violent death in a failed attempt to murder her, Kathryn worried the house would contain painful reminders. She also fretted about how things would go with Pete. He'd been her friend in the beginning, but over time their relationship had become strained. Much as she wished they could get back on their old footing, that had yet to happen. She hoped tonight's dinner, their first together at the family house, would be a step in the right direction.

As her destination came into view, Kathryn was struck again by how much the house, painted white with green shutters and door and set on a square of manicured lawn, seemed at odds with its surroundings—a slice of suburbia plopped down on the wild back side of Rattlesnake Hill. On the outside at least, the house showed no signs of change now that Millie was gone. The twin planters on either side of the front door still held flowers, though last autumn's mums had given way to pink and purple petunias. On closer inspection, some of the blossoms had withered and needed to be dead-headed, something Millie with her penchant for neatness and order would have done immediately.

Kathryn had just stooped to snap off the dead flowers when Earl strode toward her from behind the house. "You're finally here. What happened?"

She rose awkwardly to face him, feeling guilty he'd caught her doing something he might view as an intrusion. "It's a long story."

"Then I guess it will have to wait. Pete and I are starving. If I leave the chicken on the grill any longer, it won't be fit to eat."

She followed him to the back, where there was a brick patio with a grill, a metal table and chairs, and a couple of lounge chairs. Pete sprawled in one of them, eyes unfocused, and head bobbing to the beat of music coming from his earbuds. When Earl tapped him on the shoulder, he raised a hand in greeting. Earl tapped Pete again, and he removed his earbuds and said, "Hey, Kathryn."

"Hey, yourself. What're you listening to?"

He named a band.

"I'm not familiar with that one, but I noticed that Weird Grapefruit will be playing at the Paradise Rock Club later this summer. I can get tickets, if you'd like."

"I'm not into Weird Grapefruit anymore. In fact, I hate them."

His refusal surprised her. Was he just being a teenager, or was something else going on?

Earl broke the uncomfortable silence. "How about getting the salads from the kitchen, Pete?"

Pete stalked to the back door. "I'll help," Kathryn said. She started to follow Pete, but Earl put a hand on her shoulder. "Let him go. He'll come around. It just takes time."

They helped themselves to green and potato salads and barbecued chicken, which was tangy, but as Earl had predicted, on the dry side. "This potato salad is delicious," Kathryn said. "The fresh dill really makes a difference."

"I used Mom's recipe. She was a good cook," Pete said.

"Yes," Kathryn agreed.

Earl cleared his throat. "From what I heard at the general store, you had quite a bit of activity at the Farley place this morning."

She regaled them with what she hoped was a humorous account of the unexpected arrival of the delivery man with a trailer in tow, and the difficulties involved in positioning the trailer exactly where Corrigan wanted it.

"Who did you say will be living in that trailer?" Pete asked when she finished.

"Corrigan's security guard and his Doberman. They moved in today. So, there's a lot of barking whenever anyone comes or goes."

"That doesn't sound fun," Pete said. "Where's Corrigan staying?"

"He's set up an office on the ground floor of the house, but spends his nights at Maxine's."

"He's there during the day?" Pete asked.

"Right."

"That doesn't sound fun either. None of it sounds fun."

"It's not the best set-up, but I don't plan on hanging around the house all day myself. Today, for example, I went into Great Barrington to have lunch with a friend, and afterward I visited Emily."

"How she's doing?" Earl asked.

"More or less the same, although I tried something new." She told them about playing the tapes of Emily's recollections in the hopes that the old woman might respond to the sound of familiar voices.

"Did she?"

"No, but I'm going to keep trying. And listening to the tapes today, I learned some interesting stuff about Tim Waite's grandmother."

"She's a witch!" Pete exclaimed. "Creeps me out whenever—"

"Now, Pete," Earl interjected.

"C'mon, Dad, you gotta admit she has this way of looking at people, you just know she's putting a curse on 'em."

Earl chuckled. "You have a point. That woman isn't someone I'd ever want to get on the wrong side of."

The conversation moved easily to other people they knew and either liked or didn't, and both Pete and his dad seemed more relaxed. With the focus off her, Kathryn relaxed, too.

After dessert—strawberry shortcake with vanilla ice cream—Pete said he was going inside. As he left, he snagged a couple chicken legs that remained on the platter and wrapped them in a napkin.

"Eat those in the kitchen, not your room," Earl said.

Pete opened his mouth to protest, but Earl stopped him. "Mom's rules, remember." Pete made a face but didn't argue. To Kathryn, he said, "Stay out of trouble."

"What did he mean by that?" Kathryn asked after Pete was gone.

Earl regarded her thoughtfully. "He might've felt awkward, didn't know what to say, and that's what came out. Or he really thinks you could be in for trouble, if you're not careful."

"Why?"

Earl leaned toward her, his expression, serious. "You think staying at the house, with Corrigan there during the day and his security guard and an attack dog on the premises 24/7, isn't asking for trouble?"

"Speak for yourself," Kathryn flared.

"What're you talking about?"

The edge in his voice made her hesitate. But having come this far, she wouldn't back down. "Randy Plungas. You think letting a guy roam free after he might've been the one who shot at you and Corrigan in the woods, and then attacked his son in the library, isn't dangerous?"

Earl's eyes blazed. "Why do you—"

"What's going on?" Without realizing it, they'd raised their voices. Pete stared at them from behind the screen door.

"Nothing," Earl said quickly. "Star and I just got a little excited."
Pete waved a chicken leg at them and departed.

Poor kid. How many times had Pete heard his mom and dad arguing, then his dad and Diana, and now his dad and her? Her own father absent for most of her life, she'd been spared the marital discord that otherwise might have occurred. But her grandmother had more than made up for it with her constant carping at her mother for marrying a man who'd soon abandoned her and gone on to marry several more times.

"Let's go to the truck, where we can finish this without Pete eavesdropping," Earl said.

Inside the truck with the windows rolled up for extra privacy, he said, "Why do you think Randy was the shooter?"

"Gwen suggested he might be. Then I found a piece of paint-spattered denim in the pocket of your jeans. Why didn't you tell the Chief? Or me?"

Earl gave her an anguished look. "I didn't want either of you to get involved. The Chief especially. Then, he might have to take Randy into custody, Corrigan would find out, and things would get ugly."

"They're ugly now."

"I don't want to give Corrigan any reason to go after Randy."

"What's to stop Plungas from doing something else to provoke Corrigan?"

"I hope that with the serious talking-to I gave Randy, he'll quit. We've got family connections, and I felt I owed it to those folks to protect Randy from himself."

"What about protecting Robert from his dad?"

"I cornered Randy, as he was leaving the police station today. Warned him that if he beat up on Robert again, I'd turn him over to the Chief for the shooting."

"What did he say to that?"

"Started to go into another of his rants against 'New Yawkers,' but I got in his face. Told him I didn't like Corrigan either, but there were other ways to deal with him besides violence. And if he was fool enough to attack Corrigan again, he'd land in jail. Or worse."

"Do you think he heard you?"
"I hope to god he did."

*****

The barking started as soon as Kathryn turned into the Farley driveway. As she approached the trailer, Steve Reikart came out, hefting a rifle in one hand and a flashlight in the other. After shining the flashlight on her car, he spoke to the dog, waved her through and went back inside. Maxine's car was still parked near the trailer.

Kathryn felt Corrigan's presence the minute she stepped inside the house. She was aware of him in the mess of papers on the dining room table; the rumpled cushions on the living room couch; and the bottle of rubbing alcohol by the phone in the kitchen that he'd used to sterilize the handset, which had a strong astringent smell. Apparently, he had a thing about germs. But not *his* germs. He'd left the seat up and the toilet unflushed in the downstairs bathroom.

She flushed the toilet and opened the downstairs windows to let in fresh air. But she could still smell him in the room. The peculiar miasma he generated seemed to cling to her clothes. She wrenched open the heavy glass door to the patio, and stepped outside. Unfortunately, the racket made in opening and closing the door set the Doberman barking again.

Kathryn covered her ears with her hands. Reikart emerged from the trailer and trained a light on the house. She strode to the edge of the patio, where Reikart could see her, and waved. He waved back and the barking stopped.

The noise was gone, but it was soon replaced by a sense of being in a state of siege. Although free to come and go, her movements were monitored during the day by Corrigan and at night by Reikart. There was no place inside or out, where she felt entirely comfortable.

Am I crazy to remain here? Kathryn sank into an Adirondack chair, as she grappled with this question. She gazed at the pond, where the reflections of the trees were visible in the moonlight. The surface was calm, but then, as had happened a few nights ago, a breeze rippled the water, and the tree reflections seemed to reach toward her.

She had her answer. Corrigan might be the legal owner of the property, but as its self-appointed guardian, she vowed to protect it from him as long as she could. She would stay.

Chapter 19

Kathryn had set her alarm for eight AM and gone to bed, assuming Corrigan would sleep late and have a leisurely breakfast before coming to the house. That should give her time to use the phone and internet, and continue her search of the attic before he showed up. She was wrong. He was already bumping around downstairs when her alarm woke her.

Damn the man. He seemed bent on making things difficult for her. She wouldn't give him that satisfaction. She'd slip out of the house before he realized she was gone. Throwing on clothes, she tiptoed down the stairs barefoot, tote bag slung over her shoulder, sandals and cassette player in hand.

Wood creaked underfoot. Corrigan's voice reached her: "Good morning. I thought you'd never get up. But that's what burning the midnight oil will do." He rose from the living room couch and approached her.

"Midnight oil?" Kathryn stared at him blankly, then it hit her. She must have forgotten to turn off the attic light last night, and Reikart had told him about it. She tensed, half expecting Corrigan to ask what she'd been doing up there. Instead, he said, "Whatever kept you up so late, I hope it was fun."

"Great fun," she fibbed.

"Good. I'd hate to think my presence in the house has put a damper on things for you."

"Not at all," she fibbed again. "I'll be on my way now."

She turned to go, but Corrigan wasn't finished. "I hope you're not going out just because I'm here."

"I have errands to do."

His gaze strayed from her face to the cassette player. "I didn't know they still made those things. If you don't mind my asking, what's it for?"

Kathryn did mind, but at least he'd asked a question she could answer truthfully. She'd toss him this one harmless bone, then she'd leave. "I'm visiting a friend in the hospital who's in a coma. I play her tapes of her recollections of the past. Hearing familiar voices is supposed to help coma patients regain consciousness."

"Why play tapes? Why not simply talk to her yourself?"

Kathryn hesitated a moment before replying. "I wasn't all that close to this person. So, I'm not sure how familiar my voice would be, while the voices on the tape—hers and that of a close friend—will be very familiar to her."

Corrigan rubbed his chin thoughtfully. "I wish I'd known about the familiar voice thing when a dear friend of mine was in a coma. I didn't know what to do and I felt helpless."

Kathryn stared at him with amazement. Did the tin man developer have a heart, after all? It appeared so. "Was this dear friend of yours Gwen?" she asked.

Corrigan's eyes narrowed. "Why do you think that?"

"I know she was in a coma, and I know you were friends."

Corrigan seemed ready to end the conversation there, but it was Kathryn's turn to detain him. "I understand why you felt helpless while Gwen was in a coma, but once she came out of it, you must have been pleased."

"Oh, I was," he assured her. "And now, it's wonderful to see her so happy, living here in the beautiful countryside with a fine husband and two lovely children."

His hyperbole rang hollow, but before she could pursue the matter further, Corrigan gestured toward the dining room. "Time for me to get to work. Good luck with the coma lady."

Eager to avoid Corrigan, Kathryn had skipped breakfast. She stopped at the New Nottingham General Store for coffee and a muffin. Charlotte Hinckley sat at a small table in the rear, poring over a fat binder, a half-empty mug of tea and a blueberry muffin beside her.

"Good morning, Kathryn." Charlotte greeted her with a big smile. "I was just thinking about you. If you have a minute, why don't you join me?"

After her tense encounter with Corrigan, Kathryn welcomed the company of such a cheerful and energetic person. "I'd love to," she said, sitting down at the table with her breakfast.

"How's the search going?" Charlotte asked.

"With Corrigan in the house during the day, I haven't made much progress. I'm afraid he'll hear me and come up to see what I'm doing. I have to wait until he leaves for the evening, or goes back to the city, as he said he might from time to time."

"Let me know if you need help."

"I will. You'll be happy to hear Corrigan seemed a bit bent when reminded he had to get a permit for the trailer," Kathryn said.

Charlotte smiled.

"What about the wetlands restrictions?" Kathryn asked.

"I was just looking at them." Charlotte patted the binder. "And my sense is there's enough red tape here to create problems for him. Big, expensive problems."

Kathryn grinned. "Great."

They chatted until Charlotte left to check on the workmen who were re-doing her kitchen and Kathryn, to continue on her errand to see Emily. Invigorated by the chance meeting, she stood for a moment outside the store, basking in the sunlight of another perfect June day. Across the street, the library was shuttered and so silent she had a hard time imagining yesterday's uproar had ever occurred. But even as she thought this, she remembered Plungas calling Gwen a whore, and felt the sting of his words, as if they had been directed at her.

Why attack Gwen like that? Just because she was a "New Yawker"? Kathryn suspected there was more to it. The name calling was both vicious and deeply personal, insinuating that Gwen was not the virtuous wife and mother she appeared to be, but a woman with loose morals. Robert had reacted by sinking his teeth into his dad's arm.

Was there any basis for the slur? Or did it stem from sheer malice on Plungas's part? She needed answers to these questions to better understand and, if necessary, defend her friend and role model. Kathryn used the general store landline to call Gwen at home.

"Hi, I thought I'd check in and see how you're doing after what happened at the library yesterday."

"I'm okay," Gwen said, but she didn't sound okay.

"Would you mind if I stopped by at some point?"

"No, and now's a good time. Scarlett's off at her waitressing job and Billy went to work with his dad. One thing, though. Please park a few doors down, and approach the house from the back, where I'll be waiting. Grandma Waite watches this place like a hawk, and if she sees you, she's bound to come over."

*****

Shuntoll Road, where Gwen lived, turned out to be filled with potholes. Kathryn narrowly escaped hitting one and risking a flat. She parked on the street as instructed, but felt odd walking through the neighbors' backyards, until she realized she was following a well-trodden path. A neighbor woman even smiled and waved at her. Obviously, she wasn't the first person who'd come the back way to evade Grandma Waite's watchful eyes.

Dressed in jeans and a tee shirt, Gwen perched in the swing of a child-sized wooden jungle gym. Flower pots filled with impatiens hung from the ladder and from both of the rings

"Thanks for coming around the back," Gwen said. "Do you think she saw you?"

"I couldn't tell."

"Right. I'm being paranoid. Have a seat." Gwen indicated a plastic lawn chair near the jungle gym. "Unless you'd like to swing?"

"No thanks. You've done of a nice job of decorating the jungle gym with flowers."

"I probably should have thrown it out, but I couldn't bear to. Tim built it when the kids were little, and they were so thrilled." Gwen's expression turned wistful. "I've kept the gym as a memento of those days. And I've always loved to swing. I find it relaxing."

Kathryn nodded, then got to the point. "That sure was an ugly scene at the library. Plungas not only roughed up his son, but he said awful things to you. Why does he dislike you so much? Is it because Robert would rather hang out at the library than be with his dad?"

Gwen began to move slowly back and forth. "Randy's always hated me."

"Why?"

"I told you how people in town were against me, because I was a 'New Yawker.' Randy was the worst. He thought if I married Tim, he'd be losing his best buddy. Randy was having a tough time. He and Suzy had just divorced and—"

Kathryn's brows knitted. "The Suzy who's married to Earl's middle brother, Wayne?"

"The same. All this happened years ago. Randy was a senior in high school, Suzy a junior. They were hot for each other, she got pregnant, and she and Randy eloped. Her parents were furious. They wanted to have the marriage annulled, but Suzy refused. She lived with Randy and his parents for a while, then the two of them moved into a cabin Randy built in the woods. By that time, she was beginning to realize she'd made a mistake, but was too stubborn to admit it. She went ahead and had the baby, a boy. She and Randy struggled on for a couple years, until Suzy decided she'd had enough of her husband's drinking and bullying. She filed for divorce, and she and the child moved back in with her parents. They took care of him while Suzy finished high school and started taking courses at Berkshire Community College. When she got her degree, her parents threw a party for her. That's where she met Wayne."

Kathryn could understand why Wayne, a gentle, quiet man, would be attractive to Suzy after what she'd been through with Plungas. "What happened to the child Suzy and Plungas had together?"

"Suzy'd been granted full custody, so when she and Wayne married, he lived with them. But when she and Wayne had two boys of their own, Randy sued for full custody. He'd never liked it that *his* son was being raised by *another* man, especially one he considered a wuss. He must have gotten himself a darn good lawyer, because the lawyer was able to persuade the judge to give Randy joint custody."

Kathryn did some quick math in her head. "The boy is… Robert?"

"Yes."

The revelation left Kathryn speechless. Having grown up with few strong familial bonds, and a loner by nature, she marveled at the complicated web of connections that existed among the people in this town. Now, she understood why Earl, for whom family ties meant a great deal, would want to protect both his sister-in-law's ex and her son.

"That explains some things," she said, "but not why Plungas was so rude and disrespectful toward you yesterday."

Gwen began to swing faster. "I'm Suzy's friend. She encouraged Robert to work at the library to get away from his dad. As far as Randy's concerned, anything or anyone connected with Suzy is bad."

"I understand but…" Kathryn hesitated, aware she was treading into deeper water and needed to frame her next question with care. "That name he called you—do you think that's how Randy sees all women, or…?"

Gwen's expression turned somber. She stopped swinging. "Randy's a misogynist to the core. And he loves insulting people."

"It certainly seems that way," Kathryn agreed, though she wasn't entirely satisfied with Gwen's answer.

Gwen glanced at her watch. "I've got to get a move on. The library doesn't open for another hour, but I'm still behind and need to get some things done before I'm busy with patrons. Time certainly flies."

Gwen didn't add, "when you're having fun." Kathryn wasn't surprised.

On her way through the first neighbor's yard, Kathryn stopped for a minute and looked back. Gwen had begun to swing in earnest. Her legs plowed the air, and her head was titled upward toward the sun, her blonde hair loose and streaming behind her. Higher and higher she went, soaring into space like a female Icarus bent on reaching the ball of fire in the sky.

Kathryn continued on to her car. She was about to open the car door when a hand closed around her wrist with the talon-like grip of a raptor seizing its prey. She twisted around to face Grandma Waite, dressed all in black. Shirley-Temple curls dyed jet black framed a face that bore the ravages of age and anger, but in which traces of the beauty she'd once been were still visible.

"Who are you and why did you come to visit my Gwen?" she demanded.

"I'm Kathryn Stinson, and I visited Gwen because we're friends."

"A good friend?"

"Pretty good."

"Then you must warn her about the man who came to the house in a fancy car a few days ago. He is evil, and she must keep Scarlett away from him, and stay away from him herself."

"I'll do that," Kathryn said.

Gwen hadn't been kidding about the old woman's insistence that Corrigan was evil, but why did Grandma Waite think that when she'd only glimpsed him from a distance? Kathryn considered questioning the old woman but, apparently pleased with her response, Grandma Waite had released her hold on Kathryn's wrist, and was already hurrying across the street with the vigor of a much younger woman.

As she drove toward Great Barrington, Kathryn made a mental note to let Gwen know her scheme of having people park several doors down and approach the house from the rear wasn't working.

*****

Emily looked as she always did: an old woman tethered to life by an octopus of tubes. Kathryn put on a tape, and voices replaced the low hum of machines. How refreshing to listen to two people who had obviously been fond of each other. The affection in their voices was so palpable that Kathryn almost felt some of it might rub off on her. If Diana had lived longer, maybe they would have been friends. She and Emily might have been friends, too, if circumstances had been different.

Lulled by the pleasant sounds, Kathryn let her eyelids flutter, then close. She'd been up late and had arisen early. She'd just doze for a few minutes.

She awoke with a start to Emily's voice saying something about black sheep. Kathryn rewound the tape to get the full conversation.

"Seems like every family around here has its black sheep," Emily said. *"For the Barkers, it's Earl's youngest brother, Garth, and for the Plungas family, it's Randy."*

"I know about Garth, but what's the deal with Randy Plungas?" Diana asked.

"He gave his wife Suzy a hard time, but at least she had the sense to divorce him and marry a good man in Wayne Barker."

"Wayne's a good guy alright. Kinda shy, but definitely a good guy."

"And now Randy's trying to keep his friend Tim Waite from marrying that girl from New York. As far as I can tell, she's a perfectly nice young woman. A looker, too, with that long blonde hair. But that hasn't stopped Randy from spreading ugly rumors about her. Like that nonsense about Grant's Tomb."

"Grant's Tomb? What's that about?"

"It has to do with... Damnation! I can't remember the details now."

"It'll come to you eventually."

"I don't want to wait. I want it to come to me this very minute! I hate getting old!"

Gwen and Grant's Tomb? This sounded like a specific incident that had occurred while Gwen lived in New York. And rumor or not, Kathryn suspected it might be related to Randy calling Gwen a whore. Which made her all the more eager for Emily to remember the story. But after listening to more of the tape, she realized Emily hadn't—at least not on this particular tape.

Still, she knew someone other than Gwen she could ask.

Chapter 20

In the late afternoon, Kathryn headed home after visiting Emily, having lunch in Great Barrington, and doing some errands. She could have lunched at the Farley house, but even the thought of eating anywhere near Corrigan took her appetite away.

Reikart sat on a camp chair in front of the trailer. A straw hat shaded his eyes, and he was whittling a piece of wood. The sight of him reminded Kathryn of a favorite Winslow Homer painting. Titled "Boys in a Pasture," it showed two young boys lounging in the grass on a summer day. If she were to give a title to the picture Reikart presented, it would be "Man Whittling in a Field." She stopped the car and called out to him, "What're you making?"

He smiled and shook his head. "Dunno yet."

She glanced around. "Where's Solly?"

"Pulled free of her rope and disappeared. If she doesn't return before dark, I'm going in there to look for her." He gestured toward the woods.

Inside the house, Kathryn was relieved to find Corrigan gone. The dining room table was free of the papers that had been strewn there, with the exception of the trailer permit form, which had yet to be filled out. He was either at Maxine's or he'd departed for the city, as he'd said he might at some point. She welcomed the quiet that came with both the dog's absence and his.

Now that she could use the internet, Kathryn dealt with some work-related e-mails and looked up Grant's Tomb. She learned some interesting facts about the tomb, like how it came to be located in Upper Manhattan near Columbia University, but nothing that connected it with Gwen. When she finished, it was five-thirty, and she was supposed to meet Earl and Pete at six for drinks and dinner at The White Stag. She'd forgotten what a time waste the internet could be. She'd have to postpone her attic search until she returned. As she drove out the driveway, she saw that both the dog and owner were gone. Reikart must have begun his search.

*****

Kathryn pulled into the parking lot of the squat one-story building with a broken neon sign identifying it as "Th Whit tag." The last time she'd been to the roadhouse, she slow-danced with Earl to the Elvis song, "Can't Help Falling in Love," their bodies pressed so close that even now the memory of that clinch sent a flush of pleasure through her.

The bar was named for a legendary creature no one had seen— until she did, not once but twice. Earl's brother, Garth, a crazed hunter, had tried to kill the white stag, but failed miserably. She wondered if it still roamed the woods around the Farley house. If so, it would be one more piece of wild nature to either fall victim to Corrigan's bulldozers or be driven away. The loss of this beautiful, near-magical beast struck her as unbearably sad.

On earlier visits, Kathryn had found the bar tawdry with sinister undertones. It still appeared tawdry, but now with a touch of whimsy. It was definitely unique. Where else could you find a chandelier consisting of a large, metal animal trap attached to the ceiling by tire chains, with Christmas tree lights that flashed off and on, red, green, yellow, and blue? And where else would the owner of the general store, who calmly dispensed terrible coffee by day, pour beer on tap by night? From behind the bar, Lucas Rogers pointed to a table in the back, where she spotted Earl and Pete.

Earl rose and greeted her with a high-wattage smile. Pete remained seated, his smile both low-wattage and brief, gone immediately after it appeared, like a bulb that's suddenly lost its juice. Kathryn had hoped things would go better with Pete if they met on neutral ground, but now she wasn't so sure.

"We've already ordered. What would you like?" Earl pulled out a chair for her.

"A burger and a beer." Then with a mischievous glint in her eyes, she added, "And don't try to trick me like you did my friend Alan."

Pete stared at her, puzzled. "Huh?"

"Star's referring to a little incident that happened with her ex-boyfriend."

At the mention of an ex-boyfriend, Pete seemed to perk up. Hoping she'd go back to him?

"I brought two beers I thought were screw-tops," Earl said. "Then I challenged him to a demonstration of how guys like us—"

"You gave him the bottle that wasn't twist-off, didn't you?" Pete interrupted, "And when he tried to bite it off, he cut himself."

"How'd you know?" Earl asked.

"That's exactly the kind of thing you'd do." Pete shook his head with mock disapproval. "Mom always said part of your brain stayed stuck in high school. She was right."

"Hear, hear," Kathryn chimed in. She grinned at Pete, and this time got more than a ghost of a smile.

"Why do I get the sense you two are ganging up on me?" Earl pretended to be upset, but Kathryn suspected he was pleased she and Pete agreed about something, even though it was at his expense. Changing the subject, he said, "How was your day, Star?"

She told them about the visits to Gwen and Emily—leaving out mention of her strange encounter with Corrigan, and what she'd learned about Plungas from the two women. Those things would have to wait until she and Earl could speak privately. Her chance came when Pete excused himself to go to the men's room. She leaned close to Earl and spoke in a whisper. "Until Gwen mentioned it, I didn't realize Suzy was married to Plungas before Wayne, or that Robert is Suzy's and Plungas's son. Now I understand why you wanted to protect Plungas and Robert."

"I probably should've told you myself," Earl said with a pained look, "but at least you know now."

"There's more. On a tape, Emily said Plungas spread stories about Gwen to try to prevent Tim from marrying her. She mentioned some nonsense related to Grant's Tomb, but couldn't remember the details. Do you know what that was about?"

The French fry Earl had been about to pop into his mouth remained suspended in mid-air. When he finally spoke, all the jokiness was gone from his voice. "Gwen's your friend. If she wanted to share that with you, she would have."

"She hasn't, and I don't want to play The Grand Inquisitor," Kathryn said.

"Dostoyevsky, right?"

"How did you know?"

"Even country bumpkins like me read a book every now and then," Earl said.

"I didn't mean to suggest—never mind. Will you tell me about Gwen and Grant's Tomb?"

"Why do you want to know?" His blue eyes bore into her.

"Yesterday at the library, Plungas called Gwen a whore. Was he just being nasty, or does it have to do with something that may or may not have happened at Grant's Tomb? Could you please—"

"Not now." Earl jerked his head toward the men's room, where Pete had reappeared.

"When?"

"I'll find a time."

Chapter 21

When Kathryn returned to the Farley house later that evening, Reikart and the dog had not returned. Now was the perfect time for her and Charlotte to search the attic together. She hurried to the phone.

"I'll be right over," Charlotte said. Anyone hearing them might have thought they were two giddy girls planning a secret adventure.

Kathryn waited for Charlotte in the parking area. Her friend arrived and Kathryn started to usher her into the house when shots rang out in the woods. Her heart lurched. *Not again.* At least this time Earl couldn't be the target. He and Pete must be safely back at home by now.

She and Charlotte squinted into the long summer twilight, but the wall of darkening trees remained impenetrable. Impenetrable but not silent. The noise of something crashing through the brush followed the shots. The crashing rose to a crescendo, then abruptly ended. A hush fell over the woods. Moments later, a horrible howl broke the silence. In the depths of the forest, the trees and every living creature seemed to cry out in agony, as if some terrible desecration had been committed.

Instinctively, Kathryn and Charlotte drew back. Then Charlotte took off across the field toward the woods. Kathryn ran after her. She caught up with Charlotte at the start of Gordon's road. "Don't go in there, it's too dangerous!" she said, grabbing Charlotte by the arm.

"You stay here. Something or someone's been hurt. They need help." In the fading light, Charlotte's face was grim and determined. Breaking free of Kathryn's grip, she plunged into the woods. Kathryn didn't want to follow her, but felt compelled to, as if Charlotte was a magnet, pulling her deeper and deeper into the forest, over trees lying across Gordon's road, and through brush that tore at her clothes.

On and on she went, sometimes glimpsing Charlotte ahead of her, sometimes not. Kathryn kept going until she caught up with Charlotte at the end of Gordon's road. Below them in the gully, a man struggled to carry an animal almost as big as he was. The man came to a halt on the far side of the brook. His head bent over his burden, he looked like he was having a hard time staying on his feet. When he glanced up and saw them, he cried, "Help me, you gotta help me. Solly's been shot."

Charlotte raced down the bank of the gully, splashed through the brook, and was at Reikart's side in a flash. Kathryn followed more cautiously. When she arrived at the other side of the brook, Charlotte was already questioning him. "Where was the dog hit? How badly?"

"Hind quarters... bleeding somethin' fierce." Reikart gasped for breath.

The Doberman's eyes were closed. Its body hung limp, a deadweight in Reikart's arms. Dark spreading stains covered the makeshift bandage he'd wrapped around the animal. Reikart was bloodied himself. "Don't think I can..." he mumbled, swaying precariously.

The magnitude of the situation overwhelmed Kathryn. They were stuck in the woods with a dog that might die if they didn't get her out soon, but she hadn't a clue how they would do this. Reikart was on his last legs, Charlotte, while strong, might not have the necessary endurance, and she was almost certain she could barely lift the dog, let alone carry her.

Charlotte took charge. Placing a steadying hand on Reikart, she said, "I'm going to take the dog from you and lay her down." When Solly had been eased gently to the ground, Charlotte asked Reikart if he had a crate. After he said no, she turned to Kathryn. "Run to house and get a blanket for us to use as a stretcher and a couple of towels. While you're there, call this number." Charlotte pulled a scrap of paper from her pocket and wrote on it. "Use my name and ask Dr. Dinaldi to meet us at the veterinary hospital in Great Barrington."

She glanced at the luminous face of her watch. "In approximately forty-five minutes. We'll be bringing a wounded dog that needs emergency attention."

Chapter 22

In the waiting room of the veterinary hospital, Reikart paced in front of the closed door of the OR, where Dr. Dinaldi, with Charlotte's assistance, operated on Solly. Kathryn was thankful Charlotte had known exactly what to do, and that her plan for getting the dog out of the woods and to the hospital had succeeded. Obviously, Charlotte's experience in dealing with animals in Madagascar had stood her in good stead. It also helped that Dinaldi was a friend of hers. Now, all they could do was wait and hope.

But waiting wasn't easy for Reikart. Back and forth he went, his boots squeaking on the well-polished linoleum, until Kathryn became almost dizzy following his movements. To distract herself, she picked up a magazine,

"How long do you think this's gonna take?" Reikart stood over her.

"I don't know, except that it's got to be a while longer. They've only been in there about ten minutes."

"Feels like forever... You don't think they'd—" He broke off with a worried look.

"What?" Kathryn prodded.

"They'd see she was dying, but not tell me."

"Of course, not. They know you're concerned about her, and I'm sure they'll give you an update as soon as they can."

"But what if Solly goes so fast, there isn't time to get me?"

"I don't—"

Before she could finish the sentence, Reikart strode determinedly toward the OR door. "I'm going in there—now!"

"No." Kathryn leapt from her seat and got between him and the door. "You'll cause a disturbance that could be harmful to your dog. Come sit down," she finished in an authoritative voice worthy of Charlotte.

Reluctantly, Reikart returned to the seating area. He perched on the edge of a chair with his eyes trained on the OR door. To prevent him from making another run for it, she'd try to engage him in conversation. No easy task, since she'd barely spoken with him previously, and knew him only as the security guard for a man she disliked.

"So, what exactly happened in the woods tonight?" Kathryn asked. "I was so busy getting the supplies Charlotte wanted and then clearing the way for you two to carry Solly out, I never got the whole story."

Reikart turned to her. Gone was the grinning, confident man Maxine had made a play for. His eyes were red-rimmed, his chin, stubbled and he appeared jittery, as if he were still in the woods, the prey of unseen predators. "I went in there to search for her, but this area is so new to me that I soon got lost. I called and called, but no Solly. It was starting to get dark, and I didn't bring a flashlight. I thought I'd never make it outta there, let alone find her. Then I heard a faint barking in the distance. It seemed to be coming from behind me. I headed in that direction. I hadn't gone far when I heard shots. I ran toward noise. That's when I saw Solly—all bloody and dragging her hind quarters to reach me."

"Charlotte and I heard an awful howl. Was that… you?"

"Yeah."

"I'm really sorry your dog was hurt," Kathryn said. And she meant it.

"Thanks." His eyes narrowed and he said, "You got any idea who mighta done this?"

The question put Kathryn on her guard. "I don't go into the woods much myself, but I've heard hunters often do, even off-season. When I had a cat here last fall, I worried he'd get out and be hit."

"The cat was a pet?" he asked with apparent interest.

"No, I was just taking care of it for a friend while she was travelling. I've never had pets of my own," she added unnecessarily.

"Really? How come?" He looked at her as if she were a freak.

"My mother was ill most of the time I was growing up. My grandmother who took care of both of us said a pet would mean extra work for her. When I brought home a goldfish I'd won at a school fair, she flushed it down the toilet." She hadn't meant to tell him anything personal, but the words just came out.

"That's terrible. When I was growing up on a farm in Arkansas, we had all kinds of animals—dogs, cats, chickens, pigs, goats, cows and horses. I thought everyone lived like that. After I left home, I always had a dog. And of all the dogs I've had, Solstice is my favorite." He grew more and more animated as he spoke. "She was trained to be a guard dog. That's her job and she does it the best she can. But her bark is worse than her bite. If you knew her like I do, you'd know that she's got the sweetest disposition ever. Loves to jump up and lick my face and curl up on the couch with her head on my lap. This *never* should've happened."

Reikart withdrew into angry, brooding silence until the OR door finally opened and Charlotte stepped out with a big smile on her face. "Dr. Dinaldi's finishing up in there, but I wanted to let you know Solly's going to make it."

"Thank god." He rushed toward Charlotte. "Can I see her?"

"Not yet. She's still under anesthesia." Charlotte's face clouded over. "Before you do, you should know that her left hind leg was so badly damaged, it had to be amputated."

Reikart shut his eyes and gritted his teeth. "No." That single word contained so much pain he might as well have been told his own leg had been amputated.

"It'll be hard at first," Charlotte said, "but with therapy, she'll learn to manage. I've known plenty of animals that have gotten along fine on three legs."

"Yeah... sure," Reikart said without conviction. He was quiet for a few moments, then he muttered something. Kathryn couldn't make out the words, but Charlotte looked alarmed.

Chapter 23

The next morning, Corrigan showed up with another man, accompanied by a yappy brown terrier. So much for Kathryn's hopes he'd left for the city and would be gone a while.

"This is Gene Herrick," he said. "He's going to be filling in for Steve Reikart. I'm letting Steve take a few days off so he can be with his wounded dog at the hospital."

"And this is Skipper." Herrick introduced the dog, which responded with a volley of barks.

Gray-haired with a red face and a barrel chest, Herrick looked familiar. He cocked his head and squinted at her. "Aren't you the lady that was searching for a box of old letters?"

"Yes, and you kindly found it for me at the Whittemore house."

"How nice you already know each other," Corrigan said. "You might want to get settled in the trailer now, Gene. I know you're busy, Kathryn, so we won't keep you." He clapped his hands like an impresario ordering them off stage.

Upstairs in the study, Kathryn made her plans. She was anxious to resume the search for the second will, but Corrigan's presence made that difficult. Still, if he went out during the day, she might be able to steal an hour or more, then in the evening she'd try to enlist Charlotte's help.

It was another beautiful day, and since she couldn't use the phone or internet with Corrigan in the house, she decided to walk up Rattlesnake Hill to a hot spot, where she could get cell phone reception and call Charlotte. As she approached the old Whittemore mansion at the crest of the hill, she saw signs of activity. The tall wrought iron gates were open, and a truck drove in. Perhaps the current owners, whom she'd never met, had returned from their winter home in Arizona.

A short distance beyond the Whittemore mansion, she found the hot spot, called Charlotte, and left a voicemail. Her new friend might be at the general store having breakfast. She'd continue a little farther, and try Charlotte again on her way back down the hill. As she approached the trailer where Earl had lived after he and his wife split, she was surprised to see him emerge from the woods behind the trailer, chain saw in hand.

"What're you doing here? I thought you were working down in Connecticut," she said.

"I am, but..." He stared guiltily at the ground, as if he'd been caught doing something he shouldn't have. "I left some equipment up there I needed to get." He gestured toward the hill that rose above the trailer. On it was a piece of land Earl's father had given them months ago to build a place of their own. Earl had begun clearing the property, but had abandoned the effort when Kathryn made it clear she wasn't ready to make that kind of commitment. Now, the property served as a reminder of everything that remained unresolved between them.

"Reikart's dog was shot in the woods last night," Kathryn said. "I'm worried Plungas might have done it."

Earl grimaced. "I'll talk to him, see what he says, maybe knock some sense into him. You want a ride down the hill?"

"No, thanks, I'll walk. See you and Pete at The Stag tonight."

*****

At exactly 12:30 PM, Corrigan left the Farley house in his Porsche. At her post in the study overlooking the driveway, Kathryn jotted down the time in a notebook she'd decided to keep. If she could find a pattern in his comings and goings, it would give her a leg up in the cat-and-mouse game they seemed to be playing. So far, his arrivals in the morning and departures in the evening had proved unpredictable, but if she could determine how long he was likely to go out for lunch, she could plan her searches of the attic accordingly.

On the off-chance Corrigan had ventured as far as Great Barrington, where they'd run into each other at lunchtime on Monday, Kathryn headed for the attic. She'd just yanked down the ladder when she heard a car pull into the driveway. Was he back already? She looked out the window and saw Earl's sister-in-law, Suzy Barker.

Considering what she knew now, Kathryn found it hard to square the vivacious redhead with the same person who, as a teenager, had been in an abusive marriage with Randy Plungas and was Robert's mother.

"Hi," Suzy greeted her. "I thought you might like some extra-large tomato plants for the garden, so I picked up several for you. They already have fruit on them. This way, you won't have to wait until July or even August for ripe tomatoes."

Kathryn thanked Suzy and helped her lug the pots from her car to the garden, where they planted them. They were hot and sweaty when they finished, so Kathryn invited Suzy in for a cool drink and a light lunch.

After they'd settled on the porch with sandwiches and iced tea, Suzy said, "I hear my ex made trouble at the library a few days ago."

"That's right."

Suzy put down her sandwich. "I'm worried about him."

"How come?"

"Randy's always been someone who enjoys provoking people. But living alone in that cabin in the woods, he's gotten worse. He feeds on all these crazy conspiracy theories. I'm afraid he's losing his grip on reality."

"Doesn't Robert live with him part of the time?"

"Yeah, but Robert can't stand up to Randy. He's too afraid of him. I've tried to get Randy to mend his ways. So has Earl. It works for a while, but then he goes and does something really stupid." She frowned into space. "You know what he needs?"

Kathryn shook her head.

"A good woman, but she's gotta be big and strong and tough as nails. Like Wonder Woman. When Randy starts acting up, she beats him down, and she keeps doing that until he finally gets the message." Her face glowing with the vision, Suzy shadow-boxed the air. Turning serious, she said, "One day, Randy will go too far, and then... I don't even want to think about what might happen."

Suzy's Wonder Woman performance struck Kathryn as both funny and sad. Sad because Suzy was obviously concerned about her ex, but having given up trying to reform him herself, she'd created a fantasy woman who could do what she could not.

*****

Suzy had just left when Corrigan returned at one-thirty. Kathryn noted he'd been gone exactly one hour. Not enough time to get to Great Barrington, have lunch at a nice restaurant, and get back. Maybe he ate fast-food or pigged out at Maxine's. She'd have to wait a few days before she could tell if there was a pattern to his afternoon outings.

*****

Corrigan was gone and Kathryn was getting ready to meet Earl and Pete at The Stag when she finally heard from Charlotte. "Sorry I didn't return your call sooner, but it's been crazy here at the hospital."

"What hospital? What happened?"

"The veterinary hospital. I'm here because of Steve."

"Steve?"

"Steve Reikart. The man whose dog was shot last night," Charlotte said.

"Yes, of course."

"He showed up at the hospital early this morning, banging on the door and demanding to be let in. Made such a ruckus the neighbors called the police. They contacted Dr. Dinaldi. He came, let Steve in, and got him to calm down. Then he called me, and I went to the hospital. Steve was determined to remain here with Solstice, and Dinaldi agreed to let him, provided I stayed and looked after him."

"So, you've been babysitting him all day?"

"If you want to call it that. Steve did several tours in Afghanistan

95

and Iraq, and Dr. Dinaldi, who's a veteran himself, thinks Solstice getting shot in the woods may have triggered an attack of PTSD."

"Shouldn't he be getting psychiatric care then?"

"It may come to that, but right now Steve's worried about losing his job with Corrigan if he appears too unstable. I spoke with Corrigan myself, explained what had happened, and got him to give Steve a few days off while his dog recovers. I also gave him Gene Herrick's name as someone who could fill in for Steve."

"How much longer do you think you'll be tied up at the hospital?"

"It all depends on Steve. I know you're concerned about finding the will, and I still plan on helping, but this comes first."

Kathryn was disappointed. She'd been counting on the fresh pair of eyes Charlotte would bring to the search. Now that wasn't going to happen—at least not right away. She wondered why Charlotte was doing so much for Reikart. Perhaps she sympathized with him as a fellow animal lover. Or maybe Dr. Dinaldi was such a good friend she wanted to help him by staying at the hospital with Reikart. Whatever the reason, she hoped Charlotte's being on good terms with Reikart would make him easier to deal with than his boss.

*****

Earl and Pete were at their usual table in the rear of The Stag when Kathryn arrived. As she passed the bar, Randy Plungas suddenly turned and leered at her. Stiffening, she looked away. Earl probably hadn't had an opportunity to speak with him yet, and she doubted he'd do so in such a public place. Still, Plungas's presence made her nervous. Maybe it was her imagination, but the roadhouse seemed unnaturally quiet—the quiet before the storm? She hoped not.

Joining Earl and Pete, she searched Earl's face for a clue about whether anything had happened between him and Plungas. His expression was guarded, signaling to her not to mention it in front of Pete. They ordered, and over dinner, talked about how their days had gone, but Kathryn couldn't relax with Plungas there. When the roadhouse door creaked open, she nearly jumped.

Tim Waite strode to the bar where Plungas sat. His eyes hard and determined, he looked like someone on a mission. Plungas turned to greet him. Before he could get a word out, Tim's fist slammed into his jaw so hard that Plungas fell off his stool. He landed on the ground, dazed and hurting. "What the—"

"That's for insulting my wife," Tim growled. Mission completed, he marched to the door, slamming it behind him.

Kathryn was shocked. The action revealed another side of Tim she hadn't known existed. He'd been verbally aggressive toward Corrigan at the party at Maxine's, but until now she'd never seen him resort to physical violence. Plungas had obviously crossed a line by calling Gwen a whore, and when Tim had found out about it—either from Gwen or someone else—he'd become enraged.

The whole scene reminded her of something out of a Wild West movie. Men in this far corner of Western Massachusetts didn't take it kindly when their women were maligned. She'd witnessed a similar fight between Gordon and Earl in this very bar several months ago. In that fight, Earl had been the aggressor in response to provocation from Gordon. Now, he was the one who went to Plungas's aid. He helped Plungas get up from the floor, then after the squeal of tires on the pavement outside announced Tim's departure, Earl propelled Plungas to the door and went out after him.

Minutes later, Earl returned without Plungas. "What was that all about?" Pete asked.

"Randy's been acting up again," Earl said, "and I felt Tim's message needed a little reinforcement."

Kathryn could only hope Plungas finally got it.

*****

She was glad to get home after dinner. The incident between Plungas and Tim had all but ruined the evening. She'd just started up the stairs, determined to finally tackle the attic, when someone knocked on the door. Now what? It couldn't be Corrigan, could it? Surely, he wouldn't show up this late in the evening.

Puzzled, she went to the door. Gene Herrick stood on the landing, holding a large cardboard box. "Sorry to bother you, Miss Stinson, but there's something I wanted to ask you. I think I remember you saying you work with old photographs and prints. If that's correct, I've got this box of old family photos I've been meaning to get organized for the longest time. My wife was gonna do it, but then she died and I don't even know where to begin. So, I was wondering if you could maybe spare a little time." He looked at her expectantly.

"Of course, I'm happy to help." If Herrick had asked her to go to the moon with him, she might have said yes. Right now, she welcomed the company of a man who wasn't angry or violent, but probably just lonely. Plus, she owed him. He'd done her a big favor by locating the box of her ancestor's letters last fall.

Chapter 24

At exactly 12:30 PM the following afternoon—the same time he'd left the previous day—Kathryn saw Corrigan zoom out of the parking area in his yellow Porsche. Going where? Was he simply a creature of habit, or did he have a regular appointment? On an impulse, she decided to follow him.

The trick was to stay far enough behind Corrigan lest he become suspicious, while still keeping him in sight. He headed toward the center of town, but the road was so winding and he was driving so fast that Kathryn soon lost him. He'd have to slow down in the village, which had a 20-mph speed limit. Yet when she got there, she saw no sign of his car. He must have sped right through. Why was he in such a hurry? Had he realized she was following him and decided to lose her? Or was he late for an appointment?

As she drove slowly through the village, Kathryn noticed Gwen's car in one of the library spaces. Apparently, Gwen was still behind in her work, because the library didn't open for another hour. Odd. She wouldn't have thought a small-town librarian would have so much to do.

A short distance beyond the village, the road forked. If Corrigan were going to Great Barrington, he'd have turned left; a right turn would take him to Maxine's. Kathryn decided to take the latter route. Although she didn't catch sight of Corrigan on the way to Maxine's, she figured she might as well keep going until she reached the house. She'd take a quick look in the parking area, then if his car was there, she'd have satisfied her curiosity; if not, she would've at least eliminated Maxine's as the place where he went.

From Lakeshore Drive, a driveway with a mailbox at the end led to the Kepler house. Kathryn was about to turn into the driveway when she saw Maxine walking toward her. Maxine waved, so Kathryn waited until she reached the car.

"Hey, what're you doing in this neck of the woods?" Maxine asked.

"I was feeling antsy," Kathryn fibbed, "so I decided to go for a drive and wound up here."

"What a coincidence," Maxine said. "I was feeling antsy myself, which is why I came to check the mail. Come back to the house with me, and we can be antsy together. The manuscript I'm supposed to be editing is so-o boring, I'd love the company."

Kathryn glanced at her watch. It had taken her about fifteen minutes to get here. If she went back now, she wouldn't have much time to pursue her attic search before Corrigan returned. But if she stayed, she could pump talkative Maxine for more information about Corrigan and also Gwen.

"Is this where you work?" Kathryn asked as she and Maxine settled on the deck with glasses of iced tea.

"Yeah, I like being outdoors whenever I can. And now that it's summer, I especially enjoy being here instead of down in the city. That's the advantage of being a freelance editor. The disadvantage is getting manuscripts like that one." She gestured toward her laptop on a nearby table.

"What's it about?"

"Metaphysics, I think. I'm still trying to make sense of it."

Kathryn laughed. She stared at the lake, still and serene at mid-day. "You don't find it too quiet in the country?"

"Nah, if I want excitement, I can always go to the city. And right now, I've got Niall for company."

"How's that working out?"

"Fine. It's like rooming with an old friend, and the house is big enough that we don't get on each other's nerves. There's Gwen, too… although I don't see as much of her as I used to."

"How come?"

"I'm single and she's married with kids. And I don't think Tim likes me much, anymore."

"Why?"

"A lot of it has to do with Scarlett. I'm her godmother, and when she was younger, I'd take her down to the city on weekends, and we'd have a great time. But when she became a teenager, Tim called a halt to those big city weekends. He accused me of corrupting Scarlett by taking her to New York. He doesn't realize it's in her nature to be wild and rebellious." Maxine paused and studied the bright red polish on her nails. "Like her mom."

"Gwen *was* wild?"

"Yup, though you'd never know it now. I was pretty wild myself. We were both real party animals. We'd stay out until almost dawn, grab a couple of hours sleep, go to our jobs, come home and take a short nap, then the cycle repeated itself. I honestly don't know how we did it." Maxine shook her head in wonderment. "It wasn't just the hours we kept either. Sometimes we did stuff that was downright dangerous."

"Like what?"

"We'd go anywhere for a party, even if it was in the worst neighborhood. We didn't care how we got to the party or how we got home again. We'd cut through deserted parks after dark, ride the subway into the wee hours, and accept rides from people we barely knew. Once we were at the party, we usually drank too much, which made getting home even more dicey. We didn't care. At that age, we thought we were invincible. It never occurred to us we might get hurt—until Gwen almost did."

Kathryn tightened her grip on her iced tea glass. "What happened?"

"She'd taken a short cut through an alley, when all of a sudden, this guy grabbed her. He had a knife, and he would have robbed, maybe even raped and killed her, if Niall hadn't intervened. He tackled the guy to the ground, knocked him unconscious, and got Gwen home safely."

Kathryn's opinion of Corrigan rose a notch. Sleaze that he was, at least he'd done one good deed in his life. "How did he happen to be there?"

"He must have followed her. At that time, Niall was all about Gwen. I think he fell for her the moment he saw her. After that he barely looked at another woman, and his looking at Gwen included looking *after* her."

"Do you think he still has feelings for her?"

Maxine shrugged. "I dunno. Does that kind of passion, love— whatever you want to call it—last? It never has for me. And Gwen's very different from who she was then. Her 'accident' really changed her."

"Why do you always put air quotes around Gwen's accident?"

"Beats me, unless my inner editor can't resist punctuating stuff."

"C'mon," Kathryn probed, "you must have another reason for the quotes."

"Like what?"

"Maybe Gwen didn't have a car accident at all, but something else happened to her. Something that occurred near Grant's Tomb."

"That's crazy." Maxine shut Kathryn down. "I think you've been out in the sun too long. Maybe I have, also. Or it's all the talk about passion that's made me hot." Maxine pulled off the fuchsia cover-up she wore over a flowered bikini. "I'm going for a swim. Want to join me?"

"I don't have a suit."

"You could skinny dip."

I could. But even if I follow you into the water, I doubt you're going to tell me anything more. Kathryn turned to go.

"Stop by again," Maxine called over her shoulder, as she barreled toward the water. "And next time, bring a suit and that sexy boyfriend of yours."

Chapter 25

An hour later, Kathryn drove slowly up the Farley driveway. As she'd expected, Corrigan's Porsche was back in the parking area, so she was in no rush to get to the house. Her gaze lingered on the peonies in the border between the lawn and the field. The flowers she'd cut and brought inside only a few days ago were starting to shed their petals. She'd replace them with a fresh batch.

She parked by the garage, fetched clippers from the gardening supplies there, and returned to the border on foot. But finding fresh blooms was more difficult than she'd realized. The first few flowers she touched fell apart in her hands. Finally, she settled for buds that had yet to open, though some were covered with ants. The peonies' fragility reminded her of Maxine's comment about passion. Like these flowers, it was often fleeting. Still, she was determined to enjoy the peonies while they lasted. As for her passion for Earl and his for her, she could only hope it proved more long-lived than these flowers.

As she was replacing the old peonies in the vase on the screened-in porch, Corrigan spotted her through the glass door that separated the porch from the dining room, and called out, "I've got good news, Kathryn." Curious, she approached the dining room table where he sat.

"I've had it with dial-up, it's way too slow for my needs," he said. "I called a couple of internet providers down in Sheffield, where I've heard they have cable, DSL, and wireless options. I'm going to see about getting service up here. It'll be expensive, but I can afford it and it'll be worth it to have faster service. Then, the phone and internet won't be tied up while I'm here. Happy?"

"Yes."

"I bet you'll be even happier to know I'm going down to the city for the weekend."

"When will you be leaving?" Kathryn asked, barely stifling a smile.

"Sometime tomorrow, I haven't decided yet. Steve Reikart should be back on the job by then."

"Thanks for letting me know."

As she headed upstairs, Kathryn's mind raced with excitement. She'd make good use of the time Corrigan was away. And if Reikart was coming back, Charlotte's baby-sitting must be nearly over, and she'd be able to enlist Charlotte's help. Still, given the way the best laid plans could go awry, she vowed to resume her search of the attic that very evening. She'd already told Gene Herrick she couldn't help him with his family photos tonight. Now, all she had to do was beg off tonight's dinner at The Stag with Earl and Pete.

*****

Several hours later, Kathryn ascended the ladder into the attic and surveyed the jumble of boxes, old suitcases and filing cabinets. She was discouraged by how little she'd accomplished the last time she'd been up here—whenever that was. Wracking her brain, she recalled that it had been Monday evening, just before she'd gone to dinner at the family house with Earl and Pete. Now, it was Thursday evening, and she wouldn't be seeing Earl and Pete. She felt a bit guilty about that. She'd been vague about her reasons for canceling, saying only that she had things she needed to do. She hadn't told Earl about her search for the second will. She knew from past experience he didn't believe such a will existed and considered looking for it a waste of time.

She also worried Earl had accepted her excuse too readily, as if he were just as glad not to be seeing her tonight. Perhaps it was as much a strain for him to be with her as it sometimes was for her to be with him when Pete was there. But then again, maybe she was overthinking this. She needed to focus on the task at hand, for which she wouldn't have Charlotte's help. Charlotte had let her know she was still tied up with Reikart, although she expected to be free by the weekend.

At least she didn't have nearly two hundred thousand items to sort through in a space of more than eight thousand feet, like the staff at the Boston Public Library when two valuable prints, a Durer and a Rembrandt, had gone missing. Kathryn still found it amazing that the BPL had no inventory of its print holdings nor a catalog of individual items. She'd made sure the Lyceum had both. When she finished with the current search, she'd have an inventory of the attic's contents as well, but now she'd better get started.

Kathryn worked steadily, taking only three quick breaks. The first, to bandage a paper cut on her finger; the second, to fetch a box of tissues to deal with the dust motes that made her sneeze; the third, to use the bathroom. The lengthy summer twilight had long since given way to darkness when her vision began to blur and she realized she'd been reading the same page of an old tax form over and over again. Time to call it quits, even though several boxes remained.

She felt good about all she'd done, but after she left the attic and collapsed into bed, she had the nagging sense that the second will was up there somewhere, hiding in plain sight like the missing BPL prints that were discovered on a shelf top, weeks later.

Chapter 26

The next morning, Corrigan showed up as usual, dashing Kathryn's hopes he'd leave for the city directly from Maxine's. She occupied herself by taking a short walk, then working in the vegetable garden, where she could keep an eye on him. At exactly 12:30, he gathered up his papers and left. To keep the same appointment he'd had for the past two days? She was determined to find out.

Once again, she lost him in the maze of winding roads leading into town, and also failed to find him there, though she noticed Gwen's car in a library space. Her friend must have a huge backlog of work. Again, she thought how odd this was.

Continuing on to the fork, Kathryn decided to turn left in the direction of Great Barrington, rather than right towards Maxine's house. More winding roads brought her to Route 7, a larger road that was more or less a straight line from Sheffield to Great Barrington, and where she hoped to catch sight of Corrigan's Porsche.

Kathryn reached Great Barrington without so much as a glimpse of yellow. Maybe Corrigan was on his way to New York already instead of keeping what appeared to be a regular appointment. Just to be sure, she followed Main Street until it became Route 7 again. She also combed several of the nearby side streets. Then, having come this far, she paid Emily a visit at the hospital.

Emily appeared much as she had on Kathryn's earlier visits: a small, frail, silent woman connected to the machines that kept her alive. But as soon as Kathryn inserted a cassette into the player, Emily became herself again, feisty as ever. Kathryn had hoped she'd finally learn what the "nonsense" about Gwen and Grant's Tomb was. Instead, Diana brought up something else.

"A while ago, you said you were going to tell me more about Shuntoll Road," Diana said.

"Did I now?

"Yes."

"Oh, all right. Shuntoll Road intersects with a stretch of the original Sodom Road that led to a tiny hamlet by that name in Connecticut. There used to be a Gomorrah, too, but it was located across the state line in New Nottingham in an area of the township we called 'the flats,' because that's where the hills level out. So, like the Biblical cities of ill repute our Sodom and Gomorrah were cities 'of the plain.'"

"Did they go up in smoke, too?"

Emily chuckled. *"Who knows, though there is an old iron-making blast furnace over in Connecticut. But back to Shuntoll Road. It runs through part of the old Gomorrah. It may have been called the Gomorrah Road in the beginning, but I don't know that for a fact."*

"Why is it called Shuntoll? What does that mean?"

"You don't know? Emily sounded surprised.

"No."

"I suppose you wouldn't because you're not from around here. A long time ago, there was a post road between Hartford and Albany. You had to pay a toll to travel that road. But if you wanted to avoid the toll, you could take another road."

"Shuntoll Road?"

"Uh-huh. We Yankees have a reputation for being frugal, so a lot of folks took Shuntoll Road. But not everyone."

"Why not?"

"You get what you pay for, and the toll road was better than the other road. Still is. To this day, Shuntoll Road and Sodom Road are the last to be plowed in the winter, and the last to be repaired in the spring. They're roads you travel at your own risk."

"That doesn't sound fair."

"As I said before, you get what you pay for. And people who think they can sail through life doing whatever they please without paying

a toll—in other words, facing the consequences of their actions—are dead wrong."

"I didn't realize you were such a philosopher, Emily."

"Well, now you know."

Kathryn could testify to the fact that Shuntoll Road, where Gwen lived, was poorly maintained. Its surface was not only washboard bumpy but loaded with potholes. She also agreed with Emily that actions had consequences. But unlike potholes on the road, where if you hit one, the reaction was immediate, the consequences of your actions weren't always readily apparent. They could remain buried for years only to rise up and bite you.

*****

Where had the afternoon gone? Kathryn wondered as she cut up raw vegetables to go with a couple of dips, her contribution to the cook-out the Barkers were having at their compound tonight.

After leaving the hospital, she'd stopped off at the veterinary hospital to see how Solly was doing, and by extension, Reikart and Charlotte. She'd barely arrived when the staff went into crisis mode with the arrival of a cat that had been hit by a car. She waited and waited until the receptionist finally emerged to tell her the dog was getting physical therapy, and it would be better if she came back another time. Not seeing Charlotte or Reikart, she assumed they were in with Solly.

Then, she made the mistake of doing her shopping at Guido's on a Friday afternoon when the store was jammed with weekenders from New York. They acted like they owned the place, pushing and shoving, blocking the lanes with their shopping carts, pinching and poking the produce, and demanding free samples of cheese and other edibles. She even saw a man reach his hand into a plastic bin of loose granola instead of using the scoop. And she had to step quickly out of the way to avoid being mowed down by Maxine. Bent over with a fierce look on her face, Maxine propelled her cart through the throng like speed demon. Observing such behavior, Kathryn understood why some locals disliked New Yorkers.

She arranged the vegetables and dips on a platter, covered it with plastic wrap and took it to the car. On her way up Rattlesnake Hill Road, she paused at the place near Earl's old trailer where a rough dirt road led to the hillside property Earl's father had given them. Earl had carried a chain saw when she'd run into him here the other day. Did that mean he was doing more clearing? If so, did he hope they had a future together here, or was he getting the property ready for sale? She could ask him outright, but she wasn't ready to have that conversation yet. The tracks on the road looked both fresh and deep. She was half-tempted to go up and see for herself what was going on, but she was already late for the cook-out.

Kathryn zipped past the white house where Earl lived with Pete until she reached the Barker compound, a collection of dark-timbered buildings with a jumble of old farm equipment and early model cars out front. A steep, rock-strewn hill rose behind the compound, home to the family cemetery, as well as the timber rattlesnakes that had given the entire hill its name.

Beers in hand, the Barker men, Earl's dad, Roy, his brother Wayne, and Earl himself, were outside the main house, tending burgers and sausages on two large grills. Granddad sat on a bench, offering advice to anyone who'd listen. Roy gave Kathryn a hug, Earl kissed her, and his less effusive brother shook hands. Granddad demanded and got a kiss on his grizzled cheek. Pete greeted her with a nod, and his younger cousins shouted "hi" as they raced around the buildings in a raucous game of tag. After the high-pressure environment of Guido's, Kathryn was happy to be part of this friendly family gathering.

Earl's mother June and his two sisters-in-law, Suzy and Cheryl, the young widow of his brother Garth, soon joined them. They carried bowls of salad and sweet potato fries, along with a basket of burger and hot dog rolls. After they'd all settled at picnic tables and dug into their food, Kathryn said, "These sausages are delicious. Who made them?"

"I did," June said. "I used venison from the deer the men shot last fall."

The mention of deer hunting reminded Kathryn of the very first dinner she'd had with Earl's family, which had occurred during

Deer Week. Then, Roy had embarrassed her by calling her a "nice little doe," and saying she looked "good enough to eat." When he'd gone on to explain how male deer attracted females by making a scrape and urinating into it, she'd decided he wasn't just earthy, but downright crude. Now, though, she was used to Roy's sometimes salty language. It helped that she knew he was on her side and wanted things to work out between her and Earl.

"What about the sweet potato fries?" she asked. "They're yummy, too, and they look homemade."

"I can't take credit for those," June said. "Cheryl brought them."

Kathryn smiled at Cheryl and a touch of becoming color came into the young woman's normally pale cheeks.

"So, Kathryn," Roy boomed from the other end of the table. "I hear you've got a roommate down at the Farley house now."

"Not quite. I have the upstairs to myself, and Corrigan uses the downstairs for his office."

"Sounds a lot cozier than I'd be comfortable with. Especially with a security guard and a watch dog on the job 24/7."

"It's not ideal, but—"

"If you get tired of that arrangement, you could always stay with me and Derek," Cheryl offered shyly.

"Or me, Wayne, and the boys," Suzy volunteered.

"Thank you both," Kathryn said, "but it's not so bad. Corrigan's down in the city for the weekend, and the security guard and his dog haven't been around for the past couple days."

No one suggested she move in with Earl and Pete. Perhaps they guessed at hers and Earl's tacit agreement that this would not happen while Pete was still coping with his mother's death—if it happened at all. She was glad when the conversation moved on to other topics. Dinner was almost over when Roy returned to the matter of the security guard and his dog.

"Heard the dog got shot in the woods, and the guy's real broken up about it. Wonder if it was anywhere near the place you and that Corrigan fellow got shot at," Ray said with a glance at Earl.

Earl shifted uneasily in his seat. "I don't know, Dad. Maybe you should ask the security guard."

"Maybe I will. 'Cuz I got a notion as to—"

"Everyone who's ready for strawberry rhubarb pie, raise your hands?" June interrupted. All hands went up. "Good," June said approvingly. "Bring your dinner dishes back to the kitchen, and I'll give you plates of pie and vanilla ice cream."

Although both Roy and Kathryn raised their hands, neither joined the rush indoors. Instead, Kathryn took June's place next to Roy. "You were saying you had a notion about something—what is it?"

Roy shrugged. "Could be wrong but it occurred to me Randy Plungas might've been the one who shot at my boy and Corrigan, and later hit that guard dog."

Kathryn tensed. "Why do you think so?"

"Couple reasons. One, it's the kind of thing he'd do. Two, his cabin's located at the opposite end of the woods from the Farley house, and he doesn't like visitors. And three, he's supposed to have an arsenal tucked away in the forest."

"Have you actually seen it?" Kathryn asked more loudly than she'd intended. "It could be just a rumor."

"Shh—keep your voice down," Roy cautioned with a jerk of his head toward the main house. Suzy stood silhouetted in the kitchen door, so pale and still she might have been a statue. Then, wrinkling her nose, she turned away and peered into the distance. "I smell smoke."

"Sure, you do," Roy said. "From the grills."

"No. There." She pointed down the hill.

Kathryn's throat went dry. The Farley house and woods were down there. And smoke meant fire. She was halfway to her car when a siren wailed confirmation.

Chapter 27

Through the open car windows, Kathryn smelled the smoke, and the closer she got to the site of the fire, the more she felt the heat. So hot! She might as well be on fire herself. If the fire was where she thought, both the house and the woods could be burning. She pulled into the driveway and rounded the bend.

The house had yet to catch fire. But it would soon if the firefighters, whose hoses snaked from the pond, couldn't keep the flames at bay. Leaving the car, she ran to the patio to get a closer look. She counted three figures. Only three? How could such a small number of men prevail over the inferno towering over them? Especially since the fire had advanced to the front line of the trees.

The front line. The same trees whose reflections had reached out to her for help only a few nights ago. Then, their reflections had appeared as drowning swimmers; now as figures being eaten alive by flames, their bodies twisted and ghastly. Her trees were burning. She imagined them crying out in agony. And she was powerless to save them.

Hot tears scalded her cheeks.

"Hello?" A petite woman with perfectly coiffed hair, wearing country club casual clothes, approached her on the patio. "Are you the new owner?"

Startled, Kathryn said, "Yes—I mean, I'm the tenant." She had to raise her voice to make herself heard over the roar of the fire.

"Betty Phelps," the woman shouted back. "I live up the hill in the old Whittemore house. My husband and I just moved back for the summer. I was driving home with a load of groceries when I saw

112

the smoke. I used your phone to call the volunteer fire department."

"Thank you. You may have saved the house."

"The pond will save the house. And the firemen of course."

"Not with only three of them."

"Look. There's another truck coming."

A second fire truck pulled into the parking area, followed by Earl's truck, a sedan, and the Chief's patrol car. Kathryn was relieved when four additional men joined the three fighting the blaze. Earl, Pete, Roy, Wayne and Suzy piled out of the truck, and Gwen left the sedan.

Earl gave Kathryn's arm a quick, reassuring squeeze while he assessed the situation. "Luckily the house hasn't caught fire," he said

"Yes, but the woods are going fast," she cried.

"With the extra manpower, they should be able to get things under control," the Chief said, joining them. Just then, a burning branch landed a few yards away from the trailer.

"Where's Reikart?" Earl demanded.

"Still at the hospital with his dog, I guess," Kathryn said.

"Let's put that firecracker out before it hits the trailer," Earl yelled. He and Wayne grabbed shovels from the garage and hurried over to the burning branch. Roy, the Chief and Pete followed with buckets of water.

While the Barker men and the Chief attacked the smaller blaze, Gwen and Suzy moved close to Kathryn and Betty Phelps. Suzy squinted at the firemen. "There should be eight guys there, but I only see seven. Where's the eighth guy?"

Gwen coughed. "Randy didn't answer the call."

"What?! You mean he's... the... missing guy?" Suzy could hardly get the words out. Despite the glare from the fire, her face turned pale.

"I'm afraid so, but he could just be—"

"I'm going to look for him," Suzy interrupted.

Gwen shook her head. "But the fire—where will you go?"

"His cabin, for starters." Suzy headed toward Earl's truck.

Kathryn made a quick decision. She should probably remain here in case the fire advanced on the house, and she needed to remove her belongings. But she hated standing helplessly by while it devoured her beloved woods. And Suzy sounded genuinely worried about her ex. "I'll come with you," Kathryn volunteered, catching up with Suzy. "We can take my car."

"Be careful," Gwen called after them.

As Kathryn and Suzy drove out of the driveway, a truck pulled up near the trailer, and a man jumped out. "What the hell!" Reikart. He dashed into the trailer, emerging with a fire extinguisher he used on the flames of a second branch that had landed near the first one.

From Rattlesnake Hill, Suzy directed Kathryn through a labyrinth of shadowy, winding back roads until at last they came to a road that skirted the far end of the forest. To Kathryn's relief and, she assumed, Suzy's also, the fire hadn't reached this part of the woods, though thick, ugly clouds of smoke billowed in the distance. They followed the road until they arrived at a spot where a short dirt drive led to a clearing in the woods with a crude log cabin. A beat-up green truck was parked outside. "I'll go in and see if he's there," Suzy said. "You stay here."

Suzy was gone long enough to make Kathryn regret coming with her. The Farley house could be on fire, and she stood to lose at least some of her possessions, along with the second will—if, in fact, it existed. She was sorry she hadn't searched more diligently while she had the chance. With Charlotte's help, she'd hoped to do one final sweep of the attic over the weekend, but now that might not be possible.

What was Suzy doing in there? Could she and Randy be having a fight? Surely, she would've heard noise if that were so. Kathryn left the car to investigate. She'd only gone a few steps when Suzy came out of the cabin. "Sorry to keep you waiting. Randy's not there, and neither is Robert."

"Robert?"

"Randy has him for the weekend," Suzy explained. "I used Randy's phone to call The Stag and a few other places on the off chance he and Robert bummed a ride or even walked there. I also checked the cabin for clues as to where they might have gone, but no luck." Suzy waved her hands. "It's like they've vanished into thin air unless Randy's made good on his threat to take Robert on a wilderness trek to make a man of him."

"If you want to drive around some more, maybe we'll spot them along the road," Kathryn said.

"Yes. No. I don't know." Suzy was distraught. "Let's go back to Rattlesnake Hill. I need to talk to Wayne. Maybe he'll have an idea where they are."

Back on the hill, Kathryn was both glad and a bit surprised the fire had abandoned its position across the pond from the house and was headed toward a swampy area at the bottom of the hill. But, of course, it would move. Unlike a fireplace fire—the only kind she'd observed before now—this one was free to roam wherever there was fresh fuel to burn, subject only to the vagaries of the wind.

With the house and trailer no longer in immediate danger, Roy, Wayne, Pete and the Chief had joined the group on the patio, which now included Charlotte. "I came as soon as I saw the smoke," she said, giving Kathryn a hug. Suzy went straight to Wayne, and they conferred in low voices. "Where's Earl?" Kathryn asked Roy.

"Down helping the firefighters in borrowed gear. But don't worry, he'll be okay. They all will." He glanced at his watch. "The fire's starting to die down, and around midnight, they'll be able to put it to bed for the night."

"'Put it to bed?'" Kathryn asked.

"Just what Roy said," the Chief chimed in. "By midnight the temperature's dropped and the winds have died down. The fire will go to sleep and not wake up until around six in the morning when it's light and warmer again—assuming the fire wakes up at all. So, the firemen have a six-hour break to look forward to."

"And when that break comes, I bet they're going to be tired, hungry, and thirsty," Betty Phelps said.

"I can make coffee, but my larder's pretty empty," Kathryn said.

"Not a problem," Betty replied. "I've got groceries in the car."

*****

"This sure hits the spot," Earl said, digging into the plate of scrambled eggs, bacon, and toast Kathryn gave him. While Gwen and Suzy cooked and dished out the meals, she, Charlotte and Betty handed plates of food and mugs of coffee to the firemen, who looked weary and grubby, their clothes and faces blackened with soot.

"Hope we're not eating you out of house and home," Roy said to Betty.

"Not at all. I'm glad to help."

"Heard you're the one who called in the fire," Roy continued. "Lucky you saw it when you did. 'Cuz we weren't aware of it at our place farther up on the hill—until Suzy smelled smoke. And whoever was supposed to be watching the place wasn't around either."

"Gene Herrick had to leave early," Kathryn said.

"And I was still at the veterinary hospital with my dog that was shot," Reikart piped up from where he stood.

"I heard about that," Roy said. "Lost a leg, right?"

"Yeah."

"Where's Corrigan, anyway?" the Chief asked.

"Down in the city for the weekend," Reikart said.

"He know about the fire?" the Chief said.

"Not yet. I... uh... need to call him." Reikart looked uncomfortable. "I better do that."

"I wouldn't want to be in that guy's shoes," a firefighter remarked after Reikart had left.

"Me either," another man commented. "His boss isn't gonna be happy when he hears the site of his development's gone up in smoke."

"Wonder how the fire got started," a third man said.

"Could be someone got careless with a cigarette," the first man said. "It sure as heck wasn't a lightning strike."

"'Course we won't know for sure certain till the fire inspector comes, but I'm betting arson," Roy said.

Everyone stared at him. "What makes you say that?" the Chief asked.

"Think about it. The development's not popular with some people in town. There's been trouble already. My boy here," Roy jerked his head at Earl, "and Corrigan got shot at in the woods a little while

116

ago. Then the security guard's dog was shot in the woods. Now we have this fire. Seems clear to me someone wants the development stopped pretty bad."

Uh-oh. Kathryn knew where this was going. Unfortunately, Roy's wife June wasn't there to change the subject. Earl flashed his dad a warning look, and Suzy dropped her serving spoon in the fry pan with a clatter.

"Quit playing games, Roy," a fireman said. "If you think you know who this 'someone' is, why don't you just say so?"

"The same as has gone missing tonight," Roy said.

"That's enough, Roy!" Suzy flared. "Shame on you for accusing Randy when he's not here to defend himself."

"C'mon, man," one of the New Nottingham firemen drawled. "Randy's a firefighter, not a fire starter."

"If that's so, then where the hell—" Roy began.

"You heard Suzy—let it go, Roy!" the Chief commanded.

"Yeah, Dad," Earl agreed.

Roy shrugged and mumbled something into his plate. After that, no one said much, including Tim, who'd chosen not to enter the fray either for or against his former friend. With promises to return the next morning, if necessary, the firemen finished their meals and departed. Tim and Gwen were among the first to leave.

"I'll give you a call tomorrow in case you need help with *anything*," Charlotte told Kathryn before leaving herself. The emphasis Charlotte placed on the last word told Kathryn she meant the attic.

Roy and the other Barkers lingered. So did the Chief, perhaps because he felt his presence was necessary to keep peace in the family. "Why don't you spend the night up the hill with us?" Earl said to Kathryn. When she shook her head, he said, "Then I'm staying here with you. You take the others home in my truck," he told Pete.

Part II: The Cabin in the Woods

Chapter 28

Kathryn awoke with a start at dawn, as if in response to an internal summons. Beside her, Earl still slept. She would have liked to remain in bed, comforted by his body next to hers. But she needed to see if the fire had awakened from its slumber at first light.

She tiptoed to the window. A smoky mist blanketed the pond and the woods beyond. The mist began to slowly lift, revealing the ragged tops of burnt trees, then blackened trunks, and finally patches of charred ground. On the far side of the pond, she could barely make out what looked like a big animal. Putting a robe on over her nightgown and slipping into loafers, she crept downstairs and onto the patio.

It was indeed an animal, and no ordinary one. A large, light-colored deer stood by the water. *The white stag. Still alive. A blessing in the midst of the hellish scene.* He lowered his head to drink. Raising it again, he looked directly at her.

Kathryn stood still, barely breathing, lest she frighten him away. She had no idea how long she and the stag gazed at each other. Finally, he tossed his antlers, and she was sure he would turn tail and run. Instead, to her amazement, he walked around the pond toward her, every now and then pausing to paw the trampled grass, but never taking his eyes off her.

A few yards short of the patio, the stag stopped and looked at her with liquid brown eyes. Kathryn stared back, awestruck at being so close to such a magnificent creature. Then, as if in response to some internal summons of his own, the stag turned and bounded back down the slope to the pond.

Don't go, oh please don't go! Kathryn wanted to call after him. The stag stopped and looked back her. He took a few more steps, then looked back again.

He wants me to follow him. Kathryn strode forward. She half expected the stag to bolt at any moment, disappearing into the mist, as if the whole thing had been a dream. But he didn't. He was now waiting for her on the far side of the pond. When she'd almost reached him, he suddenly disappeared through an opening in the woods.

Kathryn hesitated. Did he really expect her to follow him into a place where only a few hours ago a fire had raged, and might still rage again? Peering into the dim light of the forest, she spotted the stag still looking back at her. Then, as if he'd cast a spell on her, she found herself moving ahead, her loafers crunching on undergrowth seared to a crisp.

She felt she'd be safe as long as she kept the stag in sight, a beacon of light among the black, spectral trees. A fallen branch nearly tripped her, a reminder that she needed to watch where she was going, too.

She'd just finished navigating a treacherous stretch of rocks and burned brush, when she looked up and saw her guide had vanished. Panicking, she rushed forward, determined to find him.

Her foot hit something hard and she fell. She landed half on the ground and half on the thing. It was hard in places and soft in others. As she struggled to get up, part of it clung to her. Kathryn raked her hands against her legs, frantically trying to remove whatever it was from her. She looked down, expecting to see a dead animal. Gradually, it took shape. Feet… two legs bent at the knee… arms twisted in agony… a skull. She'd fallen over the badly burnt body of a human being, a ghastly apparition of teeth, bone and tissue.

Kathryn recoiled in horror. Bile rose in her throat, threatening to choke her. The vision swam before her eyes, dissolving into a blur of black and gray. She reached out her arms to steady herself, only to flail at empty air. She had to get away, but her legs wouldn't move. At last she managed a tentative step backward, then another and another until she was able to turn and run.

Half running, half stumbling, her heart thudding and the breath rasping in her throat, she got herself out of the woods and across the field to the house. She clambered up the stairs, the noise of her entry rousing Earl. He was sitting up in bed when she burst into the room. "What is it? What's the matter?"

"There's a body…" Kathryn shut her eyes to block out the terrible image. She swayed and might have fallen if he hadn't caught her and eased her gently onto the bed.

"Slow down, Star. Deep breath. Talk to me," he said in a voice filled with concern.

"A body. In the woods. Burned by the fire."

"Okay. You stay here while I call the Chief."

Chapter 29

Kathryn lay on the bed, staring up at the ceiling. In the kitchen below, she heard Earl making the call, then it was quiet. She willed her mind to stay blank as the ceiling above. Except the ceiling wasn't entirely blank. A piece of tape, used to repair the crack she'd made when she'd almost fallen through the ceiling, had come loose and flapped in the breeze. She watched it until her attention was drawn by a fly buzzing against the window. When it had flown away, she let her mind drift, careful not to let it snag on anything remotely connected to the grisly scene in the woods.

But she couldn't avoid it forever. All too soon, vehicles rumbled into the parking area, men called out, and a dog barked. The Chief would want to speak to her, and so would whoever came with him. Kathryn wrinkled her nose. She smelled of smoke, and sooty guck stained the bottom of her bathrobe. She got up and put on clean clothes. When Earl knocked on the door, she told him to come in. He strode into the room, flanked by the Chief and another man she didn't recognize.

"This is Detective Scoville from the state police," the Chief said. "He's going to be handling the investigation."

Scoville stepped forward and shook hands with her. He was a giant of a man, so tall that his head appeared small compared to the rest of him. Craning her neck, she glimpsed brown eyes, a pointy nose, and thin lips curled into a low-wattage smile like those Pete gave her.

"I'd like to ask you a few questions, Miss Stinson," he said.

"Fine, let's go into the study," she said with a confidence she didn't feel.

He nodded and the three men followed her down the hall. Kathryn sat in the desk chair, and Scoville took a seat on the daybed opposite her. Earl and the Chief remained standing. On her level with his long legs stretched out in front of him, Scoville didn't seem so formidable.

"I understand you're the one who found a body," he said.

"That's right."

"I've got a death scene team outside with a cadaver dog. The volunteer firemen from last night are here, too, in case the fire starts up again. It would be helpful if you could give us an idea where in the woods to look for the remains."

After she told him, Scoville motioned for Earl and the Chief to leave. "Aren't you going with them?" she asked.

"Nope. We have time to talk. The death scene people don't want me there until they've finished their work." He went on to ask her some basic background questions—where she worked and where she lived when not in the Berkshires—before returning to the fire.

"Where were you last night when the fire started?"

"Up the hill having dinner with Earl Barker and his family. I first became aware of it when Suzy Barker, Earl's sister-in-law, said she smelled smoke. It seemed to be coming from below. I drove here immediately."

"Approximately what time was that?"

"Around seven-thirty."

"Before you went to dinner, were you aware of any unusual activity in the woods?"

"No, I was out most of the afternoon and only returned in time to get ready for the cookout."

Scoville jotted this down in his notebook. He studied her a moment, then said, "What made you go into the woods early this morning?"

He'd asked the one question she'd been dreading. If she told the truth—that she'd followed a legendary creature few people had ever seen—he'd think she was crazy. "I was having trouble sleeping, so when I woke up for the nth time, and couldn't get back to sleep, I thought I'd check and see if what the firemen said was true."

"What was that?"

"They said the fire goes to sleep around midnight, but wakes up again at dawn."

"Couldn't you tell it wasn't burning without going into the woods?"

"Not really. And when I saw a deer come out of the forest and go back in again, I figured I'd be safe."

"Hmm." Scoville scratched the back of his head with its buzz cut hair. "How did you happen to discover the body?"

"I became distracted, forgot to look where I was going, tripped and…" She left the sentence unfinished.

Scoville leaned toward her. "You didn't fall on the body, did you?"

"Yes," Kathryn said in a small voice.

Clasping his hands together, Scoville leaned back against a cushion. "That's unfortunate, but what's done is done. I'll let the death scene team know." Changing the subject, he said, "I understand you're the tenant here and that you share the house with the new owner."

"That's correct. He uses the downstairs as an office and I have the upstairs to myself. He spends his nights elsewhere, and at the moment he's down in New York."

"How do you feel about the development he's planning?"

Kathryn chose her words carefully. "If it were my property, I'd leave it as is, but it's not, so there's not much I can do about it." *Except find that elusive second will, if in fact, it exists.* She steeled herself for more questions about Corrigan and his development, but Scoville appeared satisfied with her answers.

Changing the subject again, he said, "Chief Lapsley told me a man's gone missing. One Randy Plungas."

"Actually, I think two people are missing," Kathryn said. "Plungas and his son Robert."

"The son's been accounted for," Scoville said.

Whew. She was relieved the body in the woods wasn't Robert's. "Accounted for how?" she asked.

"Let's stick with Plungas. Do you know him?"

"I've seen him around."

"And?"

"That's about it. I haven't been coming here for very long, so I don't know the locals all that well." Let others fill in the unpleasant details about Plungas. She wasn't about to.

"Is there anything you can tell me about him?" Scoville persisted.

"Only that he doesn't like New Yorkers, or 'New Yawkers,' as he calls them."

Scoville looked like he had more questions, but just then the Chief poked his head into the room. "The death scene people are ready for you, Detective."

From the bedroom window, Kathryn watched Scoville stride around the pond toward the woods. When he'd vanished from sight, she went downstairs and out onto the patio, where Earl and the Chief stood. "I heard Robert's been accounted for," she said. "Where is he?"

"Suzy called in the middle of the night while you were asleep," Earl said. "When she and Wayne got home, there was a voicemail from Robert. He was calling from a neighbor's house down the road, where he went after he and his dad had a fight. Wayne went to pick him up, and he's with them now."

"That's good news, but… nothing about his dad?"

"No," Earl said grimly.

"Do you think it's *him* in the woods?" she asked.

"Could be, but I hope not for Suzy's sake. Robert's too," Earl said.

"When are we likely to know?"

"Depends on what the forensics people find," the Chief said. "If they locate metal objects like belt buckles or rings that didn't burn and can be identified as Randy's or someone else's, we may find out as soon as today. Otherwise, we'll have to wait until we get the results from DNA testing that has to be done at a lab in Boston.

"In the meantime, Detective Scoville wants me to contact everyone who was either at the scene of the fire or in the vicinity last night, so he can interview them. I thought we'd do the interviews here, if that's okay with you, Kathryn?"

*****

The interviews consumed the greater part of the day. People gathered in the living room and dining room while waiting to be called one by one for their sessions with Detective Scoville upstairs in the study. Some chatted in subdued voices while others fidgeted. Suzy looked stricken, Robert frightened. Kathryn saw Wayne give them encouraging pats when their times came. Reikart appeared almost as jittery as he'd been at the veterinary hospital after Solly had been shot. He reminded Kathryn of a hyperactive child, constantly popping up and going over to the foot of the stairs, where the Chief served as gatekeeper. She overheard him tell the Chief he hoped his turn would come soon, so he could visit his dog at the hospital before it closed.

In the afternoon a light rain began to fall. The rain was good for fire prevention, but to Kathryn, it had the effect of making an already gloomy day worse.

Some of the interviews were short, others, quite long, especially those with the members of the New Nottingham volunteer fire department, the Barker men, Suzy, Robert, Gwen, and Reikart. As the interviewees came back downstairs, Kathryn searched their faces for hints of how the interviews had gone. Most wore poker faces, but a few like Suzy, Robert, and to Kathryn's surprise, Gwen showed signs of strain. As Charlotte was leaving, she repeated her promise of help the next day, and Betty Phelps said she'd also check in with Kathryn.

Before he left, Pete came up to her, and with a look that was both serious and sympathetic, said, "Hang in there, Boston."

"I will," she replied, touched by his genuine concern.

When the last person had departed, Earl said, "I'm going back up the hill to shower and change. Then let's go someplace."

She stared at him with surprise. "Where?"

"I dunno. I thought we'd just get in the truck and drive. It's been a long day, and I think it would do us both good to get away from here for a while."

*****

In the hopes of lifting her spirits, Kathryn decided to wear the one pretty sundress she'd brought. She'd just finished putting it on when she heard a vehicle pull into the parking area. Moments later, the front door creaked open.

"Is that you, honey?" she called down.

Silence.

She stepped out onto the landing. Light from the ceiling fixture above shone on the shaved head of the man in the hall below. Corrigan.

"Oh! I wasn't expecting you," she said.

"Obviously not. I thought I'd better get back here and check on the fire damage."

"Of course."

"You look like you're going out for a night on the town with Earl," he said.

"Not really."

"Well, I won't keep you. Don't want to rain on your party."

Rain on their party? What a strange thing to say. And why the note of almost bitterness in his voice?

Corrigan was gone before she could ask him.

Chapter 30

Niall sped down Rattlesnake Hill Road, pulled off onto a side road at the bottom, and turned off the lights. Get a grip. Just because she mistook you for her honey doesn't mean you have to fall apart. But damn it. Why couldn't he be the guy a certain woman was eagerly awaiting? He hated being around Kathryn when Earl was there, because he could feel the heat between them, heat he wished the woman of his dreams felt for him. Until she did, he had to console himself with small favors. Like pretending Scarlett was that woman when he held her in the water and later when she flung her arms around him after a successful run on skis.

Still, there were moments like tonight when he yearned for his ideal woman to stand at the top of the stairs, an older Juliet calling down to her Romeo. Or maybe they'd sit in his dark Porsche, making-out like teenagers, while fireflies danced around them. Yeah, he liked that picture. Pretty things, fireflies. And there sure were a lot of them around this evening. One had even settled on his windshield like it wanted to be near him. He'd read somewhere that a long time ago people in China had caught fireflies, put them in cages or containers with holes, and used them as lanterns. He'd do that with *his* firefly. Niall got out of the car and grabbed at the firefly on the windshield. He managed to catch it. But when he opened his hand, it was crushed.

Chapter 31

"You hungry?" Earl asked.

"Huh?" Kathryn snapped to attention. They'd been driving for what seemed like hours. Hitting the road with no particular destination, except to distance themselves from the fire and everything connected with it, had been fun in the beginning and a welcome escape. But now she was starting to tire. She was also ravenous.

"Asked if you were hungry."

"Yes. Where are we, anyway? I don't see any towns with places to eat. Just rolling hills and farms."

"Columbia County in New York State. I saw a sign for a diner ahead."

"Let's go."

The diner was empty except for an older couple. Kathryn and Earl slid into a booth in the rear, ordered, and when their meals came, they dug in. The older couple paid and left. Earl cleaned his plate and pushed it aside. He gazed at her with his faded blue eyes, then he said, "Something I want to ask you."

"Yeah?"

They'd hardly spoken on the drive. A lover of country western and folk music, Earl had put on some of his favorite CDs. They listened to the likes of Patsy Cline, Tom Paxton, and Pete Seeger, and even sang along with them. But now it was time to talk. And what better place than this quiet diner, so far removed from their usual surroundings they might have been strangers meeting for the first time. Except Earl probably knew her better than anyone else.

"Why'd you go into the woods early this morning?" he asked.

"Because of the white stag."

"You saw him again?"

Kathryn nodded. "I'd gotten up to check on the fire when I spotted him on the far side of the pond. For a while we just looked at each other. Then he walked to the patio where I stood. Eventually, he turned and bounded off, but he kept looking back at me, like he wanted me to follow him. So, I did. I followed him into the woods, and stumbled on the burnt body. Does that sound totally weird?"

"Not a bit. Don't forget that my great-great uncle claimed he'd seen the white stag twice. And the second time, the stag even talked to him in a dream."

"Right, but your great-great uncle was a hunter, so maybe he was meant to meet up with the white stag. I don't understand why he's appeared to me."

"It's a mystery," Earl said. "And a gift."

A silence settled over them. Earl seemed lost in thought, while she pondered the mysterious connection between her and the white stag.

"You know," Earl said finally, "I don't think I really got it about you and the woods until I saw the look on your face when those trees were burning. But nature's always on the move. If something's lost, nature steps in and fills the space with something else. Grass, bushes, and saplings will replace the trees the fire destroyed. Flowers, too. I've seen pictures of entire hillsides covered with poppies after terrible wild fires in California. Some plants are even called 'fire followers' because their seeds will only germinate in intense heat."

"But flowers are so short-lived," Kathryn said. "The peonies in the border have only been in bloom a week and already they're starting to go."

"Don't underestimate the peonies." Earl chuckled. "They're a lot tougher than they look. You could run a mower over them, and they'd still come back year after year. I'll never forget the time we got them." He paused, his face rapt with memory.

"'We'?"

"Diana and me. She'd noticed these lovely peonies in an old abandoned garden on the next hill over. Called it the 'secret garden' after a children's book. She wanted the peonies for her flower border, and asked me to help her get them. We went after dark, because it was private property, although nobody'd lived there for a long time."

"You stole them?"

"Diana didn't see it that way. Said she was rescuing the peonies by moving them to a new home. If they stayed put with no one to tend them, eventually they'd be buried in weeds.

"We set out on an October night, before the first killing frost. It comes later on the hills than down in the valley, but there was a sharp chill in the air. The stars were bright and there was a sliver of moon. Diana located the plants and I did the digging. I'd just begun when there was this loud noise. Nearly dropped the plant I was holding. A flock of wild geese flew overhead. Diana and I looked at each other and laughed. There we were, two thieves in the night, almost scared off by a bunch of geese."

"I wish I'd been with you," Kathryn said. Which was how she often felt when he told her stories about Diana and him, although she'd never admitted it before.

He took her hand and stroked it. "It was quite a night. When I'd bagged about a half dozen plants, I was ready to quit, but Diana said no, there were more and she wanted them all. She wasn't one for halfway measures."

"You gave her what she wanted?"

"That time I did. When I'd dug up every last peony plant, we loaded them into my truck and took them back to her property to be planted."

"You did that all in one night?" Kathryn was amazed.

"We had to get the plants into the ground before it froze. I was worn out when I finished, but it was worth the extra effort to see how happy Diana was. 'The peonies will be just as beautiful in this border as they were in the secret garden,' she said. 'Maybe even more beautiful. And now everyone who comes here will be able to enjoy them.'"

"They're still beautiful, and I certainly enjoy them," Kathryn said.

"I know you do. And, Star, if those peonies were threatened in any way and needed to be moved again, I'd do that for you."

His sudden pledge of devotion took her breath away. It was what she wanted and needed to hear, even though she wasn't ready to reply in kind. "Thank you," she said, aware of how stiff and inadequate that sounded. "Now, I have a question for you."

"Shoot."

"I know you've been going up to the land your dad gave us. Are you still clearing it?"

"I do a bit of that sometimes. Can't help myself. It's almost second nature." He smiled ruefully. "But mostly I just sit and let my mind wander. It's peaceful there. Quiet, too, except for the creak of the trees and the rustle of small animals. When I worked there last winter, I opened up the view. You can see the distant mountains now. I like watching them change color as the light comes and goes."

"It's a place you go to be alone?"

"Right now, it is."

Kathryn didn't ask if he'd like company. It was evident in the way he looked at her. She was glad all her rants against Corrigan and his development and sometimes against Earl himself hadn't driven him away. Knowing he loved her and would be there for her gave her an inner glow she wanted to carry with her after they left the diner.

But when she and Earl arrived back at the Farley house, her worries returned. She went into the study to look for a book, and discovered her computer was on. Odd. She didn't remember booting it up—not today when the fire and the discovery of the body had consumed all her attention. Had someone come into the house while she and Earl were out and started it? Reikart or Corrigan? If so, he would've had no trouble checking her files or her recent searches, because she was lax about protecting her computer with passwords. Still, he wouldn't have learned much from the access. Or would he? She'd done a search on Corrigan shortly after he'd arrived, but everything she'd found was public knowledge. She'd also visited the land trust website, but Corrigan already knew she and Charlotte were friends. Finally, she'd done a search on Grant's Tomb, but it, too, seemed innocuous. Nevertheless, the thought that someone had been looking at her computer made her uneasy. Even more unnerving was the realization that the light in the attic was on.

Chapter 32

Sunday morning, Kathryn awoke again to the tantalizing aroma of frying bacon and when she went downstairs, blueberry pancakes awaited her. If Earl had made them in the hopes of continuing to cheer her up, he wasn't successful. Not when she looked out the window and saw the burned trees. Nor when Corrigan called to arrange a visit later in the morning. He wanted Earl to inspect the fire damage with him, and determine when the clearing of the area could begin, as he was anxious to get started.

"At least he gave us advance notice this time," Earl said.

Kathryn frowned. "That doesn't change how I feel about him and what he wants to do."

"I know, but..." Earl held out his hands, palms up in a gesture of resignation.

As soon as the men were out of the house, she'd resume her search for the second will. Kathryn had checked the attic last night after noticing the light was on. As far as she could tell, it was exactly as she'd left it. But that was still troubling. It meant whoever it was knew something was going on up there.

*****

Corrigan showed up at the appointed hour of eleven-thirty, dressed for the outing in clothing that looked like it came from a high-end sporting goods catalog. On his head he wore the white golfer's hat he'd worn earlier. Before he and Earl set out, the three of them stood in the living room.

"Terrible thing, that fire," Corrigan said with a glance out the window at the charred forest. "Makes me wish I hadn't given Steve time off to visit his dog at the vet hospital. If he'd been on the job, the fire might not have happened. That local guy who filled in for him was next to useless." He paused, staring down at his hiking boots. Looking up again, he said, "I heard a body was found in the woods. Do you know who it was?"

"Not yet, but a local man's gone missing," Earl said. "We think it may be him. The remains are being sent to a lab in Boston for DNA testing."

"I see. Well, guess we better get started." Corrigan turned to go, but almost immediately turned back. "I almost forgot. When I stopped by the house last night, Kathryn, I noticed the attic light was on. I thought that was strange, so I came back to check on it after you'd gone. There's a ton of junk up there! When I agreed to buy the house as is, I never imagined the owners would leave behind so much stuff. It needs to be cleared out immediately. I'm calling a trash removal service first thing Monday morning, and billing the previous owners."

Kathryn was almost positive Corrigan was lying about the attic light having been left on last night. He could have heard from Reikart or Gene Herrick that it had been on other nights, and used it as a pretext to snoop around what was supposed to be her part of the house. And now she had a deadline. She needed to finish her search for the second will by tomorrow. Luckily, she only had about a half dozen boxes to go through. Then, if she didn't find the will, she'd get Charlotte's help for a second and final search. But would there be enough time for that? Not if Corrigan hung around the house after he and Earl returned from the woods.

"Ready to go now?" Earl asked.

"Yes, and I promise not to keep Earl too long," Corrigan said to Kathryn, "in case you have plans for some fun later on." He gave her a suggestive look that made her skin crawl.

She waited until the men had disappeared into the woods before going upstairs. She'd pulled down the attic ladder when the phone rang. It was Betty Phelps.

"Hi, Kathryn, I called to see how you're holding up."

"I'm okay, I guess. Though the fire was awful. And then to find out someone died in it."

"That was horrible. You discovered the body, didn't you?"

"Yes."

A moment of silence, then Betty said, "How about coming to lunch today? You sound like you could use a break from so much unpleasantness. And, since we're neighbors, I'd like to get to know you better. My husband's off playing golf, so it will be just the two of us."

"I'd love that," Kathryn said. "But I'm kind of busy right now. Can I get a rain check?"

"Oh, all right." Betty sounded disappointed. "We could make it a quick lunch if you don't have much time."

Kathryn wavered. On the one hand, she was anxious to continue her search of the attic, but on the other, she didn't feel right about refusing Betty's kind invitation. Especially since Betty had been the one to call in the fire and had been a great help providing sustenance to the firefighters Friday night.

"Okay if I come for coffee around three?" Kathryn said. That should give her plenty of time to finish up in the attic.

"You're on," Betty said, clearly pleased.

*****

At a quarter to three, Kathryn drove out the Farley driveway with a heavy heart. She hadn't found the second will, and even with Charlotte's help, she doubted she'd find it, because it seemed it simply didn't exist.

Reikart sat in a chair outside the trailer with Solly nearby. The dog was untied and teetered on three legs. When Kathryn got close, Solly growled. "Congratulations," she called to Reikart. "I bet you're glad to have her back."

"Yeah." He snapped a leash on the still growling dog.

Kathryn continued on up Rattlesnake Hill Road until she came to the tall, wrought-iron gate, now open, that marked the entry to the former Whittemore mansion. She followed a long, winding gravel driveway to an imposing brick Victorian with a turret, multi-gabled roof and a wraparound porch.

Betty greeted her at the door wearing a crisp white cotton shirt, navy slacks, and matching navy espadrilles. Kathryn guessed her to be somewhere in her sixties like Charlotte, but in appearance the women couldn't be more different. While Charlotte wore her silver hair in a simple cap around her head, Betty's chestnut curls looked beauty salon "done," and while Charlotte eschewed cosmetics, Betty's face was carefully made up.

They took their coffee, along with a plate of fresh-baked cookies, onto the wraparound porch, which offered a fine view of the surrounding landscape and distant mountains. Kathryn couldn't resist commenting on it.

"It's lovely indeed," Betty said, "and not something I take for granted either. Every time my husband and I move back here, I'm amazed by how beautiful this place is."

"You know that some changes are in store?" Kathryn said.

"I heard that a developer bought the Farley property and is planning some sort of upscale residential development." Betty sighed. "I suppose it had to happen, but I can't say I'm happy about it."

"No?" Kathryn sensed a possible ally.

"I don't know how much you've had a chance to explore, but Hal—he's my husband—and I did a lot of it when we first moved here. We still enjoy going for walks in the woods. There are all kinds of trails and old logging roads in there, stone walls, the foundations of houses hidden among the trees, and even the ruins of an old mill."

"I've seen it."

"And the swamp, too?"

Kathryn nodded.

"We liked to take our house guests to see the mill ruins and the swamp. When Diana Farley was alive, she didn't mind us tromping through her property. Now, I suppose that won't be possible." Betty looked pensive.

"You were friends with Diana?"

"We socialized, though I wouldn't say we were close. Diana was always so busy with her various causes, and as summer people, we didn't have much time to get involved in local issues."

"Did Diana ever mention plans she might have had for the woods and the swamp?"

"She spoke once or twice about possibly leaving that part of the property to the town land trust, but obviously that didn't happen."

"Other people have told me the same thing," Kathryn said. She hesitated. Should she mention the possibility of a second will? Betty seemed like she might be on Charlotte's and her side, but having just met her, Kathryn couldn't be sure. Still, it couldn't hurt to sound out Betty on the subject. "A few people have also told me they think Diana actually *did* draw up a second will, doing what you've described. Did you hear anything about that?"

"No, but..." Frowning, Betty nibbled on a perfectly manicured thumbnail, until realizing what she was doing, she withdrew it from her mouth.

"What is it?"

"Diana gave me a lockbox of what she described as private papers. At the time I thought it was odd because, as I've already said, we weren't close friends. But I knew that she and Gordon were having difficulties, so I assumed she wanted the box out of the house for that reason. And my house was convenient."

Kathryn could hardly contain her excitement. "What happened to the box? Do you still have it?"

"I think so," Betty said. "I just need to remember where I put it. Or rather where Hal put it, because I gave it to him to put away."

"Do you have any idea what's in it?"

"No. The box was locked and Diana kept the key. I assumed she'd come for it when she wanted it, but then she died and..." Betty's thumbnail returned to her mouth. Her eyes widened with worry. "Oh dear, I hope I haven't done—or *failed* to do something I should have. Diana's death was so sudden, and it came at a difficult time in Hal's and my life. My mother was dying, then Hal's brother and a niece were killed in a car accident. And neither of us were coping very well." Betty sounded distraught.

"It's okay," Kathryn said. "The box might not contain anything important, but in case it does, it would probably be a good idea if you could find it."

"As soon as Hal gets home, I'll ask him what he did with it," Betty said. "I'm sure he'll remember. I'll give you a call when we've located it."

*****

Earl was sitting on the porch with a half-eaten sandwich and a beer when Kathryn returned. "How did it go with Corrigan?" she asked. "Does he want you to start clearing the woods right away?"

"He did, but I told him he needed to get approval from the Chief and that state police detective who was here yesterday. Part of the woods is a death scene, and it shouldn't be interfered with until they're satisfied they've collected whatever evidence is there."

"But isn't the death scene just a very small area around where the body was found?"

"Not necessarily. If the body is Randy's, and I'm guessing it is, the police will need to examine a large swath of land from his cabin at the far end of the woods to where the body was found to determine how it got there. If Randy went of his own free will, or someone brought him there." Earl paused to take a drink of beer. "At least that's what I told Corrigan," he said with a grin.

"Nice work." She smiled back. "Corrigan can't have been pleased with that."

"He wasn't. Went into a rant about how inconvenient the fire and someone dying on his property were. He hopes with Reikart back on the job, he'll be able to prevent further trouble. But first he wants to get another Doberman to replace Solly."

"How come?"

"A three-legged animal isn't a very effective guard dog."

"I guess not, but Reikart's so attached to Solly, I can't imagine he'll be happy."

"He doesn't have much choice if he wants to keep his job."

"When do you think the work of clearing the land will begin?"

"As I said before, it depends on how quickly the fire inspector and the police wrap up their investigations. In the meantime, Corrigan wants me to widen the driveway, and extend the road to the edge of the woods, where Gordon's old road begins. I'm supposed to start tomorrow."

Kathryn winced.

"He also wanted me to enlarge the pond, but I talked him out of that—at least for the time being. Told him it was better to wait until fall when the water level drops."

"Good." But even as Kathryn said this, she knew they could only delay so long. All too soon, the heavy equipment would grind into gear, and the landscape she'd come to love would be destroyed. Unless...

"So that's the story with Corrigan," Earl concluded. "How was your lunch with Betty Phelps?" He gestured at the note she'd left.

"She's a nice person. And like me, she'd prefer that the woods and swamp be left as they are. She also told me something interesting. Apparently, Diana gave Betty a lockbox of private papers to keep for her. Betty doesn't know what's in it. And she and her husband need to find the box, but I think it might contain—"

"A second will you've been searching for in the attic?"

"How did you know?" Kathryn asked, embarrassed.

Earl slowly shook his head. "What else would you have been doing in the attic? But leaving a light on was kind of careless."

"I'm pretty sure I didn't leave the light on," Kathryn said. "My computer was on, too. I think either Corrigan or Reikart came into the house and went upstairs after we left last night."

Earl raised an eyebrow. "Why didn't you tell me?"

"We had a nice time last night, and I didn't want to break the mood."

"Okay, but if you're right about Corrigan or Reikart snooping upstairs, what do you think they were looking for?"

"They must've realized I was doing something in the attic, because the light's been on at night before. And now they probably know I've been looking for something, because of the way the boxes are marked and arranged. As for my computer, they couldn't have learned much from my files or the searches I've done, because there's nothing out of the ordinary. Although I learned something interesting about Corrigan."

"What?"

"All of his previous developments have been in suburban areas with access to major highways, so the present one is a departure for him. Which makes me wonder why he chose this particular spot. It's not only different from his other developments, but it's got its share of problems like the swamp, where he's up against wetlands regulations."

"I don't know what to tell you except he's dead set on going forward," Earl said.

"It certainly looks that way," Kathryn agreed. "But getting back to my search for a second will, I would have told you about it, if I hadn't thought you'd dismiss it as a waste of time."

"I might have said that, but I wouldn't have tried to stop you. I know you feel you've got to do something, and right now searching for a will that may not exist is that something. I just hope you're not too disappointed if you don't find it."

"I'll try not to be."

Earl finished his beer and took the can and his empty plate into the kitchen. "I was going to ask if you wanted to go fishing with Pete and me—they've been catching trout down at the river. But I think I know what your answer's going to be. You'd like to come, but you have other things to do—right?"

Kathryn nodded, wishing she wasn't quite so transparent. Still, it was good to know Earl didn't object to her search, and was even doing what he could to delay the development.

As he was leaving, Earl said, "I almost forgot. Charlotte Hinckley called while you were out."

"Did she leave a message?"

"She wants you to call her."

*****

"Whew. There's certainly a lot of stuff up here," Charlotte said, surveying the attic.

142

"I know," Kathryn said. "They were both packrats in their own ways—Gordon with slides of his photographs and Diana with magazines and old newspapers with stories related to her various causes. I've gone through everything once without finding a will, but I'm hoping that with your 'virgin eyes,' you'll catch what I might have missed. It's possible the will isn't here at all, but in the box of private papers Diana gave Betty Phelps. It's also possible there is no will."

"Where would you like me to begin?" Charlotte asked.

*****

After Kathryn and Charlotte had worked for almost an hour, they decided to take a break. Kathryn was halfway down the ladder when the phone rang. She took a flying leap, hit the ground running and dashed into the study, Charlotte following on her heels. It was Betty.

"We found the box! Hal opened it with a butter knife, and it does contain a will. Or rather a document that changes part of the original will. What did you say it's called, Hal?"

"A codicil." Hal came onto the line. "According to this document, Diana amended her will so that the New Nottingham Land Trust, instead of her husband, was to get the portion of her property that encompasses the woods, the swamp and the old mill ruins."

"Is this codicil signed and dated, and has it been witnessed?" Charlotte joined the conversation, Kathryn having put the phone on speaker.

"Yes," Hal said. "What should we do now?"

"Kathryn and I would like to come over and see the codicil for ourselves," Charlotte said. "Then we can discuss next steps."

Kathryn beamed at Charlotte and gave her a quick high-five, then they went outside and got in Charlotte's car. As they headed out, Reikart's truck pulled into the driveway ahead of them. Reikart and Corrigan had obviously changed vehicles at some point. Corrigan was behind the wheel of the truck while his Porsche was parked by the trailer.

As they came closer, Kathryn saw why. A Doberman sat in the truck bed. It wore a harness and a short leash, attached to the middle of a rope tether that extended the length of the back of the truck cab. The dog must be the replacement guard dog Corrigan had told Earl about. Lowering the truck's tailgate, Corrigan climbed in, released the Doberman's leash from the rope tether and led the dog out of the truck toward Reikart and Solly, also leashed. Both dogs growled.

"Maybe this isn't such a good idea," Reikart said.

"Don't be a wuss," Corrigan said. "The dogs'll be fine. They might as well get acquainted. Solstice, meet Geronimo."

Geronimo's growl became a snarl. He strained on his leash, pulling so hard he almost dragged Corrigan after him. Corrigan struggled to stay in place, but the dog was too strong for him. Corrigan dropped the leash. Geronimo lunged at Solly. Teeth bared, she reared up onto her hind leg in defense. The dogs met in midair, Solly's head twisted to one side, as Geronimo clamped his jaws around her neck. Unable to balance on one leg, Solly fell to the ground with Geronimo on top of her.

"Stand down! Stand down!" Reikart yelled frantically. Charlotte hit the brakes and left the car. Kathryn stumbled after her. Reikart continued to yell at the dogs. He circled them, apparently looking for an opening so he could wrench them apart. There was none. The dogs appeared locked in mortal combat. Corrigan added a few "stand downs" of his own, but otherwise, he was a silent observer, standing a safe distance away with his arms folded across his chest. Charlotte drew Reikart aside and said a few words to him. He disappeared into the trailer. Kathryn wanted desperately to help but fear paralyzed her.

On and on the fight went, a horror-show of snapping teeth, flailing limbs and bloody fur. Then, suddenly it was over. Reikart threw a blanket over the dogs and they stopped moving. He gathered up his wounded dog from under the blanket and carried her into the trailer. Charlotte grabbed Geronimo's hind legs, lifting them off the ground into a wheel barrow position. He tried to turn and bite her, but she dodged him until she'd secured him to the post where Solstice had been tied.

Kathryn could have collapsed from sheer relief. Only Corrigan appeared unmoved. But maybe not. Sunlight glinted on a tooth in the corner of his mouth that curled upward in a crooked smile.

Chapter 33

As she left the house Monday morning, the rumble of heavy equipment told Kathryn Earl had begun enlarging the driveway. Corrigan hadn't appeared yet. Just as well. If he'd seen her dressed in a skirt, blouse, and blazer instead of the jeans she usually wore, he might have questions she didn't feel like fielding right now.

Geronimo barked ferociously and strained on his chain as she approached the trailer. Reikart had taken Solly back to the vet to have her injuries checked out, and arranged to board her there overnight. He sat in a nearby chair, whittling. This time, his movements weren't relaxed. He tore at the piece of wood with his knife, as if bent on destruction. He stopped briefly to raise a hand in greeting and Kathryn did likewise.

Earl's front loader blocked the end of the driveway, but he moved aside to let Kathryn past. She waved her thanks, and he gave her a thumbs-up. When she'd told him about the discovery of the codicil, he'd said he was glad for her, but cautioned that she and Charlotte faced an uphill battle.

*****

The law office of Rufus Wallingford, Esquire, was located in a white colonial set on a knoll just before the first traffic light on Main Street in Great Barrington. Kathryn pulled into the parking area as Charlotte and Betty were getting out of their cars. Yesterday, they'd agreed that Betty and Hal would keep the codicil until Betty, Charlotte, and Kathryn could take it to Charlotte's family estate lawyer together. That way, each of them could explain her part in locating it.

After a brief wait in the reception area, Wallingford's secretary showed them into his office. A big man with an ample head of curly silver hair and an equally ample handlebar mustache, Wallingford reminded Kathryn of photos she'd seen of Mark Twain. He rose from behind a large, well-polished mahogany desk and came around to greet them. After Charlotte introduced Kathryn and Betty, and they'd all taken seats, Wallingford said, "So, ladies, Charlotte tells me you're here about a codicil to a will."

"That's right, Wally," Charlotte said. "Diana Farley made a codicil to her original will, leaving part of her property to the New Nottingham Land Trust instead of her husband."

At a nod from Charlotte, Betty produced the document and handed it to Wallingford, who donned reading glasses to examine it. "Well, the document does what you say. And it's duly signed and witnessed, though I'll have to have the donor's signature and those of the witnesses verified. The names of the witnesses aren't familiar to me. Do any of you know these women?"

"I don't think they're local," Charlotte said. "I'm guessing they were friends of Diana's from New York."

"I'll also need to make sure the codicil does, in fact, postdate the original will," Wallingford said. "What I don't understand is why this document wasn't filed with that will."

Good question, Kathryn thought, but she let Charlotte respond.

"We don't know the answer to that," Charlotte admitted. "We can only speculate. Diana was known to be having marital difficulties, and was considering divorce. Apparently, she changed her mind about how she wanted her property to be disposed of. But, since she didn't expect to die so soon, she failed to give the codicil to her attorney."

"How did it come into your possession?" Wallingford asked Betty.

After she'd told him, Wallingford said, "Did it ever cross your mind, Mrs. Phelps, that the box you were given might contain an amendment to Mrs. Farley's will?"

"Maybe it should've, but it didn't." Betty flushed. "I was dealing with some difficult family matters at the time, and after I gave the box to my husband Hal to hide, I forgot all about it. If Kathryn hadn't mentioned the possibility of another will yesterday, that box might still be sitting on a shelf in our garage."

Wallingford picked up a pen from the holder on his desk and tapped it lightly on the surface. "Did any of you have a clue as to what this document might contain?"

"I did," Charlotte said. "Diana mentioned she was thinking of leaving some of her property to the land trust."

"So, the organization you represent stands to benefit?"

"That's correct."

More tapping.

"And you, Ms. Stinson, as the current tenant at the Farley house, what is your interest in this matter?"

"I'd prefer that this part of the property went to the land trust."

"And you, Mrs. Phelps?"

"I'm with Kathryn," Betty said.

The tapping stopped. Wallingford said, "You realize, of course, that it would have been better if the codicil had surfaced closer to the time of Mrs. Farley's death. The fact that it's only come to light now—after her husband died, his parents inherited the property, and they've sold it to a developer—complicates things. I'll do what I can, but it's going to take time, and I can't guarantee we'll be successful. Do you still want to proceed?"

"Yes," they said in unison, though Kathryn was beginning to have qualms. Wallingford's words weren't exactly encouraging, nor was his demeanor. Although he'd greeted them cordially, as he questioned them and heard the facts of the matter, his expression had changed. Now he looked somber. She hoped they weren't setting themselves up for an endless legal battle.

She, Charlotte, and Betty decided to confer over coffee at the Brew 'N' Burger, where Kathryn and Charlotte had lunched earlier. As she walked to her car, Kathryn noticed a black pickup pull out from Main Street below. Reikart's truck? It certainly looked like it. But what would he be doing in town at this hour? He could be here to pick up Solly at the vet's—except the veterinary hospital was located on the other side of town. She felt a prickle of unease at the thought

Corrigan might have put Reikart on her tail. But then again, maybe it wasn't his truck.

When they'd taken seats at the restaurant, Charlotte said, "I think our meeting with Wally went reasonably well."

"I agree," Betty said.

Although Kathryn hated to be the lone voice of dissent, she said, "Frankly, I'm concerned about how long it's going to take and how much it's going to cost. I'd like to help pay the legal fees, but there's a limit to what I can afford."

"No need to worry about that yet," Charlotte said. "We'll have to wait and see how things unfold. And if it looks like it's going to be a long battle, I have funds I can draw upon, and the land trust can always raise money to make up the difference."

"I'm good for a sizable contribution myself," Betty said. "After all, I feel responsible. If I'd only thought to open that lockbox a lot sooner, we wouldn't be in this pickle."

"Don't blame yourself," Charlotte said. "You had no way of knowing the box contained a codicil to Diana's will. If anyone's at fault, it's Diana for not spelling out exactly what you were getting."

"I wonder why she didn't," Betty mused.

Charlotte shook her head sadly. "That's a question we may never be able to answer."

*****

This and other questions dogged Kathryn after she left the restaurant to pay a visit to Emily at the hospital. Once she got herself settled next to Emily, she put on another tape, and as she listened to Emily and Diana talk in their easy, friendly way, she imagined herself breaking into their conversation, and demanding answers from Diana.

Why didn't you tell Betty there was a codicil to your will in that box?

Why give it to her in the first place, instead of your lawyer?

Were you afraid Gordon would find out?

Did he threaten you in some way? Or were you still on the fence about leaving him for Earl?

Why won't you talk to me? I'm a novice in affairs of the heart, and I could use a little guidance.

Chapter 34

The invitation came as a surprise to Gwen. Monday morning, Maxine called to see if she wanted to come over for lunch, as the library was closed that day. "Just me without the kids?" Gwen asked.

"Yeah, figured we'd make it a grown-up thing. And bring a bathing suit, because I thought we'd go for a swim. Oh, I almost forgot. Niall's taking the day off, so he'll be joining us. Okay?"

"Fine," Gwen said, though she knew it would hardly be fine with Tim, who'd taken an instant dislike to Niall. Nor would it be fine with Grandma Waite. She'd warned Gwen he was dangerous and she should steer clear of him, and keep Scarlett away from him, too. Gwen didn't believe Niall was dangerous, however. Not in the past when he'd come to her rescue several times. And not now. The old woman was crazy. Neither she nor Tim needed to know about today's lunch anyway.

Besides, it wasn't a tryst, but a get-together of three old friends. Nevertheless, she put on lipstick, mascara, and a light foundation. Nothing wrong with looking her best. She also exchanged the jeans and tee shirt she wore for a pretty sundress. And, instead of the ratty old one-piece bathing suit that was starting to lose its elastic, she packed a new black bikini, just like the one Scarlett had bought earlier. What was it her mother used to say? "If you've got it, flaunt it." Fortunately, she still had it, thanks to daily jogs and a weekly yoga class.

When Gwen went downstairs, Scarlett was on the phone in the hall, engrossed in a conversation punctuated by gasps and shrieks of laughter. She looked up when Gwen passed. "Where are you going?" Scarlett asked suspiciously.

"Out," Gwen replied over her shoulder, delighted to have a chance to use Scarlett's standard response to the same question from her.

She avoided any questions from Grandma Waite by getting into the car and driving away before the old woman made it to the door.

*****

"Wow. It's just like old times. The three of us together," Maxine said in her amped-up voice.

"Yeah," Niall agreed.

"Mmm," Gwen murmured.

It was another perfect June day, sunny with a robin's egg blue sky, but not too hot. They'd taken a dip in the lake, and now they lingered, in nearly dry bathing suits, over a sumptuous lunch courtesy of Guido's. Gwen hadn't felt so relaxed in ages. She basked in the sun and in the admiring glances she received from Niall. She couldn't remember when a man had looked at her like that. Not Tim surely. She wondered how much he even saw her lately, so much of his attention was focused on their daughter, albeit in a negative way. Niall, on the other hand, had made eyes at Scarlett, and though Gwen hated to admit it, she'd been a tad jealous. Scarlett was young and beautiful with her whole life before her, whereas Gwen no longer had the sense of endless possibilities stretching ahead of her like a glimmering sea with no horizon in sight. A cloud blotted her pleasure. Gwen willed it away. Then, another much smaller cloud formed.

"Where's the fourth person?" she said. "I wonder what happened to him."

"What fourth person?" Maxine echoed.

"The other boy in the photograph."

Niall frowned. "What photograph?"

"Oh, sorry. The other night, I was going through some old stuff and found a photograph of you, me, Maxine, and this other guy. He was someone I was dating at the time, but I can't remember his name."

"Maybe he wasn't particularly memorable," Maxine said.

"Right, but not remembering things bothers me," Gwen said. "I can't believe I didn't recognize you at the pizza parlor," she told Niall.

"You hadn't seen him in over twenty years," Maxine said. "And during that period, he's changed a lot. Shaved his head *and* put on weight."

"What made you decide to shave your head?" Gwen asked Niall. "Was it because it's the style for some men now?"

"Nah, when he did it, it wasn't fashionable," Maxine answered for him. "Aside from that actor my parents liked—Yul something—very few men had shaved heads then."

"So, it was a while ago?" Gwen said.

Again, Maxine answered for Niall. "He did it right after you had your 'accident.' It's also when he put on all the weight. At the time, I thought you looked like a monk," she told Niall.

"You sure know how to make a guy feel good," Niall said in a mock aggrieved tone.

"Sorry," Maxine said, "but speaking of the past, I have a question for you both. When you were in your twenties, did you ever imagine you'd be living the life you are now?"

"I certainly didn't," Gwen said. "I thought I'd work for several more years, marry someone from our crowd, start a family, and move to the suburbs. But never that I'd wind up in the country, married to a local carpenter with two kids."

"This may come as a surprise to you," Maxine said, "but the life you have, Gwen, is exactly the one I've been dreaming of: living here full-time and married to a local guy with a couple kids."

"Really?" Niall said. "You've always struck me as such an urban person."

"I definitely was in my twenties, but over the years, New York's lost its luster for me. Maybe it's because I'm older now, but the city feels more dangerous. The fast pace is tiring, and the noise grates on my ears. I long for the quiet and safety of the country."

"Bad things happen here, too," Gwen reminded her.

"You mean the fire and that man getting killed?" Niall asked.

"That was awful," Maxine said. "Still, it's nothing compared to the killings that occur in New York on a daily basis."

153

"So, find a good country boy and settle down here," Niall said.

"Easier said than done." Maxine's expression turned wistful. "As you yourself said, Niall, when I asked you why you weren't married, 'the good ones are all taken.'"

"It often seems that way, but don't forget, couples split up, so good ones are added back into the mix," Niall said.

"Yeah, but if your timing's off, forget it. Take Earl Barker. He was on his own for several years after he and his wife divorced and his lover was murdered. But during those years, I was seeing a guy who turned out to be a total jerk. By the time I realized what a catch Earl was, Kathryn had already snapped him up. If I ever get another crack at him—and I just might, given the way Kathryn's dithering about marriage—I won't let it happen again." Maxine glanced at her watch and made a face. "Here I am, running off at the mouth when I've got errands to do." She rose and began gathering up their dishes.

"Let us help," Gwen volunteered.

When they'd rinsed things and loaded the dishwater, Maxine headed for the door, wearing a shift over her bathing suit. "Just because I have to leave doesn't mean you do, too. Stick around, go for another swim, and enjoy the rest of this beautiful afternoon," she called back over her shoulder.

"What do you say, up for another swim?" Niall asked.

"I don't know, I probably should be getting back," Gwen hedged.

"Why?"

"Well, the kids—"

"Surely, Scarlett's old enough to take care of herself and her younger brother as well."

"Yes, but—"

"No buts," he said in a voice that brooked no disagreement. "As Maxine said, it's a lovely afternoon, so why not enjoy it? Go for a swim, or better yet, let me take you waterskiing."

"We can go for a quick swim, but waterskiing's out. I'm sure I've completely forgotten how."

"I seriously doubt that, but I'm happy to give you a few pointers."

"No, I—"

"What's the matter? Don't tell me you're afraid. That's not like

154

the Gwen I remember. You were always so fearless. Here at this very lake, twenty years ago, you were hellbent on waterskiing. Even though it was after midnight, and the boat was in bad shape."

Gwen thought a moment, then slowly the memory came back to her. A boy with a mass of curly dark hair, and dark, intense eyes that always seemed to be watching her. That night he'd spoken. "I'll take you." Then they were out on the water together, he at the helm of the boat, she streaking behind, riding a moon beam. Darkness. Hitting something, going under, caught in a tangle of weeds. Rescued, but cold, so cold, with his thin shirt around her. Feet on the ground, running away, then back again. His mouth warm against hers.

The wild girl stepped from the wings where she'd been waiting all along. "All right, I'll do it," she said.

*****

Gwen perched on the edge of the dock, skis in the water, tips pointing upward.

"Ready?" Niall called.

"Yes!"

The wind whipped her hair back as she skimmed along the wake. When that felt too tame, she left the wake for water that was undisturbed except for the beginning of a small chop. She took two good long runs before signaling him to slow down. As they approached shore, he cut the engine, and she floated for a few moments before sinking waist-deep into the water.

"Had enough?" he shouted.

The wild girl had been cooped up so long, she was not to be denied now. "No!" Gwen yelled back. "I want to try slalom."

It took her a couple tries to get up on one ski, but the effort was worth it. She started out in the relatively undisturbed water, then decided to jump the wake. Bending her legs, she leapt into the air, straightening as she came down on the other side of the wake. She executed a second jump. What wonderful fun this was! She didn't want to stop, even though the waves were getting dangerously high.

When Niall slowed and brought the boat close to shore, forcing an end to the sport, she was furious.

"Why did you come in without a signal from me?" she demanded, as he tied the boat to the dock. "I was doing fine."

"I could see that."

"Then why—"

"It's about knowing when to quit," he said, his voice turning serious. "That's a lesson I've had to learn. The hard way."

What was he talking about? Gwen was about to ask when a cloud blotted out the sun. She began to shiver uncontrollably. Niall wrapped a towel around her, and she leaned into him as he led her off the dock, across the beach, and to the house.

Chapter 35

Niall lounged on the dock, nursing a Scotch. Gwen had left a little while ago, and Max had yet to return. He was glad to have the place to himself. Gave him a chance to re-live the highpoints of the afternoon from his first sight of Gwen in her black bikini to his last glimpse of her blonde hair cascading down her back as she hurried to her car.

Things had gone even better than he'd hoped. It was obvious from the start she'd wanted to look good for him. Why else would she have worn make-up and a revealing bathing suit? The other times he'd seen her, she'd looked almost dowdy. Now, too, he sensed her pleasure at the admiring glances he showered on her. And once she was out on the water, the years fell away, and she became the beautiful, wild girl he'd loved, and always would. He'd wanted so badly to tell her this. But he knew if he rushed things, he risked losing her. So, he'd held back, settling for holding her shivering body close. After she'd showered, she let him apply soothing lotion to her sunburnt back. How he treasured those few, brief moments of physical contact. And longed for more. But it was too soon. Still, a man could dream, couldn't he?

The sound of a car on the drive jerked Niall from his reverie. He sighed deeply. Max was back. Back with her loud clothes and even louder voice. She'd want all the juicy details about what had happened after she left. Details he'd rather not share because putting his thoughts and feelings into words would cheapen them. Still, he'd have to satisfy at least some of Max's craving to know all. He couldn't afford not to. Not when he owed her big-time for arranging the lunch and leaving him alone with Gwen. Not when he might need her help arranging more such trysts.

Chapter 36

Kathryn returned from Great Barrington in the late afternoon. Earl was still at work on the driveway. She stopped to invite him to the house for a beer after he was done. Reikart's truck was parked near the trailer, so she knew he was back from town also. On an impulse, she pulled over. Braving savage barking from Geronimo, she knocked on the trailer door. Reikart appeared. "Yeah, what is it?"

"Was that your truck I saw in Great Barrington this morning?" she asked.

"Where d'you think you saw it?"

She told him.

"Nah, couldn't 've been mine. I was in GB today to pick up Solstice from the vet's, but not in that part of town."

She glanced around him into the interior of the trailer. "Where is she?"

"Charlotte—Miss Hinckley, that is—agreed to take her for the time being. Too tense here with two dogs wanting to get at each other's throats. And Solstice likes her. That 'un," he gestured at Geronimo, who'd quieted at a command from him, "gets on my nerves also. But Corrigan says he's gotta be the guard dog, and he's the boss."

Kathryn nodded and left. She wasn't convinced Reikart was telling the truth about being near the lawyer's office. She was also surprised Charlotte had agreed to take in Solly. Apparently, Charlotte's love of animals trumped any concerns she might have about continuing to help the security guard of a man both she and Kathryn regarded as an enemy.

*****

"How did the meeting with the lawyer go?" Earl asked. He'd finished working on the driveway for the day, and now he and Kathryn sat on the patio with beers.

"Okay, I guess, though he wasn't encouraging. Said the case may take a long time, which means it'll be expensive, and there's no guarantee of success."

"I'm sorry."

She leaned over and kissed him. He looked at her, surprised. "What was that for?"

"For not saying 'I told you so.' You did warn me, after all."

"Yeah, I suppose I did."

They fell silent for a few moments, then Kathryn said, "Feels like old times, you and me drinking beer on the patio after you worked on the driveway."

A puzzled look from him, then he said, "Oh, *that* time. I remember how mad you were when you came back from the city and found I'd left a load of gravel in the middle of the drive. Did the same thing when I wrapped up today as a matter of fact."

"Whatever for?"

Earl grinned. "In case Corrigan decides to pay us a surprise visit, he won't be able to get here in his car."

"Good thinking. I was furious that other time. But you got me to calm down. And when you told me how Diana appreciated the pond you'd made when it was only a hole in the ground, my feelings about you changed. I may even have started to fall for you."

"It changed things for me, too," Earl said. "Come here." He patted his lap. He'd just begun to kiss her when the phone rang. "Let it ring," he murmured. "Whoever it is can always leave a message."

"Mmm," she murmured back, content to lose herself in his embrace.

The ringing stopped, followed by silence as the recorded message kicked in, then the caller's voice came on. Earl cocked his head, listening. "Think I better get that. It sounds like Wayne." He went inside.

A few minutes later, he returned, his eyes downcast. "The Chief stopped by Wayne and Suzy's with the news they've identified the body in the woods. As I suspected, it's Randy. Suzy's taking it hard. Robert, too."

"From what Suzy's told me, it's obvious she still has feelings for her ex, but I'm surprised Robert's taking it hard."

"In spite of how badly Randy sometimes treated Robert, Randy was still his dad," Earl said.

Plungas's mistreatment of his son brought to mind the ugly scene in the library when he'd called Gwen a whore. Kathryn had yet to find out what was behind the name-calling. Maybe this wasn't the best time to bring it up, but she was beginning to wonder if there would ever be a good time.

"Are you still planning to tell me about the rumor Randy circulated about Gwen to try to prevent Tim from marrying her?" she asked. "The one that has to do with Grant's Tomb."

Earl shifted uncomfortably in his seat. "I know I said I'd tell you, Star, but frankly I've been putting it off in the hopes you'd forget. It's such an awful story, it'll only upset you."

"Maybe so, but I'd still like to hear it."

"All right." He took a deep breath and let it out slowly, as if steeling himself for what he was about to say. "When Gwen first came here, she told people she was recovering from a bad car accident. But Randy was suspicious, as he was of all New Yorkers. He started digging in the New York papers for stories of bad things that had occurred there before Gwen's arrival in the Berkshires."

"How did he get ahold of New York newspapers?"

"With all the New Yorkers who have second homes in the area, those papers are available at the local libraries and some stores, including the New Nottingham General Store. Randy had an aunt who was a librarian in Pittsfield, so he undoubtedly got her help, too. Anyway, he fixated on one story in particular. It had to do with a young woman who was raped and brutally beaten in the part of Riverside Park that's below Grant's Tomb."

Kathryn shuddered. "That *is* awful. I hope the police found and arrested the person who did that."

"Unfortunately, they never did, despite an extensive search. The attack happened late at night in a deserted area of the park, and there were no witnesses."

"But someone must have noticed the young woman at some point in the evening before she was attacked."

"According to the newspapers, she'd been partying with friends at an apartment on Riverside Drive. A couple of them remembered seeing her leave the party, but after that, nothing."

"What about the woman herself? Did she remember anything?"

"She was beaten unconscious, went into a coma, and when she came out of it, she had no memory of what had happened."

"What made Randy think the victim was Gwen?"

"The victim's identity was never revealed. She was simply known as Jane Doe, then the Grant's Tomb Girl. Since Gwen had been in an accident and then a coma, Randy spread the rumor that she was the Grant's Tomb Girl. And Randy being Randy, he embellished the story. He claimed that instead of the victim having been at a party, she was a hooker who'd gone into the park to meet her john, they had a falling out, and he assaulted and nearly killed her."

A storm of emotions swept over Kathryn. Anger at Randy. Horror at the violent attack. And a terrible nagging suspicion that Gwen was, in fact, the Grant's Tomb Girl. A suspicion based on what Maxine had told her about both Gwen and herself when they were younger. They'd been party girls, and had often taken chances on how they got to parties, and how they returned home again. It wasn't inconceivable that Gwen might have gone into Riverside Park after a night of partying in a nearby apartment.

Kathryn focused on the pond to calm herself. But the reflections of the burned trees in the water brought no relief. Her anguish must have been apparent. Earl took her hand and squeezed it. "It's okay, Star. Try to put it out of your mind. The whole business with the Grant's Tomb Girl happened a long time ago. That girl, whoever she was— and I don't think it was Gwen—is a woman now. And hopefully, she's leading a normal, happy life."

"Yes," she replied, even though she knew she wouldn't be able to put the story out of her mind, believed the girl could have been Gwen, and wasn't sure how happy Gwen was at the moment.

The ringing phone was a welcome distraction from these gloomy thoughts. Welcome until she answered it, and the caller was Tim. "Is Gwen there?" he demanded.

"No, have you tried Maxine's?"

"Yes, but I keep getting voicemail."

"Did Gwen mention any plans she might have made?"

"Not to me, and when Scarlett asked her where she was going this morning, she just said 'out.' And left in such a hurry that Grandma Waite, who watches our comings and goings like a hawk, didn't get a chance to find out."

"I'm sorry. I wish I could help you."

"Me, too."

Tim's aggrieved tone and the abrupt way he ended the call didn't bode well for Gwen when she returned from wherever she was.

"Who was that?" Earl asked when she re-joined him on the patio.

She told him.

"I've noticed things haven't been going very well between Gwen and Tim lately," Earl said. "Tim's been drinking more, and some of it has to do with Scarlett. Must be tough having a daughter who's not only beautiful but rebellious. I was lucky with my older boys, but as you know, Pete's having a hard time dealing with his mom's death."

And with our relationship.

"There's Corrigan, too," Kathryn said. "I think he might be interested in Gwen, and Tim may have picked on that, and is angry and jealous."

Earl looked thoughtful. "If you think it would help, I could talk to Tim about his drinking. Maybe even encourage him and Gwen to see a counselor about the best way to handle Scarlett. As for Corrigan, I don't see him as a threat to Tim. Gwen loves Tim, and I don't believe she'd get involved with someone like Corrigan."

"I hope you're right," Kathryn said. But she wasn't convinced, and found herself descending into another morass of gloom. Again, her distress must have been obvious.

"Is there anything I can say or do to make you feel better?" Earl asked.

"I don't know."

"Well, I'm going to try. I'm not leaving you alone when you're this sad. I'll call Pete and tell him I'm spending the night here. Then I'm going to take you to a place you've never been. It's a lake in a nearby state forest. The swimming's good, and on our way, we'll pick up supplies for a cook-out afterward. Then we'll come back here, and, you know, enjoy ourselves upstairs. How does that sound?"

She smiled. "Good. But aren't you forgetting something?"

"What?"

Kathryn pointed at the driveway.

"Oh, *that*. Guess I better move the pile of gravel out of the way, or we ain't goin' nowhere," he finished with a grin.

Chapter 37

Kathryn lay in bed, reliving each exquisite moment of her time with Earl the previous night. The lake he'd taken her to was lovely: a sparkling blue expanse, its surface unmarred by power boats, and the woods that surrounded it, untouched by fire. A family with young children was just leaving as they arrived. Then they had the place to themselves. A rope attached to buoys marked the swimming area, but the lifeguard had gone, so Kathryn was able to swim far out into the lake. With each stroke, she seemed to shed a little more of the tension she'd been feeling. Earl joined her for part of the swim, then left to attend to their cook-out. They feasted on hot dogs and hamburgers he grilled on an open outdoor grill, store-bought potato salad, and lettuce and tomato salad, with s'mores for dessert.

When they returned to the Farley house at nightfall, Kathryn's mind was free of troubling thoughts. She was so relaxed that even Geronimo's ferocious barking didn't bother her. Their lovemaking that night was slow and incredibly tender.

Kathryn caressed the bed where Earl had lain. He'd left early so he could begin work while it was still relatively cool. She didn't have such constraints. Still, she was anxious to follow up on yesterday's phone calls. She began with Gwen.

"Oh hi, Kathryn, I'm glad it's you and not Chief Lapsley again."

"He's been in touch with you?"

"He called early this morning and said the state police detective wanted to talk to me and Tim again. Tim arranged to go in before work. My appointment is for one PM, a half hour before I open the library."

Kathryn waited a beat, then said, "When Tim called yesterday looking for you, he sounded upset. Is everything okay?"

"I guess," Gwen muttered.

"You sound unsure. Want to talk about it?"

"No—yes. But not over the phone."

"I'd invite you over, but Corrigan might show up and we wouldn't have much privacy."

"Come to me then. Don't forget to park several doors down and come the back way."

"I will, but you should know that Grandma Waite's onto the ruse. She accosted me as I was leaving your house the last time."

"I know. Several people have told me the same thing. But it's still better than nothing. Keeps her at bay a *little* longer."

*****

Swerving around a pothole in Shuntoll Road, Kathryn pulled into a parking spot. Gwen was waiting in the backyard. She sat listlessly in the jungle gym swing, barely moving. Her face and what were visible of her arms and legs were badly sunburnt.

"What happened to you?" Kathryn asked.

"Maxine invited me for lunch yesterday. We went for a swim first, and I stayed in my bathing suit the rest of the afternoon. Big mistake."

"If you and Maxine were sunbathing all afternoon, why didn't Maxine answer the phone when Tim called? Isn't there an extension near the dock?"

"There is, but we—I, that is—went back into the water to ski."

"And Maxine was driving the boat?"

"Yes."

"Tim was angry because he didn't know where you were?"

Gwen nodded.

"You didn't leave a note or tell anyone you were going to Maxine's?"

"I didn't feel it was necessary. But now I wish I had. Then maybe Scarlett and Grandma Waite wouldn't have—" Gwen broke off.

"Wouldn't have what?"

"Scarlett told Tim I was wearing make-up and a nice sundress. Grandma Waite went further. She said I acted suspicious, almost as if I was sneaking off for a tryst."

"But you weren't, were you?" Kathryn sensed Gwen wasn't telling her the whole story. "Was Niall at Maxine's?" she asked on a hunch.

Gwen stared at the ground. "Yes."

"If the three of you were there, why didn't one of you answer the phone?"

"Maxine went out to do some errands," Gwen said.

"So, it was just you and Niall at the lake for a while."

"Nothing happened!" Gwen flared, suddenly defensive. "He took me waterskiing and that was *all*."

Kathryn held up a hand, palm outward. "I'm not accusing you of anything."

"No, but Tim did when he figured out Niall and I had been alone together. He doesn't trust Niall. Me either. And when Tim found the bikini I wore wrapped in my towel, he went ballistic."

Kathryn reached over and patted Gwen's knee. "I'm sorry. What you've told me sounds a little bit like what happened with Earl at the beginning of our relationship. He was terrified I'd leave him for my old boyfriend in Boston. When I had to go back to the city for a work-related meeting and returned here late, I could tell he thought I'd met up with Alan."

"But Niall isn't an old boyfriend. We were never anything more than friends."

"Unfortunately, Tim doesn't see it that way. And from the little I've observed, Niall may be hoping for something more."

"Whether that's true or not, you'd think after twenty years of marriage—during which I've *never* been unfaithful—Tim would trust me. Instead, he told me I'd betrayed him."

"How?"

"I made the mistake of telling Tim that Randy'd called me a whore. Tim confronted him at The Stag."

"I know. I was there."

"Now that Randy's dead, Tim's under suspicion," Gwen continued.

"He defended me, and he's not only in trouble because of it, but he thinks I proved him wrong by taking up with Niall behind his back."

Kathryn flinched. Things were not looking good for Tim, *or* for the couple's marriage. But what advice could she give when she was still trying to figure out what to do about her relationship with Earl? Finally, she said. "Maybe if you and Tim had a night out, just the two of you without the kids."

"Yeah, that might help," Gwen said with enough uncertainty in her voice to make Kathryn wonder if she really believed it.

"But now, I better get a move on if I'm going to finish everything I need to do before my interview with the statie," she said.

Gwen disappeared indoors, and Kathryn took the back way to her car. She'd just emerged from behind the house several doors down, when Grandma Waite intercepted her. As before, the old woman was a study in black: black shoes, black dress, and black Shirley Temple-style curls. "So, Miss Kathryn, you are back visiting my Gwen. But you have not done a good job of persuading her to keep away from that evil man in the sports car. Only yesterday, I saw her leave the house to be with him. She did not return until hours later. My grandson is very angry about it."

"How do you know Gwen was with the man in the sports car?" Kathryn asked.

"She was all dressed up. And she sneaked out of the house. You must tell her to stop seeing that evil man immediately."

"Why do you keep calling him evil?" Kathryn asked.

Grandma Waite's talon-like hand closed on Kathryn's wrist. "Come to my house and we will have tea and talk."

The old woman could very well be crazy. Still, Kathryn wanted to hear what she had to say. "I can't do it today, but another time?"

"Tomorrow then at two PM." Grandma Waite paused, her face assuming a sly expression. "Park several doors down from my house and come the back way. I will be waiting for you."

Kathryn suppressed a smile. Perhaps the old woman wasn't so crazy after all.

Chapter 38

An hour later, Kathryn drove up the hill to the Barker compound. Suzy and her family lived in a small house constructed from the same dark timber that had been used for the other houses. Leaving her car, she was greeted by a swarm of black and tan dogs who alternated between barking and licking her hands—a welcome change from the attack dog at Reikart's trailer.

Suzy opened the door. Her face was pale, and judging from her red-rimmed eyes, she'd been crying. Kathryn gave her an awkward one-armed hug, because one hand held a tin containing cornmeal muffins. No baker like Suzy, she'd made them from a mix, but added blueberries to make them special. Suzy took the tin, thanked Kathryn, and invited her in.

The house was simply but nicely furnished. Plants on the window sill and hanging from the ceiling were evidence of Suzy's prowess as a gardener as well as a cook. Robert sat at a round kitchen table while Suzy's two younger boys played in a corner. They piped "Hi, Kathryn" in unison before returning to their game. Robert raised a hand in greeting, but remained silent, his expression glum. Normally vivacious, Suzy was subdued.

"We were just making a list of items Robert wants from his dad's cabin," she said.

"The only things I really care about are my science project and that book of Kurt Vonnegut short stories," Robert said.

"Fine, but while I'm there, I might as well get the rest of your stuff. Are you sure you won't come with me?" she asked Robert.

"No way am I going back there."

169

"Okay. I'll call the Chief and tell him I'm coming."

"I don't understand why he has to be involved. You know where Dad keeps the extra key, so why don't you just go get my stuff? It's not like you're stealing anything."

"As I've already explained, the Chief doesn't want the contents of the cabin disturbed." Suzy's tone turned testy. "He's doing us a big favor by letting me go in and take things you want under his supervision."

"*Whatever*," Robert muttered.

After Suzy'd made the call and was getting ready to leave, Kathryn offered to accompany her. She sensed Suzy's reluctance to talk about her dead ex-husband in front of Robert or her other children, and hoped this would give Suzy a chance to speak freely. She was also curious to see the inside of Randy's cabin.

"I'm sorry about Randy," Kathryn said when they were alone in the car.

"Thanks, I'm actually kind of surprised at how hard it's hit me. After Randy went missing and they found a body, I held my breath, hoping it wasn't him. Now that it's definite, I feel terrible. I know that may seem strange, given how much we fought when he was alive. But I did love him with all my heart once. And when that ended, I still liked having him in my life. My mother has always said I have a temper to go with my red hair. Randy did that for me."

"Did what?"

"Stoked my anger in a way that Wayne never could and never will, he's such a nice guy. I'll miss locking horns with Randy. Does that sound weird?"

"No, though we're different in that respect. I avoid confrontation whenever possible while you sound like you almost enjoy it."

Suzy nodded. "I'm worried life will be dull without Randy stirring things up."

"You might find someone else to get you riled up," Kathryn said.

She found herself wishing she had more of Suzy's fiery nature. Perhaps then she'd have better success stopping Corrigan from building his development. If only she had red hair.

"Right on time." Chief Lapsley tapped his watch and rose from the tree stump he'd been sitting on. His smile changed to a frown when he saw Kathryn leave the car. "Didn't realize you were coming along."

"Kathryn was at the house when I called you. She offered to keep me company when Robert refused to come," Suzy told him. "I've brought a list of things he wants, and Kathryn can help me get them."

The Chief grunted, then said, "All right, but I want you both to put on gloves, and don't touch anything aside from the things you're getting. I'm going in with you, and I'll be in charge of the list."

When they stepped inside, Suzy was suddenly overcome with emotion. She shut her eyes and gritted her teeth.

"You okay?" the Chief asked.

"Yeah, I just need a minute to pull myself together."

The cabin was as sparsely furnished as Earl's trailer, but a lot messier. One corner contained a mattress on the floor with Randy's clothes strewn on and around it, while the opposite one contained a sleeping bag, presumably Robert's, on a piece of foam, surrounded by clothing in plastic bags and other items in cardboard boxes. Robert's science project—a board covered with wires, a couple of batteries, and a switch—sat on a cardboard box in his corner.

A rickety table and two chairs stood in the middle of the room with leftover food congealing on the plates. More dirty dishes filled a small basin with a cracked mirror over it that obviously doubled as kitchen and bathroom sink. There was no separate bathroom, but Kathryn had noticed an outhouse a short distance from the trailer. *Ugh.* She felt bad for Robert having to live in such squalor, even though it was only part time.

The Chief took a seat at the rickety table and read aloud from the Robert's list, while Suzy and Kathryn located the various items in the bags and boxes. When the Chief came to the book of Vonnegut short stories, he said, "Robert's into Vonnegut?"

"Yes," Suzy said. "The stories in *Welcome to the Monkey House* are science fiction with some fantasy, and he likes that." She glanced around. "But I don't see the book here."

Kathryn looked around, too, and noticed a paperback on top of a beat-up, three-drawer file cabinet in Randy's corner. She crossed the room, picked up *Welcome to the Monkey House,* and flipped through a few pages. A piece of paper, probably a bookmark, flew out. As she bent to retrieve it, her gaze fell on the middle drawer. It was slightly open, revealing a sheaf of yellowed newspapers. She was about to pull out the drawer to get a better look when the Chief said, "Find something else interesting?"

"Just Robert's book." She held it up.

Kathryn returned to Robert's corner and helped Suzy gather the remaining items he wanted. When they were finished, Suzy pointed at the sole shotgun on the wall next to a fishing rod and a hunting trap. "I guess that scotches the rumors that Randy had an arsenal of weapons here," she said.

"Actually, those rumors turned out to be true," the Chief said. "Under questioning from the state police detective, Robert admitted his dad had an underground cache of military-type weapons. Said he'd never actually seen it, but his dad bragged about having one. We did a search and found such a cache in the woods behind the outhouse."

"Oh," Suzy said.

The discovery of the cache gave Randy an additional reason for shooting at Earl and Corrigan, and trying to block the latter's development. He didn't want anyone encroaching on his private arsenal.

As for the yellowed newspapers in the file drawer, they might shed light on another rumor associated with Randy. She'd have to come back another time to check them out when she wasn't under the Chief's watchful eyes.

Chapter 39

As Kathryn, Suzy, and Chief Lapsley walked to their cars, the Chief said, "Detective Scoville would like to talk to Robert again, Suzy. Can you bring him to my office at noon?"

Suzy looked upset. "Can't this wait? We just got the news about Randy yesterday, and Robert's taking it hard. Me, too."

"I'm sorry, Suzy, but the detective wants to do it today. You can be present when Robert's interviewed if that would make you both more comfortable. As his parent, you can also refuse to have him interviewed. So can Robert himself. But that's probably not a good idea. Detective Scoville wants to get at the truth about why Randy died, and Robert's testimony may be important in establishing that."

"Okay, I'll talk to Robert and get back to you."

The Chief nodded his approval, then turning to Kathryn, he said, "Detective Scoville would like to talk to you again also. Why don't you come around..." He paused to check his watch, "One thirty?"

*****

At a quarter after one that afternoon, Kathryn parked in the lot behind the town hall, where the police department was located. She opened the car windows to let in the soft June air and clear her head. Gwen would be halfway through her interview by now. For her friend's sake, she hoped the interview went all right, though she knew Scoville would probably probe more deeply into Gwen's relationship with Plungas.

Her thoughts returned to her earlier conversation with Gwen. On

173

the one hand, she sympathized with her friend's having to deal with her husband's jealousy. On the other, she sympathized with Tim for being jealous. A country carpenter, Tim probably felt threatened by Corrigan, a rich and apparently successful developer, much as Earl, an excavator, had felt threatened by her former boyfriend, Alan, a big city lawyer. She and Gwen were at different places in their lives, however. Gwen had been married for twenty years while she had yet to marry. And now that Gwen's marriage appeared less than happy, Kathryn wondered if the same fate lay in store for her if she married Earl. They were doing fine at the moment, but what about the future? What if Corrigan's development got underway, and Earl became the destroyer of the landscape she loved? How would she feel about him then? And while she enjoyed the country, could she really be happy living here full-time? Or would she miss the stimulation of the city, and the genuine pleasure she derived from her work as a curator of prints and photographs? After all, she couldn't very well curate the woods.

*****

Ten minutes later, Kathryn left her car and entered the town hall. The Chief's office was located on the second floor. As she climbed the stairs, she saw Gwen coming down. Gwen's sunburned face looked drawn. She acknowledged Kathryn's presence with a quick, sidelong glance before hurrying past. The Chief sat on a chair outside, apparently monitoring the flow of interviewees. At a signal from him, Kathryn entered the office. Even though it had only been a few days since she'd last seen him, Kathryn was struck anew by how tall Scoville was, when he rose from behind the desk to greet her. After giving her his low wattage smile, he motioned for her to sit and did so himself.

He began by walking her back over ground they'd covered before. Then, as she suspected he might, he zeroed in on the incident in the library when Plungas had attempted to forcibly remove Robert from the premises, and both Robert and Gwen had resisted.

"I understand you were present on that occasion."

"Yes."

"Then you must have heard Mr. Plungas insult Mrs. Waite by calling her a whore. What do you know about that?"

"Just that it happened."

"You don't know why he would say that?"

"No." Though Kathryn wondered, she didn't know for sure that Gwen was the Grant's Tomb Girl. And even if Gwen had been that girl, it didn't necessarily make her a whore.

"That's all?" Scoville said. "I would have thought that as a good friend of Mrs. Waite's, you'd be able to tell me more."

"Actually, I've only known Mrs. Waite for a few months."

"But you've known Mr. Barker for a longer period of time, haven't you?"

"What does he have to do with this?" Kathryn asked, confused by the abrupt switch to Earl.

"Answer the question," Scoville said.

"I've known Earl longer than Gwen."

"And you're in a relationship with him?"

"Yes."

"Then perhaps you can tell me why he threatened Mr. Plungas after the incident in the library."

Was Earl under suspicion too?

"All I know is that Earl felt Plungas was out of line and told him to stop." No need to mention that Earl suspected Plungas was the person who'd shot at him and Corrigan, or that Earl had used that as leverage to try to get Plungas to change his behavior.

Scoville regarded her in silence for a few moments, as if waiting for her to say more. When she didn't, he moved on. "Let's talk about the two shootings that occurred in the woods before the fire. Where were you when Mr. Barker and Mr. Corrigan were shot at?"

"In the house. When I heard the shots, I went into the woods to investigate."

"You weren't afraid of being shot yourself?"

"I was, but I was more afraid Earl—Mr. Barker, that is—had been hurt."

"But not Mr. Corrigan?"

"Huh?"

"Were you afraid he'd been hurt also?"

"Of course, I was."

"But not as afraid for him as you were for Mr. Barker?"

"I'm in a relationship with Mr. Barker, not Mr. Corrigan."

"Is it fair to say you don't approve of Mr. Corrigan's proposed development of the property you're renting?"

"As I told you earlier, I'd prefer the land be left in its natural state, but he's the owner now, so he can do what he wants."

"Where were you when Mr. Reikart's dog was shot?"

"Charlotte Hinckley and I were just about to go into the house when we heard shots in the woods. We went in to investigate and met up with Reikart carrying his wounded dog."

"How do you feel about having a guard dog on the premises?"

"I'm not thrilled about it, but I understand why Mr. Corrigan feels it's necessary."

Again, Scoville paused and looked at her, as if he expected her to continue. Then, after a quick glance at his notes, he said, "Tell me again what made you go into the woods early in the morning after the fire."

Kathryn hesitated, as she struggled to remember exactly what she'd said. "I wanted to see if the fire had woken up like the firemen said it would. And I figured I'd be safe because I saw a deer come out of the forest and go back in."

Another silent pause, longer than the previous two. Then Scoville said, "That's all for now. If I have more questions, I'll be in touch."

What a relief the interview was over. Scoville had tried to trick her into saying more than she intended with his long silences. She thanked her lucky stars she hadn't taken the bait, also that he hadn't pressed her about why she went into the woods after the fire. Because how could she have explained the strong pull the white stag exerted over her?

Before leaving town, Kathryn walked across the street to the general store and purchased a pair of leather workman's gloves. While she was paying, she noticed Reikart checking out refrigerated cases of beer. His back was to her, and she didn't know if he saw her. She left the store in a hurry.

Chapter 40

Kathryn knew she was taking a big chance visiting Randy's cabin a second time. But with the Chief occupied at his office while Detective Scoville conducted interviews, now was a good time to go unnoticed. She parked in the clearing where they'd parked earlier in the day. Having heard Robert mention his dad kept an extra key hidden outside, she searched and found it under a large rock near the entrance.

Then, with gloved hands, Kathryn unlocked the door and went directly to the file cabinet. She opened the middle drawer and pulled out a folder filled with dusty, faded papers. Some were pages from actual newspapers, others, copies of microfilm pages. A glance at the first headline told her she'd hit pay dirt. "Jogger Finds Badly Beaten, Barely Alive Woman in Riverside Park."

She read the story from beginning to end, then skimmed several accounts that followed from *The New York Times,* the *Daily News,* and the *New York Post.* Plungas had gone to a lot of trouble gathering these. He must have spent hours at the public library. But maybe not. Earl had told her Plungas had gotten help from an aunt who was a librarian in Pittsfield, so she might have done most of the work. Still, the extent of the collection showed how determined Plungas had been to prevent Tim from marrying Gwen. But so far, the stories didn't contain any evidence that the Grant's Tomb Girl was Gwen.

She read on, and a name leapt out at her. Niall Corrigan was quoted as having noticed Jane Doe, as she was called, at a party in an apartment on Riverside Drive, but then he lost track of her. He didn't think of her again until he read the story about a badly beaten and raped woman found in the park.

The mention of Corrigan made Kathryn almost positive Gwen was the Grant's Tomb Girl. But would Plungas have known that? Probably not unless he'd contacted Corrigan in an effort to learn the woman's identity. But even if Plungas had, it was unlikely Corrigan would have told him, let alone even spoken with him. From what Maxine had told her, Corrigan had been all about protecting Gwen, though he obviously hadn't succeeded the night of the party.

Pondering this, Kathryn didn't hear approaching footsteps until they were almost to the cabin. She stuffed the clippings into the folder, crossed the room to the door, and flattened herself against the wall next to it. If she were lucky when the door swung open, she could slip out before whoever it was saw her.

She wasn't so lucky. Reikart had barely stepped inside when he spotted her. He shut the door and planted himself in front of it, blocking her way. Startled by the speed of his movements, Kathryn dropped the file folder, papers spilling onto the floor.

"What the hell are you doing?" he demanded.

"I was here this morning with Suzy Barker and Chief Lapsley," she said as calmly as she could muster. "We came for some things her son wanted from the cabin. I returned to get something we forgot." She gestured at the mess on the floor.

Reikart picked up a sheet. He glanced at it and frowned. "What's this—something about a Grant's Tomb Girl?"

"I have no idea—only that Suzy's son wanted it. Now can I go?"

Reikart didn't move. "The Chief know you're here?"

"He already gave Suzy and me permission to get Robert's things."

"Yeah, sure. I bet he's gonna be very interested to know I caught you red-handed stealing stuff from the dead guy's cabin."

"And I think he'll be equally interested to know your boss put you on my tail."

Reikart scowled at her, but didn't budge.

Kathryn tried again. "I also think Charlotte Hinckley's going to be interested to know you've been following me. She might even have second thoughts about boarding Solly for you."

Reikart balled the piece of paper in his hand and tossed it across the room. He stomped on other papers on the floor and kicked at them, scattering them even more. Then he left the cabin with a savage slam of the door that reverberated throughout the room.

Shaken by the encounter, Kathryn allowed herself a few minutes to recover. Then she picked up the papers and put them back into the folder. She was about to return the folder to the file drawer, but decided not to. In her hands, she held Plungas's entire collection of Grant's Tomb Girl stories. She could try to replicate it by finding as many of the stories as she could online. But why go to all that trouble when she could take advantage of what he'd amassed? She was a curator, and she could use her skills to select and organize the contents. She needed time to do the job properly, however. She'd best take the file with her and return it when she was finished.

*****

As Kathryn pulled into the Farley driveway, she ran into Corrigan, who was just leaving. He stopped his car and called from the open window, "Earl did a great job on the driveway, don't you think?"

"Indeed," she agreed. He said nothing about the fact that she'd visited a lawyer the day before, or had just come from Plungas's cabin, information she was sure he'd gotten from Reikart, whose truck was now parked by the trailer.

Chapter 41

Back at the house, Kathryn considered reading the newspaper clippings in their entirety, but she shrank from the task. It promised to be deeply disturbing. After her run-in with Reikart, she could use a break. She hid the folder under the mattress in the master bedroom. Then she called Charlotte. She wanted to find out if Charlotte had heard anything from the estate lawyer. She also felt Charlotte should know about what had happened with Reikart.

"Would it be okay for me to stop by in a little while?" she asked.

"Of course," Charlotte said. "Solstice and I have been outdoors, enjoying the remainder of this beautiful day. You're welcome to join us."

Charlotte lived in a tall, narrow colonial with a salt box roof, perched on a hill overlooking the village. Kathryn found her friend seated on a bench in front of the house with Solly at her feet. The dog growled at her until Charlotte quieted it with a command.

"What's that you're drinking?" Kathryn pointed at a half-full glass of light brown liquid with ice cubes in Charlotte's hand.

"It's a cooler made with Madagascar rum," Charlotte said. "Would you like one?"

"Sure."

While Charlotte was getting her drink, Kathryn eyed Solly warily. Now that the dog's current mistress was gone, would she attack? Fortunately, Solly seemed to accept her presence. The Doberman remained sprawled by the bench with her head resting on her paws. Kathryn took a sip from the glass Charlotte brought her and was pleasantly surprised. "This is good."

"I've always found the end of the day to be a melancholy time," Charlotte said. "You know, 'Day is done, gone the sun.'" She hummed a few notes of "Taps." "And having a rum cooler helps take the edge off things."

They each took a few more sips, then Charlotte said, "So, what brings you here?"

"A couple of things. For starters, I'd like to know if you'd heard anything from Wallingford."

"No, and I don't expect to right away. He'll be able to determine fairly quickly if the codicil does, in fact, post-date the original will, but it may take a while to locate the people who witnessed it and verify their signatures, since neither of them are locals."

They gazed at the view of the town and the surrounding countryside in silence. Then Kathryn said, "I also wanted you to know Steve Reikart's been following me. I noticed a truck like his parked across the street from the lawyer's office yesterday. When I asked him if it was his, he said no. But the encounter I had with him today confirms he's tailing me. I went to Randy Plungas's cabin to fetch something his son wanted when Reikart burst in on me. He wouldn't let me leave until he'd grilled me about what I was doing there. When he left, he slammed the door so hard it was scary. I'm afraid to be alone with him in another situation like that."

Charlotte stared into her drink with a grim expression. "Did I mention that Steve suffers from PTSD?"

"Yes, when you told me about the ruckus he raised at the veterinary hospital. You said he developed PTSD after doing several tours in Afghanistan and Iraq."

"There's more to the story than that. Steve had a rough start in life. Father was an alcoholic who beat him and his mother. He dropped out of school, joined the Marines, and came home with a bad case of PTSD. Had trouble holding a job and finally landed his current position as a security guard for Corrigan. Steve's tremendously grateful to Corrigan for taking a chance on him, and will do almost anything for him. But it's Solstice who means the world to him. Her getting shot hit Steve really hard. He hates Geronimo, and only tolerates him because Corrigan insists, and Steve doesn't want to lose his job. I'm sure Corrigan's got him following you, too."

"I think you're right, but where does that leave us—or rather me, since I'm the one Reikart's following? You spent a lot of time with him at the veterinary hospital. Any suggestions about how to keep him from exploding?"

"Try to stay calm and don't get confrontational with him. I'll speak with Steve myself. I doubt I can stop him from following you, but I'll do my best to convince him you're not an enemy, despite what Corrigan may be telling him."

"I hope he hears you," Kathryn said.

"So do I. For your sake and for Steve's. He's in a tough place right now, but I don't think he's a bad person. Anyone who loves dogs like he does can't be all that bad."

And yet, the very quality Charlotte found so endearing could have led Reikart to commit an act of violence against the person who'd harmed his dog. But Kathryn wasn't about to say this to Charlotte without more information. Finishing her drink, she thanked her friend and drove home.

Chapter 42

Kathryn made a simple dinner and took it onto the porch of the Farley house. She wished Earl were with her, but they'd agreed he ought to spend the evening with Pete. Besides, if Earl were here, she'd be tempted to put off reading the material about the Grant's Tomb Girl. *You wanted it, and now that you've got it, you have to deal with it.*

Still, she had to force herself to climb the stairs to her bedroom and retrieve the folder from under the mattress. She took it into the study, which looked out on the driveway. That way, she'd know if she was about to have any unexpected visitors.

The newspaper accounts consisted of sometimes graphic descriptions of the discovery by a jogger of the young woman's badly beaten body, and interviews with people who'd been at the party she was said to have attended, as well as others who'd been in the general vicinity that night. They also contained information about the NYPD's efforts to find the culprit or culprits. The hardest parts to read were the descriptions of the young woman's battered body. As for the interviewees, there were other people besides Corrigan whose names were mentioned, but the only one Kathryn was familiar with was Maxine. No surprise there. The stories about the police's attempts and ultimate failure to solve the crime were depressing.

Then there was the commentary. The tabloids, in particular, mercilessly attacked Jane Doe, as she was called, for the reckless behavior that had brought her to this end, painting her as a poster girl for promiscuity. They claimed she'd been asking for it, when she'd gone—scantily clad, of course—into a deserted part of the park late at night. Some even went so far as to accuse her of being a call girl instead of a party girl, who'd been attacked by either her pimp or her john.

Talk about blaming the victim. Kathryn felt a surge of anger at the men who'd written this. Today, because of the #MeToo movement, they might think twice about airing their misogynistic views in public. But maybe not. Even in these supposedly enlightened times, she suspected that plenty of people—women as well as men—believed that when women got into trouble, it was their own fault. Which must make it very difficult for sexual assault victims like Gwen to shed the cloud of shame that hung over them. She understood now why Gwen wanted to keep her past a secret, also why she'd fled the city for the Berkshires to begin her life anew.

By the time Kathryn finished reading, her body had become a tangle of knots. She rose, stretched, and walked down the hall to the bedroom and back again. The study felt close, so she opened a window, letting in the fragrant June air. She knew from the newspaper stories that on a night like this, Jane Doe had been raped and beaten within an inch of her life.

Ever since Suzy had introduced them, Kathryn had imagined what it would be like to be Gwen, leading an apparently carefree life in the country. Now, she found herself imagining she was Gwen on the night she'd nearly died. Thanks to the pictures and maps included in the newspaper stories, she was able to recreate Gwen's journey on that fateful evening twenty years ago.

In her mind, she became Gwen standing by an open window of the apartment on Riverside Drive. Feeling the breeze that wafted in, a relief from the heat and noise of the party. She slipped through the apartment door, and once she was on the sidewalk, she stood for a moment, gazing across Riverside Drive at the massive stone monument that was Grant's Tomb. To her left, Riverside Church rose in all its Gothic glory. There were few cars on Riverside Drive this late at night, so she might have trouble finding a cab to take her home. Still, she should at least try.

But the park below beckoned. It would be cooler and quieter there. Before she knew it, she'd crossed Riverside Drive, then the plaza around the monument, and descended a steep flight of stairs to the National Park Service visitor center below. At the visitor center, a paved path took her to an entrance into the park. Street lamps lit the entrance, but after that there were none. Another flight of wide, gently sloping steps brought her into the park itself. On her right, she saw empty tennis courts, while on her left, a dirt trail ran through the woods. A large white sign designated it as "Forever Wild."

Perfect. Although she could hear the low rumble of cars on the West Side Highway below, even catch an occasional glimpse of the Hudson River through the trees, she felt as if she were in a world apart. A wild place, where her spirit could roam free, unfettered by the city around her. Her long blonde hair streamed behind her as she half-danced, half-darted forward on the soft earth of the trail, a forest nymph leading the lusty god that pursued her on a merry chase. She was having so much fun she could have laughed out loud.

But the laughter died on her lips when she realized no lusty mythical god was pursuing her, but a real man. Someone who meant her harm. And if she didn't escape, she'd be in trouble. Big trouble. But her lungs could only take in so much air, and her legs could only carry her so far. Powerful arms grabbed her and brought her down. She struggled to rise, but he beat her back with a breath-stopping blow to the chest. Then, he was on top of her, ripping off her clothes and ramming himself inside her. She screamed and screamed, but no one came to her aid. She was alone with a demon. After he'd raped her, he pounded her head into the ground and smashed her face with his fists until everything went black.

The wail of a siren pulled Kathryn out of the waking nightmare. Or maybe she was still in it, but the dream had fast-forwarded to the moment when the ambulance arrived to take her—or rather Gwen—to the hospital. Kathryn shook her head to clear it of the last vestiges of the nightmare and listened intently. The siren sounded like it was coming from above on Rattlesnake Hill. Then, judging from the loudness of the noise, she knew the emergency vehicle must be close by. In her mind's eye, she saw it barrel past the driveway and down the hill.

Her fingers were shaking so badly she could barely punch in Earl's number. Pete answered. "What happened?" she asked. "I heard a siren and it sounded like it was coming from farther up the hill."

"Robert cut himself bad," Pete said. "An ambulance is taking him to Fairview Hospital. His mom and stepdad are with him. Dad's following in his truck."

Chapter 43

Kathryn slept badly that night. Images of a girl that was sometimes Gwen and sometimes herself being beaten and raped tormented her, only to be replaced by other images of a boy that was sometimes Robert and sometimes Pete slitting his wrists. She was exhausted but wide awake at six AM when the phone rang.

"You up?" Earl said.

"Yeah, did you just get back from the hospital?"

"Couple hours ago. Didn't want to wake you. Needed some shut-eye myself."

"Had coffee yet?"

"Just about to make some."

"Come here. But first, is Robert going to be all right?"

"Lost a lot of blood, but Wayne and Suzy found him in time. They're keeping him at the hospital for observation today, maybe tomorrow, too."

"Thank god, he's okay!"

Ten minutes later, Earl showed up showered and wearing clean clothes, but with dark circles under his eyes. Comparing his circles with the ones she'd observed when she glanced in the mirror, Kathryn couldn't decide which of them had worse raccoon eyes. A toss-up maybe? But mostly, she was just glad to see him and have him enfold her in his arms.

Over hot, strong coffee and scrambled eggs and toast, Earl told her about Robert. Before beginning, he took a big swig of coffee, as if to fortify himself. Then he said, "Suzy could tell Robert was really nervous before his appointment with Scoville. But he wouldn't let her go over the questions he might be asked, or be in the room with him when he was interviewed. She went back to her car to wait but kept the windows open. The back window of the Chief's office was open. After a few minutes, she heard Robert scream, 'I didn't kill my dad! I didn't!'"

In those two sentences, Earl managed to convey the anguish Robert must have felt. Robert's denial evoked a response from deep within Kathryn. *I didn't kill my dad either. But I thought about it.* She scanned Earl's face for some sign he might have read her mind, but there was none. He paused to drink more coffee before continuing.

"The Chief came out to get her. He said Scoville had called a halt to the interview until Robert pulled himself together. Robert looked shaken, but withdrew into himself and refused to talk. Suzy was afraid to leave him alone, so she kept him with her the rest of the day.

"He disappeared into his room right after dinner, and Suzy and Wayne could hear the noise of his video games. They did the dishes, read bedtime stories to the younger boys, and tried to put them down for the night. By then, Robert had the volume up so high on his video game that it bothered his brothers. Suzy called to him to turn it down. When he didn't reply, she went to his room and found the door locked. Both she and Wayne pounded on the door and demanded that Robert open up. Finally, Wayne broke in.

"Robert was slumped on the floor, his wrists slashed and bleeding out. He was still conscious but looked like he was about to pass out. Suzy bandaged his wrists while Wayne called an ambulance. I went over there as soon as I heard the siren. Mom and Dad, too. They looked after the younger boys while the rest of us were at the hospital.

"It was a night from hell, and it's not over yet." Earl downed the last of his coffee.

"I am so sorry." Kathryn reached over and squeezed his hand. "Is there anything I can do to help? Watch the boys? Cook some meals for the family? I'd offer to visit Robert in the hospital, but he may not be ready for visitors yet. Especially someone he doesn't know that well."

"I think it's best to hold off for a while. As for meals and the boys, Mom and Dad have those bases covered. But I'm sure Suzy would appreciate hearing from you."

"I'll give her a call."

They finished breakfast, and Earl got up to leave. She walked to the door with him. As they stood on the threshold, she said, "Poor Robert, I feel so bad for him. That detective ought to be shot for giving him such a hard time!"

Earl gave her a look that was half surprised, half amused. "That's something I'd expect Suzy to say, but not you, Star. Not you." He shook his head and grinned.

"Just because I don't have red hair doesn't mean I can't get hopping mad."

Earl's grin broadened. "Hopping mad? That's another Suzy-ism."

After Earl had gone, and with him the brief flash of humor, Kathryn's anger over Scoville's treatment of Robert returned. But she'd only make things worse if she called his office and berated him. What she could do was try to get more information about other possible suspects like Reikart. He had a motive for killing Plungas, but only if he believed Plungas had shot his dog. Reikart also could've had an opportunity to commit the crime if she could establish that he'd left the veterinary hospital earlier than he claimed. Before Corrigan showed up—if indeed, he did show up today—she'd use the phone and internet to find out what she could.

Kathryn left a voicemail at Suzy's, telling her how sorry she was about Robert, and repeating her offer of help. Then she called the main house of the Barker compound. Roy answered the phone. She wasted no time getting to the point. "The night of the fire when we were having dinner at your place, you said you thought Randy Plungas had shot at Corrigan and Earl, and also shot Reikart's dog. Did you mention that to anyone else?"

"I might've," Roy said, "but I wasn't the only one who thought so."

"Anyone specific?"

"I don't recall, just that other folks shared my opinion."

Kathryn tried another tack. "Where might the shootings have been discussed—at the general store, for example?"

"They were definitely topics of conversation there. At The Stag, also."

"Did you ever notice Reikart at either of those places?"

"I don't think so, but you oughta ask Lucas Rogers. He'd remember if that Reikart fella was a customer at the store or The Stag."

Kathryn called the store. Tracy, a young woman whom Kathryn knew often helped out there, answered. She said Rogers was in the back, checking on inventory, but she'd give him the message Kathryn had called.

Unsure when the veterinary hospital in Great Barrington opened, Kathryn checked online and found it didn't open until eight AM. She had about a half hour to wait before she could speak with anyone. She also noticed that it closed at 6 PM. If Reikart had left at closing or a little before, he could conceivably have gotten back to New Nottingham, gone to Randy's, killed him, and started the fire. But it would have been tight. She hoped whoever had been on duty that night would be able to tell her when Reikart had left. Otherwise, she'd have to turn to Charlotte for answers. Which she was reluctant to do, given how protective Charlotte was of Reikart.

*****

At 7:58 AM Kathryn's hand was poised over the handset, ready to make the call, when she saw Corrigan's Porsche pull into the parking area. *Damn.* He'd not only come early, but he'd noticed her in the window. He held up a hand in greeting. She was tempted to call the hospital anyway, but the sound of his footsteps on the stairs told her not to. Double damn! He usually went to work downstairs, but not today.

"Good morning," he said with a heartiness she was sure was phony. "I'm glad you're up. I have a couple of things I'd like to talk to you about."

He settled on the daybed, and she swiveled her chair around to face him.

"I understand you and some others visited a lawyer in Great Barrington. I don't know what that was about, but I hope you won't try to hold me up. I own this property and I'm going to develop it

190

no matter what. Good," he said without waiting for a reply. "I'm glad we understand each other." His voice was calm, and his posture suggested a man at his ease.

She, on the other hand, was steaming inside. "What else is there?" she asked.

Corrigan studied her a moment, then in the same calm voice, he said, "Those papers at Randy Plungas's cabin—did you take them?"

"What papers?" She stonewalled.

"The newspaper clippings."

"Why would I want newspaper clippings?"

"I don't know. You tell me. Does the Chief know you were there?"

"Why don't you ask him?"

"Maybe I will, but I wanted to ask you first. You told Steve Plungas's son needed those papers, but that struck me as strange."

"Why?"

"Because of the content."

"What content?"

Corrigan smiled and shook his head. "You're being difficult, Kathryn. So, I suggest we continue this conversation another time. But on the off chance you *do* have those papers," he said as he walked toward the door, "you might want to think about returning them to the cabin. Or why not simply dispose of them? They are, after all, old news."

But old news can still be damning. That must be why Corrigan wanted the papers destroyed. To protect Gwen? Or himself in some way, since his name was mentioned in one of the stories?

Her first impulse was to retrieve the folder from under the mattress and hide it somewhere else. But where? The attic was out. It would soon be emptied. And she didn't dare leave the house to hide the folder elsewhere. Corrigan probably figured that if he waited long enough, she'd break down and do one or the other.

Well, she could play that game, too. She didn't have to be any place until her two PM tea with Grandma Waite. While she hoped the old woman had something important to tell her, she could always postpone the meeting until another time. The question now was how to occupy herself until Corrigan left.

*****

Kathryn's eyes had closed and her head had drooped over the book she'd been struggling to read for the past few hours, when engine noise snapped her to attention. Corrigan pulled out of the driveway at twelve-thirty, the very same time he'd left the house on several days last week. Apparently, keeping whatever appointment he had was more important to him than playing cat-and-mouse with her. Again, she was tempted to follow him, but decided against it. She waited a couple minutes in case his leaving was a ruse. When he didn't reappear, she retrieved the folder, now secured with rubber bands, flew down the stairs and out of the house. Then she roared out the driveway and up Rattlesnake Hill. She didn't slow down until the parking area at the former Whittemore mansion came into view.

Hal Phelps was just leaving the house with his golf clubs. He shot her an astonished look. She felt a bit silly behaving in such a cloak-and-dagger manner, but she couldn't help it.

"I'm sorry to bother you," she told Phelps, "but I'm afraid I have some other papers I'd like you to hide for me."

He frowned. "This isn't another will, I hope."

"It's just some pages I need to take a closer look at when I have time. I'd tell you more, but it's… well… complicated."

"Oh-kay," Phelps rolled his eyes. "I'll do it, but promise me you'll come for these papers before Betty and I return to Arizona. I don't want us involved in another situation like what happened with that codicil."

"I promise," she said, handing him the folder. "And don't worry, I'll return for them shortly."

Back on Rattlesnake Hill Road, Kathryn was relieved to see no sign of Reikart. She hoped that meant he hadn't followed her, but she could be wrong. He could be hiding someplace. In any event, she'd done what she could. She'd just have to trust Phelps to find as good a hiding place for the folder as he had for the codicil.

As Kathryn drove through the village center on her way to Grandma Waite's, she noticed Corrigan's Porsche parked next to the library. So, that's where he'd gone. And those other times, too? What was Gwen thinking, meeting him at the library when she was already in trouble with Tim over being alone with Corrigan at Maxine's? Was she actually tempted by him? Or did he have some kind of a hold over her? Whatever the reason, Kathryn wasn't going to find out while he was there.

Kathryn arrived at the block on Shuntoll Road where Grandma Waite's house was with time to spare. She used the extra minutes to travel the short distance from Shuntoll to Sodom Road. A pothole the size of a crater marked the juncture. Steering carefully around it, she followed Sodom Road until it ended at the border with Connecticut. As she drove, she looked for traces of the dens of iniquity that had once lined the road, but found none. The road itself was in even worse shape than Shuntoll Road, as if the highway crews on either side of the state line each claimed the other was responsible for maintaining it. Returning to Shuntoll Road, she parked a few doors down from the house, as Grandma Waite had instructed her.

The old woman was waiting for her in the back, an area that looked like it might have been a garden once, but was now filled with weeds except for a clear patch where a very old, maroon Dodge Dart was parked. As before, Grandma Waite was dressed all in black.

"Why did you come by way of Sodom Road?" she asked sharply.

"After all the stories I've heard about the hamlet that used to be there, I wanted to see what it looks like now."

Grandma Waite humphed. "Come inside and we will have tea and talk." She led Kathryn through a kitchen with appliances from the 1950s—now they'd be called vintage—then, a dining room with a dusty table and chairs into what must be the parlor. Judging from the first two rooms, housekeeping wasn't Grandma Waite's forte, but the parlor with a sofa and two high-backed arm chairs in a faded floral pattern was immaculate. The old woman motioned Kathryn to sit on the sofa. "I will make tea now."

"I've already drunk so much coffee today, I'd better skip tea, but thank you anyway," Kathryn said.

"Would you like anything with your tea? Lemon or milk and a little sugar?" Grandma Waite acted as if she hadn't heard Kathryn.

Kathryn was on the verge of repeating that she didn't want tea, when Grandma Waite said. "Neither? That is the way I like it also. I will be back in a few minutes."

Kathryn glanced around. One of the armchairs was turned so that whoever sat there had a good view of Gwen and Tim's house across the street. This must be where Grandma Waite did her surveillance. A small round table by the armchair held framed photos. Kathryn got up to inspect them. One was a wedding picture of Grandma Waite and her husband Henry. She wore a triumphant smile while he looked solemn and even a bit baffled, as if he was already beginning to wonder what he'd gotten himself into. There were other photos of family groupings over the years, but Kathryn was struck by how many featured Grandma Waite and the great granddaughter who bore her name. She was further struck by the strong resemblance between the two Scarletts.

Kathryn returned to her seat just as Grandma Waite emerged from the dining room bearing a tray with a teapot, two cups and saucers, and a plate of biscuits that looked rock-hard. The old woman placed the tray on the table between them, and sat in the armchair angled toward the window. Pouring two cups, she handed one to Kathryn and took the other herself. She took a sip and smiled. Kathryn followed suit, except that instead of taking a sip, she merely pressed the cup to her lips and pretended to drink the tea, which had a sickeningly sweet smell like Lemon Pledge.

Kathryn took a few more pretend sips, then she said, "I know you're worried about Gwen and Niall Corrigan, the man in the yellow sports car. And I'm worried, too. He's supposed to be an old friend of hers, but I'm unsure exactly what their relationship was. Has Gwen ever mentioned him to you?"

"She does not talk about her past. But I have looked deep into her heart, and I know she is a broken person."

Kathryn put down her tea and leaned toward the old woman. "Broken, how?"

"She was badly hurt many years ago. Maybe by this Corrigan. And now he has come back for her."

Kathryn's pulse quickened. "What do you think he did to her?"

"I can only see so far into the past. But what I see now makes me afraid for her, and for my Scarlett, too."

"Are you referring to the time you think Corrigan tried to kidnap Scarlett and her brother?"

There was a cracking noise, as Grandma Waite bit into one of her rock-hard biscuits. She put the remains back into the tray and rubbed her teeth. "No, before that. I do not sleep well at night. When I wake up while it is still dark, I turn on the light and watch at the window in case there are evil spirts or evil people afoot. And what did I see but a yellow sports car parked on Shuntoll Road, a short distance from my grandson's house? Not once, but several times now. I cannot see who is in the car, but I know he is up to no good."

"Are you certain it was Corrigan's car."

"Yes." Grandma Waite looked out the window and scowled. "A black truck has just parked on the opposite side of the street, a few doors down. I do not recognize it. Tell me if you do."

Even before she went to the window, Kathryn had a pretty good idea whose truck it was. "The driver is Corrigan's security guard. He's been tailing me for the past couple days."

"He has his guard following you? That is outrageous! I am going to give that man a piece of my mind!"

Before Kathryn could stop her, Grandma Waite rushed from the house, waving an unopened black umbrella. Kathryn couldn't see Reikart's face, but she could easily imagine his astonishment and fright as the old woman, who resembled an angry crow, descended on him, shrieking, "Go away, go away, you are not welcome here!" When he didn't immediately respond, Grandma Waite beat the cab of the truck with her umbrella.

The truck lurched forward and sped away toward Sodom Road. Moments later, they heard a loud bang. Grandma Waite returned to the house with a satisfied smile. "If I am not mistaken, he has hit that big pothole and blown at least one tire, maybe more. He will not be going anyplace soon. He has paid the toll for today."

"The toll?"

Grandma Waite chuckled. "In spite of the name of our road, we do sometimes charge unwelcome strangers a toll in the form of a mishap."

With Reikart temporarily stuck, Kathryn thanked Grandma Waite for the tea and conversation and departed. She was glad Reikart had gotten his comeuppance for following her. As for Grandma Waite, she wasn't sure what to make of the old woman's belief that Corrigan might have harmed Gwen in the past. It didn't square with what she'd heard about him protecting and even rescuing Gwen from dicey situations. But the revelation that Grandma Waite had seen Corrigan's car parked on the street late at night, before he made his presence known, had sinister implications.

Chapter 44

Before returning to New Nottingham, Kathryn stopped at the veterinary hospital in Great Barrington. The last time she'd been there, she'd noticed sign in/sign out sheets for visitors attached to a clipboard at the reception desk. On the off chance the sheet for last Friday was still there, she went in. A fresh-faced young woman whose name tag identified her as Jenn stood behind the desk.

"Hi, can I help you?" Jenn asked.

"My cat's having a problem, and I wondered if there was a vet I could talk to," Kathryn said.

"Let me see if anyone's available," Jenn said.

While she was gone, Kathryn grabbed the clipboard and flipped through the sheets, and found the one for Friday. It showed that Reikart had left at five PM instead of the closing time of six. She put the clipboard back on the desk just as Jenn returned.

"No one's available right now, but if you don't mind waiting a few minutes."

"Thanks, but I'm in kind of a hurry," Kathryn said. "I'll come by another time."

*****

As she drove through the town center, Kathryn noticed Corrigan's Porsche was no longer parked at the library. That was a relief, though the fact that he'd been there at all was worrisome. Time to approach Gwen.

Gwen stood behind the desk, entering a pile of returned books into

197

the computer. She looked up at Kathryn's approach, her expression guarded. "Hi, Kathryn, what can I do for you?"

Kathryn glanced around. Satisfied the library was empty except for her and Gwen, she said, "I saw Corrigan's car in the library parking area when I drove by earlier. I couldn't help wondering why he was here."

"It didn't occur to you he came to the library for the same reason other people come—to check out or return books?"

"Not when he timed his visit to arrive before the library was officially open."

"Maybe he wanted to beat the rush."

"Maybe, but I doubt it."

Gwen pulled a face. "All right, he did come just to visit. Maxine told him about all the frantic messages Tim left on her voicemail. Niall wanted to see if everything was okay."

"That's all?"

"Did anyone ever tell you that you have a *suspicious* mind?"

"No, you're the first one."

Gwen held Kathryn's gaze a long moment, then returned to the pile of books in front of her. "If you don't mind, I have work to do."

Maybe it was only her suspicious mind, but Kathryn continued to wonder *what* was going on between Corrigan and Gwen. She found it interesting Gwen had made no mention of the Grant's Tomb Girl papers, which Corrigan might have told her about. But if Gwen had broached the subject, it would have been tantamount to admitting she was that girl.

Following up on another question that nagged at her, Kathryn crossed the street to the New Nottingham General Store. Lucas Rogers was in the back at the deli counter, fixing a sandwich for a workman. When he finished, Kathryn asked for a sandwich like the one he'd just made. As he sliced ham, she said, "Did Steve Reikart ever come in here, or show up at The Stag?"

Rogers sliced Swiss cheese without replying, then began slathering mustard on two pieces of rye. Kathryn was about to repeat the question when he said, "He was in here a couple times. Usually late in the day around closing time to buy beer and sometimes a sandwich."

"Did he talk to you or anyone else?"

"He pretty much kept to himself."

"When you say 'pretty much' does that mean he never spoke to anyone?"

Ignoring the question, Rogers piled ham, cheese, a sliced tomato and lettuce onto the pieces of bread, slapped them together, and cut the whole in half. "You gonna eat this here, or do you want it wrapped?"

"Wrap it please, then would you answer my question?"

"Persistent, aren't you?" Rogers observed. Lowering his voice, he said, "You didn't hear this from me, but Reikart did speak with me once."

"About his dog that was shot?" Kathryn asked eagerly.

Rogers wound plastic wrap around the sandwich with maddening slowness. "Yeah," he said finally.

"Did he ask who you thought might've done it?"

Rogers gave her a steely look. "Remember, you didn't hear this from me, but yeah, he asked that question."

"What did you tell him?"

"I just repeated what everybody else'd been saying."

"That it was probably Randy Plungas?"

"I might of told him that. You want anything else to go with your sandwich—a drink or bag of chips?"

"Just the sandwich."

At the register, Kathryn realized Rogers had charged her an extra dollar. When she pointed this out, he said, "Did the same for that detective when he came around asking questions, so why not you?"

Why not, indeed? Kathryn smiled as she left the store. There was no sign of Reikart's truck when she drove up the driveway. Nor of Corrigan's Porsche in the parking area. Good. She listened to the one voicemail she'd received, which was from Suzy thanking her for her call. Then, she called the Phelps' house. Betty answered the phone. She said Hal was out but she expected him back shortly and would give him the message Kathryn had called. "Is this about the folder of papers Hal said you asked him to put in a safe place?"

"Yup."

"Wow, lately I've started to feel I'm living in a spy novel," Betty said.

"I hope it's not upsetting you."

"Quite the contrary. Our life is usually pretty dull so I'm enjoying the excitement. Speaking of that, do you have any news about what's happening with that amendment to Diana's will, or whatever it's called?"

"Not yet, but while I've got you, would you mind if I came over later today? I want to have another look at the papers in that folder. I'd do it here, but I can't be sure no one will walk in on me."

"Ohhh!" Betty exclaimed, "This definitely sounds like something from John Le Carré."

*****

Ensconced in a small room on the second floor that Hal used as his office, Kathryn settled down with the Grant's Tomb Girl stories, while the couple watched TV downstairs. Again, she marveled at the size of the collection. She also found herself wondering what Plungas had done with it once he'd assembled it. Had he simply put the folder in the drawer and forgotten about it? She doubted that. From her curatorial work, she knew that just as some collectors accumulated certain items to the point of obsession, so they were compulsive in their handling of them, arranging and re-arranging the items, and generally fretting over them. She could easily picture Randy alone in his cabin at night, reading the stories over and over again and feeling—what? Did he derive a sick thrill from the descriptions of the violence done to the girl?

She skipped over those parts now, focusing instead on the interviews with people who'd either been at the party or in the neighborhood that night. She found the place where Corrigan was quoted as having noticed Jane Doe at the party, but not thinking of her again until he read the story about a badly beaten woman in the park. She also found the place where Maxine was quoted. She read Maxine's words more carefully: "I was standing near the door talking with some friends when Jane Doe brushed past me.

'Leaving already?' I asked. 'No,' she said, 'I'm just going out for a breath of air.'"

In another paper dated a couple days later, Kathryn found a quote from Corrigan she'd missed earlier: "I remember seeing Jane Doe leave, too, but I didn't think twice about it, because she told my friends and me she was just going out for a breath of air. In hindsight, I regret I let her go out alone. I wish I'd accompanied her, even if it was only to get some fresh air myself."

Why the discrepancy? Had Corrigan been too ashamed to admit he'd seen Jane Doe leave and done nothing about it when he was first interviewed? And then changed his story after Maxine's interview because he knew others, including Maxine, could identify him as being among the friends who saw Jane Doe go out? Whatever the reason, he obviously felt guilty about what he'd failed to do. Although no Catholic but a staunch Methodist, Kathryn's grandmother had drummed into her the fact that there were sins of omission as well as commission. In this instance, Corrigan appeared to be confessing to the former.

She discovered a much more glaring example of a sin of omission in another article. A man walking his dog on the sidewalk above Riverside Park reported having heard screams from below. He said he hadn't wanted to go down into the park to see what was happening for fear of getting hurt himself.

"Didn't it occur to you to call the police?" the interviewer asked.

"No, I didn't want to bother them," the man said.

"But isn't it the job of the police to help people in trouble?"

"Yeah, but I didn't know for sure that something bad was going down. The screams could've been from someone just having fun, you know, playing games, rather than from someone who was in trouble. And when they stopped, I figured the game was over."

It was over all right, you dummy. But it wasn't a game, and because of what you failed to do, a woman was nearly killed. Kathryn wished she'd been around when the dog walker was interviewed. Then she could have throttled him. She liked to think she would have called the police if she'd heard the screams, but as for what she would have done if a friend, known for taking chances, left a party alone, she honestly didn't know.

She separated the pages with mentions of Maxine and Corrigan from the rest, put the folder in her tote, and went downstairs.

"Are you taking those papers back with you already?" Betty sounded a tad disappointed.

"Yes, I'm done with them," Kathryn said. "But thanks again for keeping them for me."

"Anytime," Betty said. Hal merely rolled his eyes.

*****

Kathryn returned to the Farley house to find a voicemail from Earl, asking if she'd like to meet him at The Stag for a drink after he finished work around four-thirty. It was past that time now. And there was something else she wanted to do.

Chapter 45

Kathryn called Charlotte to make sure she was home, then got in her car and started out the driveway. Reikart's truck was parked near the trailer, so he must be back, though she didn't see him. Inside nursing his wounds after the encounter with Grandma Waite?

Charlotte met her at the door, holding Solly's leash in one hand and a rum cooler in the other. "Would you like a drink, too?" she asked.

"Thanks."

Charlotte fixed her drink and they settled in the living room. The walls were covered with paintings and photographs of Madagascar from Charlotte's years there, while the comfortable, well-worn furniture looked like it dated from Charlotte's grandparents' time.

"I heard from Wally," Charlotte said. "He's been able to authenticate the codicil. It was definitely drawn up by Diana after the original will, and witnessed by two friends of hers in New York."

"That's wonderful news. Now we can contest the original will?"

Charlotte's gaze strayed from Kathryn to a photograph of dancing lemurs. "Wally advises not," she said quietly.

"What? I thought he said we had a chance, even though it might take time and money."

"True, but apparently he's changed his mind. He told me there's a statute of limitations on contesting a will. It's usually four years in many states, but in Massachusetts, it's shorter. And since Diana's been dead for five years, and the property has already passed from her to Gordon, then to his parents, and has now been sold to a developer, it's just too complicated. We'd be throwing our money away with virtually no hope of success."

Kathryn felt as if the ground had fallen out from under her. "But…"

"I'm sorry, I had high hopes for that codicil, too, but the battle to stop the development is by no means over. We've still got the wetlands restrictions to use against Corrigan, and there may be other things we can do as well."

Kathryn didn't doubt this was so. She did doubt, however, if Charlotte's friend Wally was the right lawyer for them. He was old and perhaps too tired to put up a fight on their behalf. Maybe what they needed was a younger and more aggressive attorney. "I think we should consult another lawyer," she said.

"Do you have someone in mind?" Charlotte asked.

"Not yet. My ex-boyfriend is an attorney at a large and well-respected Boston firm. I can get a recommendation from him."

"I suppose there's no harm in consulting another lawyer, but I'll be very surprised if he doesn't give us the same advice as Wally," Charlotte said. "Was there something else you wanted to talk to me about?"

"Steve Reikart."

Charlotte swirled her rum cooler so jerkily that liquid spilled onto her lap. She mopped it ineffectually with her free hand. "He hasn't been giving you more trouble, I hope?"

"He's still following me, and today he got into trouble himself." She told Charlotte about Grandma Waite's attack on Reikart, and how he'd driven into a giant pothole trying to escape.

Charlotte's mouth compressed into a thin line of disapproval. "That woman knows no bounds when it comes to going after people she dislikes."

"Maybe so, but that's not what I wanted to talk to you about. Lucas Rogers told me Reikart asked him who he thought might have shot his dog. Rogers repeated what a lot of people in town had been saying—that it was probably Randy Plungas."

Solly emitted a low growl, as if she understood what Kathryn had just said.

"So?"

"Reikart had a motive for killing Plungas. He also had an opportunity. According to the sign-in sheet at the veterinary hospital, he left there at five PM last Friday evening. Which would have given him plenty of time to—"

Another low growl.

"Hold on a minute, Kathryn," Charlotte interrupted. "You're accusing Steve of killing Plungas when the police haven't even established it was murder."

"I'm not accusing him. I'm just saying that if Plungas was murdered, Reikart had a motive and the opportunity."

Solly growled again, and this time Charlotte reacted. "She's upset because we're arguing. We need to lower our voices and stay calm." Addressing the dog, she said, "It's okay, Solstice, Kathryn and I are having a friendly discussion." To Kathryn, she said, "But why single out Steve when plenty of people in town had grudges against Plungas? Is it because he's been following you? You know he's only doing it because Corrigan's ordered him to. And why are you playing detective when it's the police's job to find out what happened to Plungas?"

"I only wanted to—"

"Shh—" Charlotte put a finger to her lips. "That may be Steve now."

"Following me again," Kathryn grumbled.

"No. Since I started boarding Solstice, Steve's been coming in the evening to visit her. That's undoubtedly why he's here."

"I should go." Kathryn rose.

"Don't. I think it would be good for the two of you to talk, face to face. Might help clear the air."

Kathryn wasn't convinced that was such a good idea, but she sat down while Charlotte went to the door with Solly, wagging her tail and hobbling along as fast as she could on three legs.

"What's *she* doing here?" Kathryn heard Reikart say. She didn't hear Charlotte's reply, but Charlotte must have persuaded him to stay, because he followed her into the living room.

"Hello, Kathryn," he said gruffly, settling into an arm chair with Solly at his feet.

"Steve."

An awkward silence followed. Reikart busied himself with the dog, scratching her ears and murmuring endearments. Kathryn stared into space, not knowing what to say and wishing Charlotte would return with the beer she'd offered Reikart. When Charlotte did return, she seemed at a loss herself. "So, Steve," she said finally, "I understand you had a bit of an accident today. I hope your truck's all right."

"It is, no thanks to *her*." He jerked his head at Kathryn.

"I didn't—" Kathryn began.

"Sure, you did." Raising his voice, he jabbed a finger at Kathryn. Solly looked at her and growled. "Led me right into a trap with that crazy old lady," he continued. "You should have seen her," he said to Charlotte. "Looked like a witch dressed all in black. Yelled at me to leave. When I didn't, she beat the cab of my truck with her umbrella. Afraid she was gonna break the windshield. I was in such a hurry to get the hell outta there, I drove right into—"

"I didn't know Grandma Waite would go after you like that," Kathryn protested, raising her voice to match his.

Another growl from Solly.

"The hell you didn't!" Reikart shouted back.

"That's enough," Charlotte intervened. "It's time to dial things down. If you can't speak civilly to each other—"

"I'll leave." Kathryn stood. No point staying while Reikart seemed determined to attack her, and the dog's growling made her nervous.

"Yes, do," Reikart cried. "I don't understand why you came here in the first place. Unless it was to try to poison Charlotte against me."

Solly growled a third time.

"Kathryn and I are friends," Charlotte said calmly but firmly.

"Well, she ain't no friend of mine. She's hoping if she badmouths me enough, you'll stop taking care of Solstice for me."

Charlotte looked at Kathryn, askance. "Is that true?"

Kathryn squirmed inwardly. "I might have said something to that effect. But it was to get him to stop blocking my way so I could leave Plungas's cabin."

"No one's blocking your way now." Reikart gestured toward the door.

Kathryn headed in that direction. But she couldn't resist a parting shot. "You know, Steve, none of this would've happened if you hadn't been following me."

"I was only doing my job," he retorted, "while *you*..." He left the sentence unfinished, anger rendering him momentarily speechless. Solly growled and bared her teeth. Reikart glanced at his dog, then at Kathryn. "Lightning strike, Solstice, lightning strike," he yelled, letting go of the leash and stabbing a finger at Kathryn.

The Doberman torpedoed at her, a blur of furious motion. Kathryn froze, too terrified to move. "Stand down, Solstice, stand down," Charlotte commanded. The dog crumbled to the ground. Kathryn's terror changed to wonder. Solly had done what she hadn't thought possible for an attack dog. Obeyed one master over another.

Reikart looked stunned himself. "What have you done?"

"Try that again and I'll sic her on *you*," Charlotte said.

"You wouldn't—" Apparently thinking better of it, he bolted.

Chapter 46

"I need to call Chief Lapsley and tell him what just happened," Kathryn told Charlotte. "Where's your phone?"

"Do you think that's a good idea?"

"Reikart just sicced his dog on me! I could have been badly hurt, even killed if you hadn't called Solly off. This is a police matter. It's too serious not to call him."

Charlotte looked glum, but resigned. "The phone's in the kitchen."

The Chief picked up on the third ring. He listened to Kathryn's story, then said, "Where are you now?"

"At Charlotte's."

"And Reikart?"

"He stormed off a few minutes ago. I don't know where he went, but if he returned to his trailer, I don't feel safe going back to the Farley house."

"Stay where you are. I'll find Reikart and take him into custody, if necessary. I'll let you know if and when I do."

Returning to the living room, Kathryn told Charlotte what the Chief had said.

"You're welcome to spend the night here if the Chief doesn't find Steve."

"Thanks. Since I may be here a while, I'd love a cup of coffee."

"I'll make some." Charlotte disappeared into the kitchen, Solly following at her heels.

Kathryn plopped into an armchair. The adrenalin that had gotten her through the near-attack by Solly and the phone call to the Chief was gone, leaving her limp. She would have been happy to crawl into bed right now. But she and Charlotte needed to talk.

While waiting for her to return, Kathryn rose and looked more closely at the lemur pictures. She especially liked the ones that showed them cavorting across the jungle floor like dancers in a chorus line. Another favorite was a photo of a smiling Charlotte with a lemur draped over each shoulder eating bananas she'd given them.

"These are amazing photos," Kathryn said when Charlotte reappeared with the coffee.

"I'm glad you like them." Charlotte's expression brightened. "They were taken by a dear friend who—" She broke off, her face clouding over.

"What is it? Did something happen to your friend?"

"Let's sit." Charlotte set the tray with coffee mugs, sugar, and a small pitcher of milk on a low table. She seated herself on the sofa, facing Kathryn in the armchair. Kathryn added milk to her coffee and took a drink. Instead of following suit, Charlotte finished her rum cooler. "It's a long story and I won't bother you with it now."

"We have time and I'd like to hear it." Kathryn really wanted to discuss what had happened with Reikart, but if they started out with this story, perhaps she could find a way to segue into the other one.

Charlotte picked up her rum cooler again, realized it was empty, and took a sip of coffee. "Edino was a young boy when I first met him. I'd recently arrived in Madagascar to study lemurs, and he was quick and eager, and very helpful. However, he stole from me in the beginning. Like many on the island, his family lived in abject poverty. I explained that theft was wrong, and said I'd pay him for his help. I also let him borrow things that belonged to me, provided he returned them.

"He was particularly fascinated by my Leica. I showed him how to use it, and he caught on so quickly, I let him take pictures. Over time, he became such a first-rate photographer that the other researchers and I used him for our photography. He also started a business, photographing lemurs for tourists.

"That's how the trouble began. By then, Edino had made enough money to buy his own camera. One day when his camera had gone on the fritz and was being repaired, he asked if he could borrow my

Leica. Of course, I said yes. He was taking pictures for some tourists when an obnoxious woman in the group noticed the Leica and decided it must be stolen. Because how could a poor Madagascaran own such an expensive camera? She reported the possible theft to the police.

"A young man new to the force confronted Edino about the Leica. Edino tried to explain he'd borrowed it from me, but the policeman wouldn't listen. He kept calling Edino a thief. In frustration, Edino took off to find me. The policeman chased him down, confiscated the camera, and took him to the station, where he was badly beaten. When I finally found him, he was close to death from his injuries. Despite my efforts to nurse him back to health, he died a few days later. Edino's death was a great blow to me. I've never had children myself, and he'd become like a son to me."

"I'm so sorry," Kathryn said. She wondered if Steve Reikart had become another substitute son for Charlotte, but couldn't think of a tactful way to ask. Fortunately, Charlotte brought up Reikart herself.

"I owe you an apology for tonight," she said.

Kathryn opened her mouth to protest, but Charlotte cut her off. "Let me finish. I wanted so much for you and Steve to get along. I thought if you got to know him as well as I did, after all the time we spent together at the veterinary hospital, you'd at least understand where he was coming from. But I went about it all wrong. I should have realized he might still be mad about Grandma Waite's attack on him, and blame you. Shouldn't have mentioned it in the first place. Then, when things started going south, I should have ended the evening. But I was so sure I could get him to calm down. I'm disappointed in myself, but also in Steve. I never imagined he'd sic Solstice on you. His behavior tonight shook my faith in him."

"I'm partly to blame, too," Kathryn said. "You warned me to stay cool with him, but when he started yelling at me, I gave it right back to him. I was terrified when he sicced Solly on me. And very glad you were able to stop her. I was also surprised. I thought an attack dog will only respond to a command from its master."

"That's what I thought, too," Charlotte said. "I asked Steve about it when I agreed to board Solstice. I wanted to know if I'd have any control over her. He told me Solstice was conditioned to follow a particular command no matter who gave it. For that reason, when police and soldiers retire, they can transfer their dog to another handler and the dog will follow commands from that person."

"Even to the point of attacking their former master?"

"Apparently so, if their master is the designated target. Still, I'm glad I didn't really have to test that with Steve."

Charlotte sank back into the sofa and closed her eyes for a moment. The excitement of the evening, combined with all the talking she'd done, seemed to have tired her. She excused herself to go upstairs and lie down. In parting, she said, "If the phone rings and I don't answer, feel free to pick up. It will probably be the Chief calling you back."

After Charlotte had gone, Kathryn thought about what she'd just heard. If she had spent more time with Reikart, would she feel differently about him? She'd certainly sympathized with him after Solly was shot, and they'd waited together at the hospital while the dog was being operated on. She remembered their conversation about how he'd grown up on a farm surrounded by animals, but he hadn't said anything about his abusive father or his tours in Afghanistan or Iraq. And any closeness she'd felt toward him had evaporated when he started tailing her.

She also found herself wondering if she'd end up like Charlotte, if she didn't settle into a relationship with Earl and have a family of her own. Would she, like Charlotte, create a surrogate family from people who seemed to need her help, only to lose them or have them betray her? True, Charlotte had her work with the land trust and friendships with people like Dr. Dinaldi and Wallingford, but at the end of the day, she was alone, nursing a rum cooler with a dog at her feet as night approached. Would that be her fate, too? And even if she did settle down with Earl, would that be enough without satisfying work? Difficult questions to which Kathryn didn't have answers. To lift her spirits, Kathryn rose and looked at the photos of Charlotte and her lemurs in better times.

She was still staring at the photos when the phone rang a few minutes later. She waited four rings before picking up. As Charlotte had predicted, it was the Chief.

"I didn't have any trouble finding Reikart," he told her. "He'd gone back to his trailer."

There was a loud whoosh of air on the line. Charlotte must have picked up the phone. And was obviously relieved Reikart hadn't fled and been chased down and harmed like her surrogate son, Edino.

"Seeing as how he was still pretty worked up, I took him to the lock-up in Great Barrington," the Chief said.

"Great Barrington?"

"We don't have a jail in town, so we pay Great Barrington a monthly fee to use their lock-up. When Reikart's had a chance to cool off overnight, we'll see how things are. In the meantime, I need to have a chat with you about some papers you took from Randy Plungas's cabin."

She might have known the Chief would find out about that. "Do you want me to come to the station?"

"Nope, we can talk at the Farley house. Matter of fact, that's where I am now."

Chapter 47

It was starting to get dark and the first stars had come out when Kathryn headed back to the Farley house. Geronimo's ferocious barks made her tense up as she drove past. She had to remind herself Reikart wasn't there to issue an attack command.

The Chief was waiting outside the house, his head craned up at the sky. "Gonna be a real planetarium night," he said as she walked toward him.

"What?"

"When it's so clear you can see the stars as good as at a planetarium. You know much about astronomy?"

"No."

"Me either. Let's go inside."

They settled in the living room, the Chief on the couch, Kathryn in an armchair. In the lamplight, the Chief looked cherubic with his round, ruddy cheeks.

"How was Reikart?" Kathryn asked. "Did he go with you willingly?"

"He wasn't happy about it. Used some pretty salty language about you, but I was able to convince him it was in his best interests to spend the night in jail."

"And tomorrow, you'll let him go?"

"Depends. I warned him you could take legal action against him. And that if he doesn't behave himself and stay away from you, he'd be in big trouble."

"What did he say to that?"

"Claimed you're the one who's up to no good, and that's why his boss had him following you."

"Do you believe him?"

"I wouldn't go so far as to say you're up to no good, but you *did* do something you shouldn't have."

"I know I shouldn't have gone back to Plungas's cabin without your permission," Kathryn said.

The Chief's expression changed from cherubic to stern. "Why did you?"

"I heard Randy had spread rumors about Gwen when she and Tim were dating to try to keep Tim from marrying her. The rumor that she was the Grant's Tomb Girl intrigued me. While I was at the cabin earlier, I noticed old newspapers in a file drawer. I thought they might have some bearing on that rumor. I figured I'd read them at the cabin, but there were so many, I ended up taking them with me. I'm planning to return them, however."

"Where are they?"

"In a folder upstairs."

"Get them."

As she handed him the folder, the Chief said, "You know you could be charged with tampering with the evidence in a murder trial, if it comes that?"

Kathryn nodded.

"One more thing," the Chief said, holding up his index finger, as if to emphasize the importance of the point he was about to make. "This is a police investigation, and the *last* thing we need is folks like you going around asking questions. Understood?"

Kathryn met his gaze steadily. "Yes."

The Chief's expression softened. "Good. I'll be going now."

Chapter 48

After the Chief left, Kathryn went out onto the patio and stared up at the stars. They were so clear and bright it was indeed a planetarium night. Star gazing had calmed her in the past. And now that she needed to unwind, she hoped it would help.

She was relieved she'd confessed to the Chief about taking the Grant's Tomb Girl papers. She was also glad they were now in his possession. He would safeguard them, unlike Corrigan who seemed to want them destroyed. As for Reikart, at least he was behind bars for the time being and couldn't harm her. She was starting to feel better when the phone rang. She hurried inside and picked up.

"Hey, Star, where you've been all day? I called to see if you wanted to meet at The Stag after work, then a couple times afterward. Is everything okay?"

She sighed. "Now it is."

"What happened?"

Kathryn gave him an abbreviated version of the day's events, including Reikart's attempt to sic Solly on her, and her visit with the Chief.

"Thank god, you're okay!" he exclaimed about the aborted attack, then "Jeez, Star, whatever possessed you to lift those papers from Randy's cabin?"

"Ever since you told me about that rumor, I've wondered if Gwen was, in fact, the Grant's Tomb Girl. I hoped the papers would answer that question."

"Did they?"

"Based on what I read and some things Maxine told me, I think she was."

"Poor Gwen. I feel bad for her."

"Me, too."

"Where are those papers now?"

"I gave them to the Chief." She waited a beat, then said, "Anything new with you?"

"I got a call from Emily's older daughter, the one who lives in Springfield," Earl said. "She told me she'd heard from the hospital that Em's showing signs of coming out of her coma."

"That's wonderful!"

"I knew you'd be pleased after all the time you spent with Em when she was alive, and after she was hospitalized. Looks like playing those tapes of her recollections helped. I was thinking you and I could visit her tomorrow morning, so we can see for ourselves how she's doing. Okay if I pick you up around seven-thirty?"

"Fine."

Liar. You don't feel at all "fine" about visiting Emily when there's a chance she'll wake up from her coma. Not when you were the one who caused her stroke. You dread being in the room when she opens her eyes, sees you, and says, "It's you. You're the person who did this to me."

And how would Earl react if he knew Kathryn's words were responsible for Emily's stroke? Would he recoil from her in horror? She could only hope and pray Emily wouldn't remember the argument that had brought on her stroke.

Gwen had also been in a coma and had come out of it with no memory of her attacker. Had Gwen ever tried to recover that lost memory—through hypnosis perhaps? Or had she preferred to let it go? Still, the trauma of that night probably remained with her, despite her refusal to talk about it.

And what about Gwen's attacker? If it was a stranger, he'd worry Gwen would remember him or an eye witness would come forward. But he could disappear into the shadows more easily than if he were someone Gwen knew. If the latter, he'd have to feign concern for her as Kathryn did for Emily, all the while hoping that if she did recover, she wouldn't remember him as her assailant.

Chilling to think she had a certain kinship with Gwen's assailant in their shared dread of discovery. Yet, having lived so vividly Gwen's experience of being raped and beaten in her imagination, Kathryn also felt a deep, visceral fear of the person who'd attacked Gwen. Even more chilling was the realization he might still be at large, and given the right opportunity, could strike again.

Chapter 49

When Earl showed up at 7:30 the next morning, Kathryn was in the middle of her third cup of coffee. As if caffeine could make her brave. She took a final gulp and followed him to the door. For the second night in a row, she'd slept poorly, haunted by visions of Emily accusing her of having caused her stroke. Now, all the coffee she'd drunk made her so jittery, she found it hard to concentrate on what Earl was saying as he drove to the hospital.

"You okay, Star?" he asked.

"Sorry, afraid I'm still waking up. Last night when Reikart tried to sic Solly on me was so intense, I had trouble sleeping."

"No wonder. Reikart's still in jail, right?"

"The Chief said he'd let me know if and when he'll release him."

"Hope the Chief keeps him there as long as he can."

Changing the subject, Kathryn said, "What signs of recovery can we expect to see when we visit Emily?"

"According to Em's older daughter, Em has begun to react to her surroundings. For example, she now tracks movement with her eyes. She also responds to simple commands. If you tell her to stick out her tongue, she will."

Kathryn smiled and nodded, though this didn't sound good to her. But maybe if she stayed in the background and let Earl do the talking, she'd be okay.

Still, she had to force herself to leave the car, follow him into the hospital, and down the corridor to Emily's room. The old woman was staring into space when they entered, but immediately trained her laser-sharp blue eyes on them. Earl strode over to Emily, pulled up a chair next to her bed and sat. Kathryn hung back, wishing she could vanish into the woodwork.

"Hello, Em, it's Earl—Earl Barker," he added. "It's great to see you with your eyes open, noticing things. Can you stick out your tongue for me?"

Emily's tongue worked in her mouth, then her lips parted and her tongue protruded.

"Good," Earl said. "I'm glad you haven't lost your spunk. You can put your tongue back."

Emily did.

"I'd like to hold your hand now. Can you give it me?" Emily grasped his outstretched hand.

Watching them, Kathryn was reminded of a trainer putting an animal through its paces, but Earl must know what he was doing. She just hoped she wouldn't be expected to interact with Emily very much—if at all.

Emily and Earl held hands for a long moment, then Earl said, "You can let go now, Em. There's someone else here who wants to say hello." He gestured for Kathryn to take his place. Emily's eyes remained on Earl, as if unwilling for him to go. It was all Kathryn could do to leave her post by the door and walk the few steps to the empty chair. When she was almost there, Emily's gaze shifted from Earl to her. The old woman's eyes seemed to drill deep inside Kathryn to her guilty heart.

Then, abruptly Emily broke eye contact. She turned her head emphatically away from Kathryn—or so it appeared.

She's still angry at me, and she's shunning me. Anyone who sees this will wonder why. Kathryn wanted to flee the room, but remained frozen in place.

"Thank you both for coming," a nurse said from behind. "But now I think it's time for you to leave. Emily's obviously tired and needs to rest."

"Sure," Earl replied for both of them. "We'll come back another time. Bye now, Em." He reached over and patted Emily's arm. Emily's eyes sought his, but she didn't look at Kathryn again.

I can't go on like this, pretending nothing happened between Emily and me right before her stroke. At some point, she's going to look directly at me and denounce me.

Kathryn half wished Earl would remark on Emily's turning away from her, but he seemed to accept the nurse's explanation. "Guess I shouldn't have worn Em out," he said. "Then, you could've talked to her."

"I'll have other opportunities."

As they drove through Great Barrington and still had cell reception, Kathryn's phone rang. It was the Chief. "I left a message on the landline, but wanted to be sure I reached you. Corrigan came to the lock-up to get Reikart this morning. I decided to let him go after getting assurances from them both that he'd leave you alone. Corrigan made it clear he'd fire Reikart on the spot if he bothered you again. You can still file a restraining order, but that's up to you."

She needed to decide what to do about Reikart. But all Kathryn could think about right then was how hard it was pretending she'd played no part in Emily's stroke.

There was no sign of Reikart as they drove past the trailer, but she assumed he was inside, because Corrigan's Porsche was parked by the house. Before she faced either of them, she had to unburden herself about Emily.

"There's something I need to tell you," she said when Earl had parked his truck.

"Yes?" The edge of worry in his voice gave her pause. Was he afraid that "something" had to do with their relationship?

"It's about Emily." Maybe it was her imagination, but he seemed to relax. "I went to see her right before she had her stroke. I was angry because I'd just learned about a wrong done to my ancestor. I said things I shouldn't have. She became so enraged that she got up and came at me with her cane. Before she could hit me, she collapsed.

"I never should have gone to see her when I was so worked up. I believe I'm guilty of causing her stroke. All the time I've been visiting her, I've been afraid she'd come out of her coma and accuse me. I think that's why she turned away from me today."

Earl put his arm around Kathryn and pulled her close. "Oh, Star," he began. He broke off at a loud rapping on the truck door.

"I hope I'm not interrupting anything," Corrigan said.

"You know perfectly well that you are," Kathryn snapped.

"Give us a minute," Earl said tightly.

Corrigan moved away from the truck, where he was joined by Reikart, who'd apparently been waiting in the wings. "We'll talk more later," Earl said, turning back to her. "Now, let's hear them out." Exiting the truck, Kathryn and Earl stood side by side facing Corrigan and Reikart.

Reikart stared at the ground while Corrigan spoke. "Steve has something he wants to say to you, Kathryn."

"I'm sorry about last night, Miss Stinson," Reikart said, eyes still on the ground. A nudge from Corrigan, and he looked up. "I was way out of line, and I apologize. I promise it won't happen again." His voice was flat and robotic as if he were repeating a prepared speech.

"Good," Corrigan said briskly. "Steve knows he'll lose his job if he so much as looks at you the wrong way. Now that's settled, let's shake on it." He held out his hand with a phony half smile.

"Not so fast," Kathryn said. "I need *your* word you'll quit ordering Reikart to follow me."

"Follow you?" Corrigan feigned surprise.

"You know what I'm talking about. Do I have your word?"

Corrigan shrugged. "Okay. No more joyrides, Steve. Now can we wrap this up? I have a busy day ahead of me."

"After you, if that's where you're headed." Kathryn gestured toward the house. She had no intention of shaking either man's hand. Perhaps realizing this, Corrigan withdrew his after motioning for Reikart to return to the trailer.

When both men were gone, Earl said, "You comfortable staying here?"

She nodded.

"I'll check in with you later."

When Kathryn went inside, Corrigan was seated at the dining room table, seemingly absorbed in some papers. She'd planned to slip upstairs without speaking to him, but he heard her and called her over.

"There's something I forgot to ask you," he said. "Did you return those old newspapers to the cabin, or better yet, dispose of them?"

"I gave them to the Chief after Reikart told him I'd been there." No need to tell him that she'd kept the pages in which his name was mentioned.

"Ah," he said with a smile she suspected would turn to a scowl the moment her back was turned.

The rest of the morning passed quietly, if slowly. As noon approached, Kathryn wondered if Corrigan would leave the house to pay another visit to Gwen at the library before it was officially open. But noon came and went without him stirring. She waited until one-thirty when the library opened to the public. When Corrigan still hadn't departed, she left the house to call Earl herself from a hot spot up the hill.

"Everything okay?" he asked.

"So far. Corrigan's working downstairs and I haven't seen Reikart since this morning. Can we meet someplace when you're finished for the day?"

"How about Cameron Falls? I don't think you've ever been there. It's a nice spot not far from Rattlesnake Hill. In the late afternoon, I doubt anyone'll be there. If there is, we can sit in the truck and enjoy the falls from a distance while we talk."

*****

The afternoon passed like the morning—slowly. Kathryn read some, then went outside to weed the flower border where the peonies were. Geronimo barked at her, but she didn't see Reikart. When she was finished there, she walked around to the other side of the house and went to work on the vegetable garden. Absorbed in the task, she didn't notice when Corrigan left his place at the dining room table. Not until she heard the rev of a car engine did she realize he was leaving. It was almost four-thirty, quitting time for most workers in the area, including Earl. She'd go inside, wash up, and get ready for their meeting.

Indoors, she caught a whiff of aftershave. Earl's? No, the scent was different from his cologne. She followed it to the half bath on the first floor. By the sink, she found a shaving kit with a gold-finished double-edge razor, a brush with a tortoise shell handle and real bristles, a bottle of Old Bond Street aftershave lotion, a toothbrush and tube of toothpaste.

It looked like Corrigan had been preparing for a rendezvous of his own. The library didn't close until five, and Gwen's husband would be home from work shortly, so he couldn't be meeting with her. Or could he?

Chapter 50

A little after four-thirty, Gwen entered the library restroom, locking the door behind her. She'd already locked the main door and posted a sign that the library would close a half hour early. She didn't need to lock the restroom, but did so out of habit. And sheer nervousness.

Gwen studied herself in the mirror over the sink. Dark circles under her eyes gave her a haggard look. She'd lain awake most of the night, hoping and praying she hadn't made a terrible mistake by agreeing to meet Niall one last time. She was tempted to cover the circles with foundation. No. Let him see her as she really was: a woman in her forties, married with two children. A woman with an ugly scar on the left side of her face, a reminder of the reckless girl she'd been. Her long blonde locks obscured the scar. She pulled back her hair into a bun so it was plainly visible.

The scar was an emblem of her secret shame. Niall and Maxine were among the few people who knew what had really happened that June night twenty years ago. Maxine had promised to keep her secret but, drama queen that she was, Maxine couldn't resist using air quotes when talking about Gwen's accident. Which must have made Kathryn wonder if something other than a bad car accident had put Gwen into a coma. And now that Kathryn had stumbled upon Randy's file on the Grant's Tomb Girl, she'd probably figured out what that "something" was.

She needed to make Kathryn understand the importance of keeping her secret until she was ready to tell Tim. Whenever that would be. Gwen had always promised herself she'd do it when the time was

224

right. But the time never seemed to be right. Especially now, when Scarlett was causing Tim so much grief. He blamed their daughter's wild ways on Maxine and sometimes Grandma Waite. But how would he feel if he knew the wildness came from her? Would he regard her with the same anger and disgust with which he regarded their daughter? Maybe not, but Gwen wasn't ready to put this to the test.

First, though, she needed to settle things with Niall. She wished she hadn't agreed to this meeting, but he wouldn't take no for an answer. "If you're not comfortable meeting at the library anymore," he'd said, "why don't you suggest another place and time? I'll take care of the rest." She'd come up with the idea of Cameron Falls, and they'd decided to meet around 5 PM. Ordinarily, Tim would be home from work then, but Niall had arranged with Maxine for a friend of hers to have Tim come over to look at her dock and give her an estimate for rebuilding it.

Remembering how pleased Tim had sounded when he told her about the opportunity, Gwen felt a guilty pang. If he ever found out it had been a ruse. That was the trouble with lies, one always seemed to lead to another until you found yourself caught in a web of falsehoods with no easy way out.

But she mustn't worry about this now. She needed to focus her energy on the meeting ahead, which promised to be difficult. She had to make it clear they weren't going to become lovers. At the same time, she had to let him down gently, lest he become angry and reveal her secret to Tim.

Gwen gave herself a last once-over in the mirror. A lock of hair had fallen loose from her bun and partially covered her scar. She pushed it back in place and redid the bun, pulling her hair tightly away from her face. As she did, a ghost memory of someone yanking furiously at her hair slipped into her mind. Who? When? The memory vanished into a black hole in her brain, leaving her staring into the void. Frustrating, though maybe it was just as well.

Chapter 51

By the time she arrived at the parking area for Cameron Falls, Gwen had composed herself. But the sight of Niall's Porsche in the lot, then Niall himself at the base of the falls below unnerved her. He waved when he saw her. She didn't wave back.

Gwen started down the trail to a level area at the foot of the falls. As she came closer, she could smell his aftershave. The fact that he'd shaved and wore a new lime green polo shirt over his khaki pants suggested he viewed the meeting as a tryst. She'd sent the wrong message when she'd picked this spot. Or had she? Had part of her secretly wanted a tryst? Perhaps, but she didn't want it now. She could only hope the pains she'd taken to make herself less attractive would help him realize her expectations were different.

"Glad you could make it," Niall greeted her. He had to raise his voice to make himself heard over the rush of water from the falls. He smiled, then frowned slightly, as he took in the dark circles under her eyes, her pulled back hair, and the faded sundress she wore. "Rough day at the library?"

"It was okay."

He looked away, then back at her. "You're wearing your hair differently."

"The better to show my scar."

"Why would you want to do that?"

"It's part of who I am. I'm not the wild, free girl you knew twenty years ago in New York. When I was raped, and beaten nearly to death, it changed me."

He seemed taken aback by her words. Obviously, he hadn't

expected their meeting to take this turn. When he spoke, his voice was filled with regret. "Oh, Gwen, if only I could have rescued you like I did those other times."

"I'm not blaming you. It was my own damn fault I went into the park that night."

"I still blame myself. And I—I want to make it up to you."

"Make it up to me?"

"Let's sit." He gestured toward a wooden bench that faced the falls.

"I'd rather stand." Best to keep this short, if not sweet.

"Please." He looked at her so imploringly that she relented.

They sat in silence for a few moments, watching the water cascade downward. Then he said, "You weren't meant for the life you have now. Buried in this backwater town. With a husband who drinks too much and doesn't understand you or your lovely daughter."

"Stop." She must not have spoken forcefully enough, because he went right on talking.

"You were meant for better things. Things I can give you if you'll only let me. We'll travel around the globe. Home will be a luxury apartment in Manhattan and a big house in Connecticut. We'll give lots of parties, and entertain the best people. Our life together will be rich and full."

As he spoke, visions of the glamorous, exciting life he was offering flashed through Gwen's mind. But then they were replaced by an image of something very ordinary: the jungle gym in the backyard when it was fresh and new, Tim standing proudly beside it, while the kids shrieked with delight. "Get your mom, I want her to see this," he said. The kids returned with long faces. "We can't find her. She's gone." Tim looked bewildered and sad. "She can't have gone. I built this for the whole family, built it to last a long time."

"No, Niall," Gwen said, "The life I have is the one I chose and I want to keep it."

"But can you honestly say you're happy in your marriage?"

"I admit things have been less than great lately. But I think that's true of many marriages. They're bound to have their rough patches. 'Happily ever after' is a myth. But you wouldn't know that. You've never been married."

"I came close a couple times, but in the end, I couldn't go through with it."

"Why not?"

"You don't know?" He looked at her incredulously.

She shook her head.

"Why do you think I came to the Berkshires in the first place?"

"You got a nice deal on a property, and it seemed like a good site for another of your upscale developments."

"No." Niall pounded his fist into his open palm. Startled by the sudden gesture, Gwen moved slightly away from him.

"It wasn't such a nice deal, and the property's a mess," he continued. "It's going to take millions to turn it into a decent development. I came to be close to you, Gwen." He leaned toward her.

"Then you're here for the wrong reason." Gwen leaned away.

"*No,*" he repeatedly stubbornly. "The times we spent together in New York and now here have been some of the best in my life."

It was Gwen's turn to be incredulous. "Secret meetings at the library and that one time alone at Maxine's?"

"Don't tell me they haven't meant something to you?"

Let him down gently, Gwen reminded herself, seeing his growing agitation. "I like you, Niall. I've enjoyed reminiscing about the fun we had in the past, and sharing something of our present lives. But the meetings have to stop. They're creating problems in my marriage, and I don't want that."

"If it's the scandal of an affair or divorce you're worried about, we could—"

"I don't think you heard me. I don't want to end my marriage."

"You really want to spend the rest of your life with a man who doesn't understand you? Who might not love you, let alone even like you, if he knew the truth about your so-called accident?"

So that was it. He was willing to use emotional blackmail to get what he wanted. "Are you threatening me?"

"I don't have to. At some point, your knucklehead husband is going to realize that with your daughter Scarlett, the apple doesn't fall far from the tree."

Whether he knew it or not, Niall had hit on one of her worst fears.

But she couldn't let him see this. "That remains to be seen," she said evenly, "but in the meantime, no more meetings."

"Fine. We can stop seeing each other for a while, but I hope you'll change your mind. I've waited twenty years for you, Gwen, and I'm willing to wait a few more, if that's what it takes."

His eyes pleaded with her, but she couldn't give way. She needed to make a clean break.

"You'd only be wasting your time. As I said, I like you, Niall. I'm grateful to you for rescuing me when you did. And I don't hold it against you for the time you didn't. But as for love, it isn't there. And it never will be."

Perhaps she imagined it, but Niall seemed to suddenly swell with rage. Gwen wanted to turn and run, but knew it would be a bad move. She didn't want him to know how much he frightened her. She held his gaze a moment longer, then said, "I'm going home now."

She rose and walked slowly and deliberately toward the trail up the hill. She'd only gone a few steps when he grabbed her roughly by the arm and spun her around, yanking her close. The stink of his cologne nauseated her, and the falls roared in her ears, almost drowning out his words: "You haven't changed a bit, Gwen. You were a tease then and you're still a tease, making me think you cared for me when all along you didn't give a shit!"

She struggled in his grip, but he held tight with one hand while raising the other to strike her. She opened her mouth to scream, but the cry caught in her throat.

"What's going on?" A man's voice shouted from above.

Niall let go of her so quickly she nearly lost her balance. Righting herself, Gwen ran. Up the trail, past Kathryn and Earl, her sole thought to put as much distance between her and Niall as possible. Flinging herself into her car, she drove away in a cloud of dust.

Part III: Cry Wolf

Chapter 52

"Looks like we have company," Earl said as they pulled into the parking lot at Cameron Falls. "Want to go someplace else?"

"No, let's stay." Kathryn was surprised and dismayed to see Gwen's sedan parked next to Corrigan's Porsche in such a romantic spot. Did this mean they were lovers, or…? She left the truck and walked to the viewpoint with Earl.

They could see Gwen and Corrigan sitting on a bench facing the falls, talking. Kathryn couldn't make out what they were saying over the roar of the water. She could only guess at what was going on from their body language. Corrigan leaned toward Gwen, but she moved away. A few minutes later, Gwen rose and began walking toward the trail to the parking area. Kathryn turned to go. If Gwen was leaving, she and Earl might as well leave, also. She did not want to talk to Corrigan right now. Happening to glance back, she saw Corrigan get up and go after Gwen. He grabbed her by the arm, jerking her close. Gwen twisted in his grip.

Kathryn returned to the viewpoint and signaled frantically to Earl. "Gwen's in trouble," she called, even as Corrigan raised a hand to strike her friend.

Joining Kathryn, Earl called down to the couple. Corrigan let go of Gwen immediately. She ran up the trail, got into her car and drove away with barely a glance at Kathryn and Earl. After Gwen had gone, Corrigan strode up the hill, his face a mask. She thought he might ignore them completely if neither she nor Earl spoke up. "So, what *was* going on down there?" Kathryn demanded.

He smoothed the dirt in front of him with his shoe. "Nothing much. Gwen didn't like something I said, so she left."

"That's not how it looked," Kathryn spoke for both herself and Earl. "You were about to hit her."

"Well, I didn't, did I?" Corrigan said.

"No, but I think you would have if Earl hadn't called down to you."

"You're jumping to conclusions. What went on between Gwen and me is none of your business, anyway." He stalked to his car.

Kathryn was tempted to go after Corrigan and wrench the truth out of him. Earl must have read her mind. He shook his head emphatically.

"Why did you let him go?" she demanded as Corrigan left.

"We weren't going to get anything more from him."

"But we have to do something. He was going to strike Gwen, maybe beat her up. I think we should at least call the Chief, tell him what we saw, and let him take it from there."

"Okay. We'll go back to the house and make the call. But I think I know what he's going to say."

In the kitchen at the Farley house, Kathryn was about to call the Chief when she saw the voicemail. It was from Gwen asking—or rather, *begging*—her and Earl not to say anything about seeing Corrigan and her at the falls.

Frustrated, she turned to Earl. "What do you make of that?"

"Just what she said: she doesn't want us talking about what we saw."

"But he almost hit her!"

"That's just it. Because nothing actually happened, Gwen doesn't think the incident's worth reporting."

"I called the Chief when Solly almost attacked on me."

"That was different. You had nothing to lose by reporting the incident, but Gwen obviously feels she does. Do you think Tim's going to like it if he finds out Gwen met Corrigan in secret?"

"Of course not."

"Well, then."

Kathryn pursed her lips. "I wish there were something we could do. I'm worried Corrigan might really hurt Gwen another time."

"I'm hoping that since he knows we're on to him, he'll stay away from her. And that she'll have the sense to steer clear of him as well."

"I hope you're right."

"Yeah. Want to talk more about Em, or save it for another time?"

"Let's go out onto the porch."

They settled into chairs facing away from the pond and burned woods, which Kathryn still couldn't bear to look at.

"I'm glad you told me what happened between you and Em before her stroke," Earl said. "I don't want us to have secrets. Em's stroke was probably an accident waiting to happen. If you two hadn't argued, something else would've set her off."

"I wish I could believe that."

"And I wish I could convince you. I do admire you for visiting Em when you were worried about the outcome."

"I care about her, and I wanted to do something to help her get better. Playing the tapes let me be in the room with her without her knowing. But now that she's started to come out of her coma, I'm afraid."

"It's still early. We don't know how much she'll recover. Would it help if I spoke with the doctor?"

"I'd appreciate that." She reached over and gave him a quick kiss.

They talked until it was time for Earl to leave. He'd promised Pete they'd have dinner together, and Kathryn wanted him to keep that promise. She felt better, having shared her feelings of guilt about Emily with him. Yet, she continued to think about comas and how they affected not only the comatose patients, but the people around them.

She knew how she felt when she visited Emily, but what had it been like for Corrigan when Gwen was in a coma? In a moment of uncharacteristic candor, he'd told her how helpless he'd felt. Helpless and afraid Gwen would wake up and blame him for not rescuing her when he could have? He *had* seen her leave the party, according to what he'd told a reporter. Had he harbored feelings of guilt, even though his sin was of omission rather than commission. She tried to picture him in the room with Gwen when she'd been tethered to the tubes that kept her alive, her prognosis uncertain. But the image remained blurry, and another image kept intruding. It was of Corrigan, hand raised against Gwen.

Chapter 53

When Kathryn woke up the next morning, questions about Corrigan were still on her mind. She wasn't about to ask him when—or if—he showed up at the house. She waited until 9 AM, then called the only other person she thought would know.

"Yeah, who's this?" a groggy Maxine answered.

"It's Kathryn. I remember you telling me how Niall was so upset after Gwen's accident that he shaved his head and gained a lot of weight. Did he also visit her at the hospital?"

"Sure did," Maxine replied. "He went every freakin' day."

"It must have been hard for him, seeing her like that and not being able to do anything."

"It *was* hard—unbearable, in fact. That's why he didn't go into her room, but stayed in the reception area. I'd see him when I went in, and he'd still be sitting there when I left."

"When Gwen started to come out of her coma, he must have gone in to see her."

"I don't recall that he did. At least not while I was there. He seemed to prefer getting news about her progress from others." Silence on the line, then Maxine said, "Is this important?"

"Not really. I was just curious."

"I'm hanging up then. I need to get some caffeine into my system, or I'll fall back asleep."

And I better get some caffeine in me, too. Kathryn went to the kitchen and made coffee. Cup in hand, she headed back upstairs. As she passed the half bath, the faint odor of Corrigan's aftershave reached her. His shaving paraphernalia, toothbrush and tooth paste

236

were still there, a reminder of his preparations for yesterday's meeting with Gwen. He'd obviously had high hopes for it. And if those hopes were for a romantic relationship, she must have quashed them. Why else would he have raised his hand against her? If Earl hadn't called out, would Corrigan have hit her?

Kathryn took her coffee into the study, where she had a view of the driveway. She'd make a few more calls before Corrigan arrived, assuming he did.

"Hello?" Scarlett said. The eagerness in her voice told Kathryn she'd been hoping the call was for her, followed by disappointment when Scarlett realized it wasn't. "Okay, I'll get Mom. MOM!" Scarlett yelled.

"Oh, hi, Kathryn." Gwen's tone was guarded.

"I just wanted you to know that I got your message and—"

"You can hang up now, Scarlett," Gwen interrupted.

At the sound of a click, Kathryn finished what she'd been about to say: "I did what you asked. But if you feel like talking, I'll be around until late afternoon on Sunday when I return to Boston."

"I'll think about it," Gwen said, her voice still guarded in case Scarlett had picked up again.

Next, Kathryn phoned her ex-boyfriend, Alan, at his law firm in Boston. After a brief and somewhat awkward conversation, she got a recommendation for an estate lawyer at the firm and made an appointment for the following week. She was just about to make another call when she heard a car engine in the driveway. Corrigan had arrived. Tired of tiptoeing around him, she punched in the number anyway.

"Hi, Suzy, I'm calling to see how you and your family are doing."

"Okay, I guess." Suzy sounded stressed.

"What is it?"

"I can't talk now. I'm just heading out the door. Robert has an appointment with a therapist at the Berkshire Medical Center in Pittsfield."

Kathryn thought a moment, then said, "Would it help if I took Robert to Pittsfield?"

"That's kind of you to offer, but it's probably more of a time commitment than you want to make."

"I can do it."

"All right, you're on. Thanks, Kathryn."

As Kathryn headed for the front door, she heard Corrigan clear his throat in the dining room, as if about to speak. She didn't wait to hear what he had to say.

On the drive to Pittsfield, Robert was mostly silent, replying with monosyllables to the simple questions Kathryn asked. At the Berkshire Medical Center's mental health clinic, she sat in the reception area and tried to read a magazine, while Robert saw the therapist. Flipping aimlessly through the pages, her thoughts wandered to Corrigan sitting in the hospital reception area while Gwen was in a coma. What had been going on inside his head as he sat there day after day? More importantly, what was going on in his head now if Gwen had rejected him? But it was useless to speculate. What she should do was figure out a way to get through to Robert.

As someone who'd had a difficult relationship—or rather non-relationship—with her own father, she felt a surge of sympathy for the boy. Having an abusive dad like Plungas couldn't have been easy. There must have been times when Robert wished his father were dead, just as she had her father. Now, he probably felt guilty for having such thoughts, much as she did. Unlike Robert, she hadn't suffered abuse from her father, but rather from his complete abandonment of her and her mother, until her mother took him back when he was ill and alone. And despite her fellow-feeling for Robert, she wasn't sure how to get him to open up.

The answer didn't come until he emerged from his session, red-faced from crying, his body slumped and emotionally drained.

"Hey, Robert," she said, "I don't know about you, but I'm starving. How about we grab a bite to eat before we head home?"

"Whatever," he replied dully. Once they were in a burger place on North Street, his attitude changed. He ordered a cheese burger with fries and a chocolate shake. When the food arrived, he dug in with the gusto of someone who hadn't eaten in days.

"Feel better?" she asked when he was done.

"Yeah," he said with a shy half smile.

"Me, too, but now that I've got some food in me, I'd like to stretch my legs before the drive back. Is that okay with you?"

He nodded, and they set off down North Street. After they'd gone almost a block, Kathryn said, "Have they given you any idea how much longer you'll be seeing the therapist? I ask because I know Gwen misses you at the library."

"She does?" Robert stopped in his tracks and stared at her.

"Yes. She told me you've been such a help, it's hard without you." Although Gwen hadn't said this in so many words, Kathryn believed it wasn't far from the truth.

Robert's eyes lit up, then he frowned. "She has other help," he muttered.

"What other help?"

"The developer guy—Corrigan. I don't know if he was actually helping her, but he stopped by the library several times to see her."

"I noticed his car parked by the library a few days ago when it wasn't open yet," Kathryn said.

"That's when he usually goes," Robert said. "I know because when I'd show up a little before opening time, he was already there."

Kathryn hesitated before asking her next question, trying to think of the best way to frame it. "What was Corrigan doing at the library?"

"Sitting in the back talking to Gwen."

"If they were in the back, how did you happen to see them?"

Robert flushed. "The first time, I knew she was inside because her car was parked in its usual spot, so I walked around the building until I saw her... and him."

"Did they see you?"

Robert's flush deepened. "I don't think so."

"And this happened, how many times?"

"Almost every day the library was open until I had to go to the hospital."

Clearly, Robert had spied on Gwen and Corrigan. Because he had a crush on her? It was certainly possible. "You like Gwen, don't you?"

"I think she's cool," Robert said more to the sidewalk than to her.

"In spite of what your dad said about her?"

"Yes!" Robert cried with sudden fury. "I hated him for that."

239

"Did he ever tell you why he thought she was a whore?"

"No, just that he had a lot of dirt on her, and one day, he'd share it."

"But he didn't?"

"The night he was killed, he said he was gonna. The minute I walked in, he started in about Gwen—what a horrible person she was, and how he was gonna show me evidence to prove it. I told him I didn't want to see it. We argued. When I couldn't take it anymore, I gave him a shove and ran out the door."

"He didn't try to follow you?"

"No. Looking back, I think he deliberately picked a fight because he didn't want me around. Dad loved provoking people. Mom gave it right back to him, but he knew I'd choose flight over fight."

"Why do you think he didn't want you around?"

"Isn't it obvious? So he could start that fire without any witnesses."

"You believe he was the arsonist?"

"Dad was a troublemaker. He enjoyed it. From where I was hiding, I could hear him laughing as he went deeper into the forest."

"Did you hear anyone else in the woods?"

Robert shook his head. "I didn't want to be there when Dad got back from wherever he was going. I walked to the road and tried to hitch. Several cars passed, but none stopped. I kept walking until I reached a house where I could call Mom."

The flow of words ended abruptly. Robert looked around, confused. "How'd we get on this anyway?"

"Gwen and the library," Kathryn reminded him.

"Oh, yeah. You won't tell her I sort of spied on her and Corrigan, will you?"

"No, but I hope *you'll* tell the police detective what you just told me about the night of the fire—if you haven't already."

Robert looked uncertain. "I think I told him at least some of it the first time I spoke to him. The second time, I broke down before I could. I doubt he would've believed me anyway."

Kathryn put a hand on his shoulder. "I believe you, Robert."

*****

240

Corrigan wasn't at the Farley house when Kathryn returned. Papers were still scattered across the dining room table, but he'd taken his shaving paraphernalia with him. There was no voicemail from Gwen, though if she'd called when Corrigan was there, he would've picked up, and Kathryn doubted Gwen would leave a message for her with him. She still hoped Gwen would confide in her about what was going on between her and Corrigan, but her conversation with Robert made her wonder if perhaps things weren't as bad as they appeared. While the fact that Corrigan and Gwen had been meeting secretly in the library was worrisome, at least all they'd done was talk.

As for what Robert had told her about the night of the fire, she was more and more convinced the boy hadn't killed his dad. Pity he hadn't heard anyone else in the woods, though. She could only hope the police would find evidence that another person *had* been there. Unless, as Charlotte had pointed out, Plungas's death was an accident.

Kathryn was still mulling over these and other matters when Earl showed up for dinner with two steaks for the grill and a foil-wrapped plate, containing fresh-baked brownies. "They're from Suzy," he explained, "to thank you for taking Robert to his therapist appointment. He came home in a much better mood than he's been in lately, and she thinks you're responsible."

"All I did was take him to lunch afterward, and then we talked a bit." She told him about her conversation with Robert. "But if that helped him, I'm glad," she finished, "Especially after all Suzy's done for me... and for us."

Kathryn couldn't help but think of the irony in the fact that Gwen wasn't the perfect role model of a city-bred woman happily married to a local man, as Suzy thought. Rather, Gwen was someone who'd been sitting on a big secret for years—a secret that might threaten her marriage, if Tim was as unbending toward his wife as he was toward their daughter. Still, Kathryn hoped Gwen would find the courage to tell Tim she was the Grant's Tomb Girl. Then Corrigan wouldn't have anything to hold over her, if that's what he was doing. And, as a keeper of secrets herself, Kathryn knew how, in the end, it was better to come clean. That had certainly been the case when she'd confessed her guilt about Emily to Earl.

"Star, are you there?"

"What? Oh, sorry, I was just thinking."

"Want to tell me?"

"Not right now. Let's have dinner and enjoy the rest of the evening."

While Earl grilled the steaks, Kathryn made a salad with lettuce and radishes from the garden, along with tomatoes and cucumbers she'd picked up at a local farm stand. But try as she might, she couldn't shake a lingering feeling of unease.

Chapter 54

"Don't come. Getting ride w/ Annie." Alone in the restaurant restroom, Scarlett texted her mom and waited. Moments later, the reply came back: "OK."

Scarlett smiled. That was easy. She already had her boss's approval to leave a half hour early from her waitressing job at the Brew 'N' Burger. Now, all she had to do was wait another thirty minutes for Niall to arrive.

She'd been surprised and excited when he'd texted her at the restaurant: "Pick u up @ 9:30 tonite?" She knew he liked her. That had been obvious when they'd first met at the pizza parlor and she'd snatched his glasses from his head. The way he'd looked at her then, eyes lingering on her breasts and hips as he gave her a once-over, had sent her heart racing. She hadn't been attracted to anyone so much since... well, Jason. At the thought of Jason, Scarlett felt a pang, but pushed it to the back of her mind. He was gone, and Niall was the one she'd be seeing tonight.

So what if he was old enough to be her dad? Jason had been older, too, though Niall was at least twice his age. But Jason paled next to Niall, who was unlike any man she'd ever known. Cool and sophisticated with a hint of danger. No country bumpkin like her dad, Niall belonged to a world she barely knew, but wanted desperately to be a part of. Her godmother, Maxine, had taken her on trips to New York City when she was a child, but when she became a teenager, her old fogey dad called a halt to the trips. Dad even accused Maxine of corrupting her.

If a few visits to New York could corrupt her, she wanted more.

She'd had a taste of what it would be like to be with a *real* man—and a New Yorker to boot–that afternoon at Maxine's when Niall taught her how to waterski. He'd pressed his body against hers as he held her in the water with her skis on, and whispered in her ear, "So beautiful!" Sweet-nothings, Grandma Waite would've called his words, but to Scarlett, they were thrilling. Grandma Waite was crazy, anyway. Imagine thinking Niall was trying to kidnap her and Billy when all he was doing was giving them a ride to Maxine's. Of course, her dad bought right into the kidnapping idea, and insisted her mom go to Maxine's to chaperone. As if *that* were necessary.

Since then, Niall had whispered more sweet-nothings in her ears when he came to the restaurant during her shifts. She'd been hurt when she wasn't included in the second invite to Maxine's for swimming. Why should her mom have all the fun while she was stuck at home? She knew Niall was an old friend of her mom's, but that was it. When asked, her mom refused to talk about that time in her life. Scarlett could only guess if there'd been something more between her and Niall.

And now, how could he possibly be interested in her *mom*? Sure, there were moments when she caught glimpses of the beauty her mom must have been, mostly from a distance or when the lights were dim. But up close in broad daylight, her mom looked all of her forty-some years. There were wrinkles around her eyes, and white hair mixed in with the blonde. Why didn't her mom pull them out? Or get a better dye job? Her mom had always had that ugly scar running down one side of her face, but lately it seemed more noticeable than before. Because her mom no longer went to great lengths to hide it? If *she'd* been cursed with a scar like that, she would've insisted on plastic surgery to remove it. Even if her mom *had* kept her looks, Niall couldn't be interested in her, because didn't older men always prefer younger women?

That was fine by Scarlett. She *so* preferred older guys to the pimply-faced jerks in her class. Pete Barker was kinda cute, but when she'd smiled seductively and said "hi," in her super sultry voice, he'd blushed, turned tail and run.

A loud pounding on the restroom door pulled Scarlett out of her reverie. She flushed the toilet, waited a moment, then exited. Annie, a fellow waitress who was several years older, glared at her. "What were you doing in there?"

Scarlett glared back. "Wouldn't you like to know?"

At a little after nine, the restaurant was nearly empty. There were a few couples at tables, and some stragglers at the bar. One of them, a regular with longish gray hair and a full gray beard, called out to Scarlett: "Hey, honey, I'm feeling kinda lonesome tonight. How 'bout keeping me company?" He patted the stool beside him.

After checking to make sure her boss wasn't watching, Scarlett gave him the finger and walked away. The downside of working Friday nights was being hassled by guys like him. The upside lay in the generous tips she received—money she needed for a move to New York as soon as she turned eighteen.

*****

At exactly 9:30, Scarlett left the restaurant and stepped into a black SUV that was double-parked outside. Niall had told her he'd be driving it without explaining why. After greeting him in her super sultry voice, Scarlett said, "What happened to your Porsche?"

"It needed some work," Niall said. "So, I rented this. Like it?"

"Nice," Scarlett said, taking in the fresh, nearly-new car smell, and the smooth leather seats.

"The Porsche is more fun to drive, of course, but I find these big cars more comfortable. You know you can adjust your seat to turn it into a recliner?"

"Cool."

"How was it at the restaurant tonight?"

"Busy like it always is on weekend nights. I'm glad to be off my feet."

"I brought some nips in case you want to take the edge off. You've had nips before, right?"

"Sure, lots of times," Scarlett fibbed. No need to tell him she had to get older friends to buy them for her.

Niall handed her a small bottle. "What kind is this?" she asked.

"Fireball whiskey."

Scarlett opened the bottle and downed the contents in one gulp. The whiskey burned her throat, and the alcohol went straight to her head. She shook herself and blinked. That was when she realized they were headed in a different direction from her home. "Where're we going? This isn't the way to my house."

"Relax, we're taking the long way around to give us more time to talk. Would you like another nip?"

Scarlett hesitated. She knew she should probably say no, but didn't want to appear uncool. "Okay, thanks." This time, though, she only took a small drink.

"If you're tired of whiskey, I've got tequila, too," Niall said.

"Whiskey's fine, I just want to… savor it." *Savor*, was that the right word? It wasn't part of Scarlett's normal vocabulary, but she vaguely remembered someone in a movie using it. Now, speeding along in a black SUV with Niall, she felt like she *was* in a movie, made all the more exciting by the thought that her parents would be furious if they knew what she was doing.

"So, Scarlett," Niall said after a few moments, "Who usually gives you a ride home at night?"

"Sometimes I get a ride with one of the other waitresses, but mostly my parents pick me up," she admitted, wishing he hadn't asked that particular question, because it made her feel like such a dependent child.

"No boyfriend?"

"Not at the moment."

"That surprises me. I would've thought the boys would be all over a beautiful girl like you." He placed a hand on her thigh and moved it in ever widening circles toward her crotch.

Scarlett's brain told her she should remove his hand, but her body said no. It was enjoying the massage and wanted it to continue. In the end, her brain won and she removed his hand, but only after she'd pretended it belonged to a pimple-faced jerk in her class.

"I'm not interested in boys my own age," she said.

"Your former boyfriend was older?"

"Twenty-seven." The words were no sooner out of her mouth

246

than she realized how ridiculous she must sound. Ridiculous and impossibly young to a man in his forties.

"I suppose twenty-seven would seem old to you," he said. "Tell me about this boyfriend."

"He was just a guy I met." Scarlett hoped they could leave it at that and talk about something else. Like the fact that Niall had turned off the main road and was now navigating a maze of side roads, none of which led to her house.

"At the restaurant?" He persisted.

"Yes, now can we—"

"What is it, Scarlett? You sound upset." His hand was back on her thigh again, moving in lazy circles that were driving her crazy with desire.

"I'm not upset," she said shakily. "I don't want to talk about my old boyfriend. I want to go home."

"I'll take you home," he said, "But not right away. Not in the state you're in. I'm going to find a quiet place where we can talk. Then you're going to tell me all about that boyfriend and why talking about him is so upsetting."

His refusal to take her home was a clear sign of trouble. But there'd been other hints that, flattered by his attention and determined to impress him with her worldliness, Scarlett had ignored. She knew she couldn't ignore them now. Not if she wanted to arrive home safely. She needed to keep focused on that goal, and not let Niall lead her astray. No more nips, no more touching, and definitely no more talk of Jason.

"I can't talk while you're touching me," she said. "It's too distracting."

"Fair enough," he said, removing his hand to grasp the steering wheel, as he pulled off onto a dirt road.

"Where're we going?" Scarlett demanded.

"Calm down. I thought we agreed—"

"There was no agreement."

"Okay. But just as you find it too distracting to talk while I'm touching you, I find it too distracting to drive while we're having a serious conversation. That's why I suggested we find a quiet place."

He drove a short distance farther and brought the car to a halt. "This all right?"

"I guess," Scarlett said, "as long as you promise that as soon as we've talked, you'll take me home."

"You have my word. About the boyfriend?"

"There's not much to tell. My parents didn't approve of him, so we ended it."

"That's all?"

"Yes."

"I don't think so. I think you were very much in love with this guy, and when your parents made you break it off, you were devastated."

"No, that's not how it was."

"Then *how* was it? You can confide in me, Scarlett. After all, I'm an old friend of the family and—"

"An old friend of *mom's*," she corrected. "And while we're talking about her, were you really just friends, or was there something more between you?"

Niall's face was in shadow, so Scarlett couldn't see his reaction. Yet judging from his silence, she thought she'd caught him off guard. Anything to get him to stop prying into what had happened with Jason.

"All right, if you must know, your mother and I were lovers," he said at last. "But after her accident, she broke off with me and just about everyone else from her past, moved to the Berkshires, and married your dad. I was heartbroken. It took me years to get over her, but finally, I did."

Scarlett was genuinely moved by his words. She'd never dreamed Niall would open up to her like this; he'd always seemed so in control of himself and his feelings.

"I'm sorry, Niall," she said. "I had no idea Mom hurt you."

"Of course not, sweetheart," he said, "but if there's one thing I've learned, it's that time heals even the deepest of wounds." He fumbled in the compartment between their seats and produced two more nips, one of which he handed her. "To time's healing power," he said, raising his nip in a mournful toast and downing it.

Swept up in the emotional tide of the moment, Scarlett joined him in the toast. And then another, until she did what she'd promised herself she wouldn't—told him about Jason—how handsome he was, and how she'd fallen hard for him, only then to discover he was an addict and have him overdose before her eyes. She'd called 911, an ambulance had come and taken him to the hospital, but after the doctors determined he was brain dead, his family had them pull the plug. "It was horrible, just horrible." She broke into sobs.

"There, there," Niall soothed, stroking her hair. "I'm sorry I brought it up. But it's over. You're going to be all right."

Woozy with alcohol and drained from crying, Scarlett was dimly aware of him leaving the car to come around to her side. Opening the door, he adjusted the knobs on her seat so she lay almost flat. Then he said, "I'm going to give you something that will help you relax. Be a good girl and open your mouth."

He had to repeat the last three words several times before Scarlett did what he wanted. Moments later, darkness overcame her.

Chapter 55

By quarter of eleven when she and Earl ended their stargazing on the patio, Kathryn had pretty much decided nothing bad was going to happen that day. Then the phone rang.

"Has Niall been to the house today?" Gwen sounded distressed. In the background, Kathryn heard raised voices. Tim and Grandma Waite were having an argument. A *heated* one.

"He came in the morning a little after nine," Kathryn said.

"When did he leave?"

"I can't say for sure, but when I got back from some errands around one, he was gone."

"Did he say anything about going to the city?"

"We didn't speak, so I don't know his plans. Have you tried Maxine? She'll probably have a better idea where he is."

"I just got off the phone with her. The last time she saw him was before he came to you."

"What did I tell you?" Grandma Waite's voice came through so loud and clear, she had to be standing next to the phone. "That evil man has kidnapped my Scarlett and taken her god only knows where!"

Kidnapped? Kathryn would have dismissed Grandma Waite's words as more "crying wolf" but for the scene at the falls yesterday. Could Corrigan have taken Scarlett to get back at Gwen for rejecting him? Kathryn couldn't very well say this over the phone. Definitely not while they were all yelling at each other.

"We never should have agreed to let Scarlett waitress Friday nights," Tim shouted. "She's already shown poor judgment, taking up with that druggie. For all we know, she's hanging out with someone just like him."

"No, you are wrong," Grandma Waite cried. "She has been kidnapped by that evil man!"

"Will you both stop it?" Gwen pleaded.

Kathryn exchanged looks with Earl. He rolled his eyes. "Gwen, listen," Kathryn raised her voice to make herself heard over the continuing din in the background, "how about Earl and I come over? Our presence may help dial things down. Then, when everyone's calmer, we can put our heads together and try to figure out where Scarlett's likely to be."

"I don't know. It's late and this is our problem, not yours."

"It is *her* problem, too," Grandma Waite chimed in. "If she had warned you like I told her to, this wouldn't have happened."

"Grandma, you're like a broken record, and it's not helpful. I want you to go home now," Tim ordered.

"I am *not* leaving until you call the police and tell them my Scarlett has been kidnapped," the old woman shot back.

"Ohhh," Gwen moaned into the handset. "Yes, come, Kathryn," she said.

"It sounds like a madhouse over there," Earl said when Kathryn ended the call. "Are you serious about going?"

"It *is* a madhouse, and that's exactly why we're needed."

They were silent on the drive to the Waites' house, but before they left the car, Kathryn said, "The plan is to get some basic information— like when Scarlett was expected home and what friends she might be with. Depending on what they tell us, I may need to speak with Gwen in private."

"How come?"

"I'll explain later."

Gwen opened the door for them and practically fell into Kathryn's arms. "Thank heaven, you're here. I don't think I could've taken another minute of this. Tim and his grandmother have been going at each other and me, too, for hours, it feels like. And while we're quarreling, Scarlett's still missing." She began to cry.

"I know," Kathryn soothed. "But we're going to find her."

They went into the kitchen, where Tim and Grandma Waite continued to argue. Earl stepped between them, clapped his hands, and called for quiet. "If Kathryn and I are going to help, we need your cooperation. She has some questions for you, and instead of everybody talking at once, she'll call on you one at a time. Okay?"

Grandma Waite opened her mouth, presumably to protest, but Earl shook his head vigorously. "You'll get your turn, Mrs. Waite, but now Kathryn has the floor."

Kathryn was impressed. She'd never seem him take charge like this before. She knew he'd coached his three sons' teams, so maybe he'd learned these techniques then.

"How does Scarlett usually get home from the restaurant?" she asked Gwen.

"Either Tim or I pick her up, but sometimes she gets rides from friends or one of the wait staff," Gwen said. "That's what was supposed to happen tonight. I was just about to take a computer game to Billy, who's having a sleepover at a friend's house, when Scarlett texted me she was getting a ride from Annie, another waitress."

Through another set of questions and answers, Kathryn established that when Scarlett hadn't shown up at the expected time of ten-thirty, two things had happened. Grandma Waite, who kept track of the family's comings and goings, had rushed over and insisted Corrigan had kidnapped Scarlett. Gwen had called Annie's house. Annie told her she hadn't given Scarlett a ride, but she said Scarlett had left earlier, around nine thirty. Annie hadn't seen who Scarlett had gotten a ride with. "One minute, Scarlett was there, and the next she wasn't," Annie said.

Kathryn's heart sank. She felt there was a strong possibility Scarlett was with Corrigan—either she'd gone willingly or she'd been abducted. Gwen, however, might be reluctant to point the finger at him, because she might feel she'd have to reveal she'd been meeting him in secret. It was also possible that both Gwen and Tim would continue to resist pinning the crime—if that's what it was—on Corrigan, because when Grandma Waite had accused him of kidnapping Scarlett and her brother Billy earlier, he hadn't actually done so. In any case, Kathryn felt they should exhaust other possibilities before she said anything.

Kathryn got the names of Scarlett's friends and co-workers, then Gwen called them all, but with no luck. "So, here's what I think," Kathryn said. "Scarlett could have gone off with some unknown person she met at the restaurant, or she might have left with Corrigan. Why don't you call the restaurant owner," she said to Tim, "and see if he noticed Scarlett spending an unusual amount of time with any patron?" To Gwen, she said, "I'd like to speak with you in private for a few minutes."

Upstairs in the master bedroom, Gwen perched on the edge of an old-fashioned four-poster bed with a canopy and a white chenille spread. Kathryn sat in an armchair. "I hate to say this," she said, "but this time, I think Grandma Waite may be right about Corrigan taking Scarlett."

Gwen paled. "You've gotta be kidding. I can't imagine Niall doing something like that. Grandma Waite is just plain crazy."

"She is a bit strange, but sometimes so-called crazy people can sense things others don't. And she's had a bad feeling about Corrigan from the get-go."

"She doesn't *know* him. She's never even spoken to him. She only glimpsed him from afar that one time he came to pick up the kids."

"Not so. She told me she'd seen his Porsche parked on Shuntoll Road several times late at night *before* he made his presence known to the rest of us. That says to me he might've been stalking you. Also, I've been around him enough to believe he won't take no for answer. So, if you turned him down at the falls yesterday, he might've taken Scarlett to get revenge."

"That's ridiculous," Gwen flared. "You just don't like him because of the development he's planning."

"I admit the development set me against him, but there's more. When he almost struck you at the falls, I found myself wondering what might have happened if Earl hadn't called out."

"He wouldn't have hurt me, if that's what you're thinking. He rescued me from a guy who *was* about to attack me twenty years ago."

"Maxine told me about that. I know from personal experience how rescuing someone creates a strong bond between the rescuer and the person who's rescued. Corrigan may even have thought he was going to rescue you again, when—" Kathryn broke off, horrified at what she'd almost said. She mustn't voice the suspicion lurking in the back of her mind when it was still so nebulous.

"When he *what*?" Gwen's eyes drilled into her.

"Nothing."

"No, you were going to say something about Niall."

Kathryn hesitated a long moment, considering how to respond. Finally, she said, "He may have told you I found a file of newspaper stories about the so-called Grant's Tomb Girl at Randy Plungas's cabin. From what I read in those stories, and what Maxine told me about how wild you and she were in your younger days, I think you were probably that girl."

Gwen swallowed hard. "I was, but what does that have to do with Niall?"

"He's quoted in one of the stories as having seen you leave the party."

"So? I'm sure there were others who saw me leave."

"I'm sure there were, too, but those other people weren't in the habit of following you."

"Following me? What're you talking about?"

"Did you ever wonder how Niall happened to be there when that other guy attacked you?"

"He must have been nearby. Lucky for me he was. Otherwise, I could've been badly hurt, maybe even killed."

"It didn't occur to you that he'd followed you?"

"No. Even if he did, what harm was there in it? He protected me."

"*That* time he did," Kathryn said carefully.

Gwen's eyes widened with alarm. "Are you suggesting that… ?" She moved closer to the head of the bed, as if to distance herself from Kathryn. "No, Niall would never hurt me like that." She worried a nub on the spread, tugging at it until it looked ready to come off. Looking up again, she glared at Kathryn. "You're as crazy as Grandma Waite."

"I could be wrong, but consider his behavior when you were in the hospital in a coma. He came every day, but he never went into your room. There could be other reasons for this, but I think he might've been afraid you'd wake up and recognize him as your attacker. As you started to come out of your coma, don't you think he would've come into your room to offer words of encouragement? No. He stayed outside."

"He sent flowers and a card."

"But kept his distance. He also changed his appearance—shaved his head and gained a lot of weight. So, twenty years later when he showed up here in the Berkshires, you didn't recognize him at first."

Gwen shook her head slowly. "I just can't believe Niall would have attacked me like that. Or that he's got Scarlett now. But if you are right, I can't face telling Tim about my shameful past, or that I've been meeting Niall in secret."

"There is *no* shame in being a rape victim," Kathryn said.

"But the newspapers painted me as this awful, immoral woman who was just asking for trouble," Gwen said. "They did it enough that I started believing it. My parents weren't exactly supportive either. Especially my dad. I overheard him telling my mother I was damaged goods, and it was important to keep my identity under wraps. He was thinking of running for a local office at the time, and was afraid the scandal would hurt his chances. I think he was relieved when I left the city and married Tim. And Tim's such a straight-arrow guy, I don't think he'd understand."

Gwen looked so miserable that Kathryn went to the bed and put a comforting arm around her. "I read those newspapers also. It was terrible what some of them said. And what your dad said as well. But times have changed. Thanks to the #MeToo movement, women are coming forward with their stories of sexual assault, and people are starting to recognize it for the crime against women it truly is. Still, if you're not comfortable telling Tim yet, wait until you are. The same goes for your secret meetings with Niall. For now, it's enough if we both say we've noticed Niall coming on to Scarlett at various times, and leave it at that."

When they returned to the kitchen, Tim said, "I just got off the phone with the owner of the Brew 'N' Burger. He can't think of anyone in particular who's shown an interest in Scarlett, aside from a few regulars at the bar who hassle all the waitresses."

"I guess that eliminates that possibility," Kathryn said. "Gwen and I have talked and—" She broke off when the phone rang. Gwen made a dash for it, but Tim beat her to it. He picked up and listened intently. Kathryn searched his face for a sign of whether the caller had news about Scarlett. She hoped against hope the girl had turned up safe at someone's house.

"Thanks," Tim said, his face grim. "That was the owner of the Brew 'N' Burger calling back to say he'd noticed an older guy with a shaved head chat up Scarlett a couple times. If she wasn't waiting on him, he'd motion for her to come over. Then, he'd whisper in her ear and she'd smile and even blush a little."

Chapter 56

"Scarlett's missing. We think Corrigan's taken her," Tim told the Chief over the phone, then gave him the make and model of Corrigan's car, and the time Scarlett was last seen at the restaurant. The Chief said he'd contact the State Police to put out an Amber Alert.

"We really appreciate your help," Gwen said to Kathryn and Earl, "but for now we've done everything we can. Why don't you both go home and get some sleep?"

It was almost midnight, and Kathryn was exhausted. Earl seemed tired, too. Gwen and Tim looked stricken; Grandma Waite, angry. Observing the furious gleam in her eyes, Kathryn could almost believe the old woman was a witch. The idea of sleep was tempting, but she wanted to be there for Gwen.

"You go," she told Earl. "I'll stay here."

"If you stay, I will, too," he replied.

"I'll make coffee," Gwen said.

The shot of caffeine revived Kathryn, but also made her restless. She couldn't just sit and wait. "Mind if I use the phone?" she asked.

"Help yourself," Tim said.

The phone rang and rang before Maxine picked up. Kathryn hit the speaker button so they could all hear. Maxine sounded even groggier than she had that morning. Kathryn had to repeat herself a couple of times before Maxine got it about Niall and Scarlett. Then Maxine couldn't believe he'd actually taken the girl. When Kathryn had finally convinced Maxine, she said, "You know Corrigan better than any of us. Where do you think he might have gone with Scarlett?"

"I don't know. He certainly wouldn't bring her here."

"I doubt he'd bring her anywhere near the Farley house either. But is there any other place in the area where he liked to go? The boat ramp on Lake Clyde, perhaps?" She'd been to the public boat ramp with Earl months ago, and knew it as a place where couples sometimes went at night.

"I don't think Niall even knows it exists," Maxine said. "He isn't much of an explorer. He wouldn't take Scarlett into the woods for fear *he'd* get lost."

"Could he have taken her all the way to New York?"

"Maybe. If the police don't find him soon, they should look in the city. Unless…"

"What?"

"Give me a minute."

Kathryn waited, and so, she imagined, did everyone else in the room. It was as if they were all holding their collective breath.

At last, Maxine said, "Long before Niall and I renewed our friendship, I'd see his name in the "Sunday Styles" section of *The New York Times* in connection with various parties and charitable benefits. Several of these events were held at an estate in Westchester County—Croton or Katonah? Niall told me the estate belongs to a wealthy friend, and he often rents a guest house on the property. Sometimes he gives small parties there. He invited me to one a while ago, but I couldn't go. From what he said, the estate is a big rambling place. That's where I think he might take Scarlett, if the cops don't nab him first."

"Does the estate have a name? If not, what's the name of the owner?" Kathryn asked.

"It does, but I can't remember it, or the owner's name."

Kathryn's excitement gave way to disappointment. Without more information, it would be almost impossible to find the place.

Earl moved closer to the phone. "Hi, Maxine, Earl Barker here."

"Oh, hi." Maxine's tone turned sultry.

Unbelievable. In the midst of a crisis, Maxine was flirting with Earl.

"You said you were invited to a party at the estate. Do you still have that invite?" he asked.

"Let me check."

They heard Maxine move around the room, followed by silence, then her returning footsteps. "Found it! The address is 21 Dutchmans Hill Road in Katonah."

If Maxine had been in the room, Kathryn would have hugged her. "Thanks, Maxine, you've been a huge help."

Tim called the Chief so he could relay the information to the Katonah police. Then Tim booted up the family computer and mapped the location for them all to see. The estate was more than seventy miles away, a drive of nearly two hours. Tim printed the map, stuck it in his pocket, and disappeared into another room. He returned with his shotgun.

"What do you think you're doing?" Gwen demanded.

"Going after the man who's got our daughter." Tim bolted for the door.

"No!" Gwen grabbed at him, but he pulled free. She dashed after him. Grandma Waite started to follow them, but Earl blocked her. "You'd best stay here, Mrs. Waite." She scowled at him, muttered something, and reluctantly returned to the computer, glowering at it as if the machine itself held her namesake captive. Earl ran outside, Kathryn on his heels.

Tim had started up his truck in the driveway and was about to leave. Gwen flung herself into the passenger seat and the truck roared off.

"This is crazy," Kathryn said. "We have to stop him!"

"I'll go after them," Earl said.

"I'm coming with you."

"Do you remember the address on Dutchmans Hill?" Earl asked when they were in the car. She told him and he typed it into his GPS device.

They drove to the intersection of Shuntoll Road with Sodom Road, then headed south to the Connecticut border. From there, they sped down dark winding roads until they picked up Route 22 South in New York State. Kathryn spotted Tim's truck a couple of times only to have it disappear around a bend. Eventually, they lost him completely. He seemed to be going a lot faster than they were, even through towns, where she insisted Earl slow down in case any police were lurking in the middle of the night. More winding roads brought them to Interstate 684. Fortunately, Katonah was located in northern Westchester County. Signs for the northernmost towns flew past, then Katonah. Almost there.

A siren shrieked and blue lights flashed behind them. Earl slowed to just under the speed limit. The police car shot past them in pursuit of a red pickup. Tim's? Earl hit the gas. The police car tailgated the pickup until it veered from the left lane into the middle lane. Then the police car forced the pickup from the middle lane into the right lane. With nowhere else to go, the pickup swerved from the highway. It zoomed off the breakdown lane, nosediving into a ditch.

Kathryn gasped. If Tim and Gwen were in that truck, she hoped and prayed they were all right.

Chapter 57

When Kathryn and Earl arrived at the spot where the pickup had gone into the ditch, the state police officer had already left his vehicle. He shone a flashlight into the pickup. Kathryn was close enough to identify the pickup as Tim's, but too far away to see what shape their friends were in. She was about to get out when Earl put a hand on her arm. "Let the officer do his job. He'll find out soon enough if Tim and Gwen are all right. If they're not, he'll call an ambulance."

Kathryn was relieved when Tim and Gwen slowly exited the truck. Gwen joined Tim on the driver's side, where they raised their hands over their heads while the officer patted them down.

"Who does he think they are—Bonnie and Clyde?" Kathryn demanded indignantly.

"Calm down, Star. It's dark, they're strangers who were speeding, and he probably saw the shotgun in the back. You rush down there now, you'll only cause trouble."

"We're just gonna sit here?"

"Before we do anything, we'll let the officer know we're here." They left the truck, positioning themselves in its headlights, so they were plainly visible when Earl called down to the statie, "Everything okay down there, officer?"

"Move along," he replied gruffly.

"Those folks are friends of ours," Earl said. "We want to be sure they're okay."

"You can see for yourselves they are. Now, move along!"

"We're *not* okay," Gwen cried. "Our daughter's been kidnapped! Didn't you get the Amber Alert?"

261

"That's no excuse for doing ninety with a gun in back," the officer shot back.

"We were with our friends when they realized their daughter was missing," Earl shouted. "Can we come down and help explain?"

"No, stay where you are. You, too." He gestured at Tim and Gwen. He strode to his patrol car, presumably to run Tim's plate, and maybe also check the information on the Amber Alert. When he returned, he said, "All right, if you can get your truck back on the road safely, I'll let you continue, but stick to seventy-five max. I'll be following to be sure you do. I'm also confiscating your gun, Mr. Waite, before you get in serious trouble."

Tim opened his mouth to protest, but Earl cut him off, "Fair enough, officer. Right, Tim?"

Tim nodded grudgingly.

"Now, let's get this baby out of the ditch," Earl said. "I've got a hitch in my truck we can use. If that doesn't work, we'll have to call a tow truck."

After several tries and a lot of maneuvering, Earl pulled the pickup from the ditch. Although the front end was dented, the pickup was still drivable. They formed a caravan in the middle lane with Tim and Gwen in the lead, the patrol car, then Kathryn and Earl.

Kathryn glanced at the clock on the dash. It was almost 2 AM. If Corrigan had picked up Scarlett at 9:30 and driven straight to Katonah, he would've arrived around 11:30. It had been close to midnight when they'd called the Chief, the Amber Alert had gone out, the police in Katonah had been notified, and they'd gotten on the road themselves.

She could only hope the Katonah police apprehended Corrigan before he harmed Scarlett, if that was his plan. But surely, she and the others would have heard by now if Corrigan had been arrested. The silence was troubling. She remembered how Corrigan had almost hit Gwen at the falls. She and Earl had been able to stop him from hurting her then. But who would stop him now?

Chapter 58

A rustling outdoors drew Niall to the bedroom window. Pushing aside the curtain ever so slightly, he peered out. Nothing. Must have been the wind. Besides, he doubted they'd think to look for him here—if they thought to look for him at all. No, they'd start with the woods around Great Barrington and the roads leading out of town. They'd waste valuable time in both places. It would take them forever to search in the dark. They'd be looking for his Porsche, not the black SUV he'd rented. He'd been smart about the car, about giving himself at least an hour's head start before Scarlett's parents even realized she was missing, and about turning off her cell phone and tossing it into the woods, so it couldn't be used to track them.

He'd also been smart to bring her here, and lucky the owner was out of the country at the moment. The staff lived off the premises and did only minimal upkeep while he was away. The guard was on duty at the gate, but after Niall assured the guard he wasn't needed—that Niall would let himself in and out with his key card—and gave him an overly generous tip, the guard had departed for the weekend.

Even so, Niall had taken care to make the guest house appear deserted. The doors were locked, the curtains closed, and the bedroom where he'd carried an unconscious Scarlett lit only by a night light, plugged into a wall socket.

Niall returned to his vigil by the bed where the girl slept. "So beautiful," he whispered. How many women had he murmured those same words to after he'd brought them here, only to realize they were all wrong, and only Gwen would do? But Gwen—damn her to hell— didn't want his love. Hadn't wanted it twenty years ago when he'd followed her into the park, and still didn't want it now. She'd made that painfully clear yesterday at the falls. Her rejection of him then, delivered with chilling calmness, was so much worse than her half-drunken rebuff the first time. He'd been so furious he could have struck her. Probably *would* have if Earl Barker hadn't intervened.

Just as well he hadn't. There was another way to hurt her. At first, he'd thought only of revenge. Not until later did it occur to him that revenge could be so sweet, because Scarlett bore such a strong resemblance to Gwen in her younger days. Same beauty. Same wild spirit. The difference being that she was attracted to him in a way Gwen apparently had never been. Scarlett also wanted the things he could give her. She longed to live the high life in New York instead of remaining cooped up in a backwater town.

Niall's gaze traveled down the girl's prone figure, taking in the fullness of her breasts and the flare of her hips, before returning to her shadowy face. "So beautiful," he murmured again. But what was he waiting for? Time to make her his. The sedative he'd put in her drink wouldn't last indefinitely. He'd take her while she was still unconscious, and unable to protest. Afterward, he'd tell her the sex had been consensual, and she had initiated it. With no memory of what had actually happened, she'd be forced to agree.

He kissed her mouth and neck, then began to slowly undress her. Their coming together would not be a frenzied struggle like that other time with Gwen. It would be leisurely and tender. When he'd removed her blouse and bra, he lingered over her breasts, sucking her nipples and even giving one a little bite with his teeth. She moaned and turned her body slightly. *You want it, don't you? But you gotta be patient. I've waited a long time for this, and I'm not gonna rush it.* His mouth moved down her torso to her navel. He tickled it with his tongue before easing her out of pants and panties. He spread her legs gently apart, pressing his lips into her. Might as well get her ready for him to enter. She moaned again. *I know, baby, I know. And oh, am I gonna give it to you, Gwen.*

He'd barely unzipped his pants when the quiescent girl became a whirling, yelling fury. "Where am I? What're you doing?" She twisted away from him, kicking at him until he lost his balance and tumbled to the floor. He sat there, dazed, while she jumped off the bed and ran to the door. He caught her just as she was turning the knob, caught her and spun her around. "Let me go! I hate you, you're disgusting!" He slapped her hard across the face. Her once perfect nose was scrunched to one side, blood spurting from it. He saw fear in her eyes, but also cold anger.

"Slut," he said between clenched teeth.

She showered him with bloody spit.

Grasping her tightly with one hand, Niall raised his fist to strike again. And again, and again. He beat her to the ground, but when he looked into her battered face, he saw Gwen as she'd appeared that night all those years ago in the park.

It's about knowing when to stop, a voice in his head said. *His* voice. *That's a lesson I've had to learn the hard way.*

Stop, yes, that's what I'll do. If I let her go now, there's still a chance she'll forgive me and we can begin anew. I can't lose her a second time.

Niall lowered his fist and let the hand holding her drop to his side. "Go," he hissed. She stared at him with the wonder of a caged animal that can't believe it's being released. "Go!" he repeated. He grabbed a sheet from the bed and tossed it to her to cover her nakedness. "Go. Before I change my mind. Follow the path to the front gate. Use the phone. Call for help." She hesitated a moment longer. Then clutching the sheet to her body, she bolted.

There. She was gone now. Better get the hell out of here himself. Niall tossed the few belongings he'd brought into a bag and hurried downstairs. He'd use the estate's rear entrance for his escape. First, he peered out a window in front to be sure she was on her way. The path was empty.

When he was halfway to the back door, a voice called his name. He turned around. "Who's there?"

"Scarlett. Let me in."

"Scarlett?" He was confused. Only a moment ago, Gwen had been with him.

"Please let me in."

"No. Go!"

"Please, I'm begging you."

Was this really happening? Could she have had a change of heart? Did she want him after all? Part of Niall was skeptical, but the other part wanted desperately to believe she'd come back. He went to the front door and glanced out the window. The path was empty. Had she given up and left? "Where are you?"

"Here," she whimpered. Niall looked out the window again. A figure crouched in the bushes to one side of the house. Dark curls covered her bowed head. He opened the door.

A woman dressed all in black rushed in, slamming the door behind her.

Whoa. Who was this? He'd been expecting Gwen, then Scarlett, not this stranger. She had dark curls like Scarlett, but the face of an old woman. Was she wearing a mask? Were his eyes playing tricks on him. *What* was going on?

"Who…?" He could barely get the word out.

"You do not know me, but I know you for the evil you have done," she snarled. "Time to pay the toll." She whipped out a butcher knife and charged.

Hurling the bag with his belongings at her, Niall fled. If he could just reach the rear door before—

A searing pain in the back of his right thigh. No good running, he needed a weapon. He swerved into the living room, grabbed a lamp on an end table and threw it at her. She was stunned momentarily, but when he tried to dash past her, she slashed his arm. He stumbled backward, leaving a trail of blood. His hand closed on the edge of the table. He picked it up and held it in front of him like a shield, legs pointing outward.

She thrust right, then left, then right again, looking for an opening. Each time he managed to fend her off. But he couldn't keep it up forever. Blood poured from him. He was starting to feel weak. *Have to disable her long enough to escape.* He moved in closer with the table. Aiming a leg at her chest, he rammed it into her, even as she reached around and slashed his arm.

She staggered backward and fell. The table crashed to the ground. Carried forth by his momentum, Niall fell, too. He sprawled, face down on the floor, hurting bad. Slowly he lifted his head. She lay motionless. Down for the count or...? He wouldn't wait to find out. But when he tried to stand, he couldn't. The pain was too great. Gritting his teeth, he dragged his body forward.

Out of the living room into the hall, every move he made was agony. The door lay ahead. If only he could get to it. Footsteps behind him. Niall made one final, frantic push for the exit. He levered himself up, straining to reach the knob. Then, it was as if a burning hot iron had been raked across his back and onto his outstretched arm. He collapsed, his screams filling the echo chamber of his brain until it went silent.

Chapter 59

The gate at 21 Dutchmans Hill Road was open, but two police cars with flashing lights blocked the way. Sirens screamed from below. A cold sweat drenched Kathryn. It was just as she'd feared: they were too late. Gwen must've had the same thought. She jumped from the truck before it came to a complete stop, dodged the policeman who tried to stop her, and dashed in the direction of the sirens.

Kathryn raced after her, ignoring calls from the police ordering her and Gwen to come back. The driveway twisted and turned until at last, a small house came in view. Two fire trucks, more police cars, and an ambulance were parked in front. As Kathryn got closer, she saw EMTs carrying a stretcher from the house. Gwen lunged at the stretcher, but the police caught her. The EMTs loaded it into the back of the ambulance and closed the doors. Breaking free from the police, Gwen ran to the ambulance and beat her fists against the doors. "That's my baby in there! You've got to let me ride with her to the hospital."

Kathryn joined Gwen at the ambulance. "It's her daughter for heaven's sake. Let her in."

"Listen to me, both of you," a policeman roared. "Your daughter's not in that ambulance. The man in there's badly hurt. Back off!" After the ambulance had left, the policeman said in a normal voice, "You'll find your daughter in that police car. Aside from some bruises and a broken nose, she's okay."

Gwen and Kathryn rushed toward the police car. Wrapped in a sheet with a police jacket around her shoulders, Scarlett met them halfway. She collapsed into her mother's outstretched arms. "Oh, honey, are you really all right?" Gwen asked.

"Sort of, I guess." Scarlett's voice shook. "I mean, he was gonna rape me, but I came to in time."

"What happened to your face?" Gwen held Scarlett at arm's length.

"He hit me when I was trying to escape. Was gonna hit me again but then suddenly changed his mind and let me go."

Tim and Earl joined them. "Where is the bastard?" Tim demanded. "I'll make him pay for this."

"I think Corrigan was in the ambulance that just left," Kathryn said. "A policeman said he was badly hurt."

"Serves him right," Tim muttered. "You didn't...?" He frowned at Scarlett.

She shook her head. "I just ran."

"Then who?"

"Grandma Waite ran past me when I was heading for the gate," Scarlett said. "She must have gotten into the house somehow and gone after Niall. I heard him screaming, then it was quiet. The police came, and everything went crazy again."

"Where's Grandma Waite now?" Tim asked.

"In the other police car." Scarlett pointed at it.

Gwen and Tim exchanged glances, but almost immediately returned their attention to Scarlett. They alternated between hugging her and peppering her with questions about the kidnapping and its aftermath. They stuck close to her, as if to protect her from further harm. Kathryn listened and asked questions, too. Then, on an impulse, she went to the patrol car with Grandma Waite.

The old woman sat in the back, with a police woman in front. Grandma Waite stared straight ahead. When Kathryn peered in, she slowly turned and met Kathryn's gaze. Her features were hard and set, as if cut from cold stone. There was no trace of remorse in the look she gave Kathryn. Instead, her eyes burned with defiance. *Vengeance is mine, saith the Lord* was what her expression conveyed. On a night of many terrors, that look was the most terrifying of all.

Chapter 60

"Barring any last-minute snafus, that's how the process is supposed to go," said Mrs. Braithwaite, Kathryn's boss at the Lyceum. It was late on a Tuesday afternoon, and Mrs. B had called a meeting to discuss the library's move out of temporary quarters and back into its recently remodeled building. "Any questions?"

Oh please, let's just end this. Kathryn scanned the gathering of staff members, seated like her on uncomfortable metal folding chairs, and was disappointed when a few hands went up. She was tempted to leave anyway, but forced herself to wait until the Q and A was over before bolting.

Ever since Sunday when she'd left the Berkshires for Boston, she'd missed being in the thick of things in New Nottingham. Although Scarlett had been reunited with her parents and the family could begin to heal, another pressing matter remained unresolved. No one had been charged for Randy Plungas's death, if, in fact, he'd been murdered. And, after learning from Earl that Robert had been called back for questioning today, Kathryn was eager to know how that had gone.

As she hurried to her car, she punched in Earl's number. "Hi, have you talked to Suzy yet? Do you know how Robert's interview went?"

"Well, hello to you, too, Star," he said. "I'm doing okay, thank you very much. As for Robert, Suzy said he didn't fall apart, but answered all the police detective's questions the best he could."

"That's a relief. What about Reikart, do you know if he's been called back for questioning yet?"

"Suzy said she saw him enter the police station with a man in a suit

270

when she was leaving with Robert. I'm assuming the guy with him was an attorney."

If Reikart had lawyered up, he must in trouble.

"There's something else you should know," Earl said. "I heard at the general store Reikart's moved in with Charlotte Hinckley."

"What? He could be a murder suspect."

"I don't understand it either, but she must have her reasons. Maybe she believes he's innocent."

"But..."

"If you want to find out more, you probably oughta speak with Charlotte directly," Earl said.

Changing the subject, she said, "How are Gwen, Tim, and Scarlett holding up?"

"All right, I guess. There's been a big outpouring of sympathy for them in town. Folks have brought food and offered to help in any way they can. Suzy and my mom spoke briefly with Gwen. She said Scarlett's having a tough time, but she and Tim have found a therapist for her. They're hopeful that with time and counseling, she'll get better."

After they hung up, Kathryn debated phoning Charlotte but decided against it. She had an appointment the next day with an estate attorney at her ex-boyfriend's firm about the feasibility of challenging Diana Farley's will. She'd use that meeting as an excuse to contact Charlotte, then ease into the subject of Reikart.

Chapter 61

An inner door of the law firm opened and a tall, boyish looking man stepped into the reception area. "Sorry to have kept you waiting, Ms. Stinson," he said with a warm, welcoming smile.

This was James Lambert III. Kathryn did her best to hide her surprise. When Alan had described Lambert as a shark, she'd pictured a scowling older man with large, gleaming incisors used to bite off his words. She and Lambert shook hands, and she followed him to his office, a spacious room done in understated elegance with an Oriental rug, a couple of high-backed armchairs, and a mahogany desk. Behind the desk, a large window offered a fine view of Boston Harbor.

Kathryn sat in the chair Lambert indicated. After she'd declined his offer of coffee or tea, he said, "I've reviewed the documents you sent, and everything seems to be in order. As I'm sure you've already been told, it's going to be difficult to challenge Mrs. Farley's will, since the deadline for doing so expired several years ago."

She nodded, perched on the edge of her seat, ready to leave, in case, as she feared, the meeting was about to end.

"However," Lambert continued, "It's not impossible."

Not impossible. Kathryn allowed herself to relax ever so slightly.

"Some judges, though by no means all," Lambert continued, "are serious about honoring the wishes of the deceased, even if it means bending the rules a bit. If we're fortunate in getting a sympathetic judge, we may be able to make a case that leaving a portion of the property to the town land trust was what Mrs. Farley truly wanted when she drew up a codicil to her will. We'll need witnesses who can testify to that. We'll also need witnesses to testify to her distracted state of mind that apparently prevented her from taking the necessary steps to ensure the codicil was duly attached to her will.

"I confess I have a hard time understanding why the neighbor mentioned in Attorney Wallingford's notes didn't come forward with the codicil at the time of Mrs. Farley's death or shortly thereafter. She sounds like a bit of a flake."

"I'm afraid she is, but in all fairness to her, she and her husband were going through a difficult time then."

"We'll want them both to testify before the judge as well. Although..." He let the word hang while he rose from his desk and stood with his back to her, staring out at the harbor.

Kathryn wished she could see into Lambert's head and find out what he was thinking. Having second thoughts about taking the case? Wishing he were sailing in the harbor instead of cooped up in this office with her?

She was about to finish his sentence for him when he turned. "This developer who bought the property you believe should have gone to the land trust—is he the same person who's been accused of kidnapping and attempted rape? I ask because there was a story about him in *The New York Times* on Monday. When I looked at Wallingford's notes, his name sounded familiar."

"It's the same person."

"Interesting." Lambert left her to gaze out the window again. Again, she wished she knew what was going on in his head. This time, the turn-around came faster. "If you're willing to hold off a little, I suggest we wait and see what happens before contesting the will, a process which could take a long time and be costly. I think we can strike a deal with Mr. Corrigan to sell the property to the land trust for a sum not to exceed the land trust's original offer to the previous owners. Possibly *substantially* less."

"But why should the land trust have to pay for something that was supposed to go to it in the first place?"

"There's no guarantee a judge will rule in the land trust's favor. But once Mr. Corrigan realizes what he's up against in terms of medical bills and legal fees, not to mention a jail sentence, he's going to be desperate for cash."

"But he could get more from a buyer other than the land trust."

"True, but we'll let him and any other prospective buyers know that his ownership is in question and likely to be challenged. How does that sound?"

"Okay, though I'll have to run it past the land trust board and get their approval."

"Of course." Lambert's smile was different from the one he'd used to greet her—the smile of a gambler about to play his ace in the hole. Or a shark about to chomp down on its unwitting victim—in this instance, Corrigan.

Chapter 62

Just short of the New Nottingham general store, Kathryn turned up the hill to Charlotte's house. When she'd called Charlotte on Wednesday to tell her about her appointment with James Lambert III, Charlotte had been open to his idea of the land trust making Corrigan an offer on the Farley property. "We'll need to do some serious fundraising before we approach him, but it's certainly worth a try," she'd said. She had, however, refused to discuss Reikart over the phone. "That's a conversation we should have in person." They'd arranged to meet at Charlotte's late Friday afternoon.

Kathryn wondered if Reikart would be there. She hoped not. His truck wasn't in the parking area, but he could still be in the vicinity. As she left her car, Charlotte appeared with Solly on a leash. The dog growled at her, but quieted at a word from Charlotte. "Thanks for coming," Charlotte said. "Steve's not here," she added in response to Kathryn's unspoken question. "He's off doing errands. Let's go inside."

Charlotte motioned Kathryn into the living room. "I was just about to make myself a rum cooler. Would you like one, too?"

"Sure."

They sipped their drinks quietly for a few moments, then Charlotte said, "I know you probably think I'm crazy to have taken in Steve, but I want you to understand why I did." She stared into her glass, a finger circling the rim. Meeting Kathryn's eyes again, she said, "I'm not a cougar, chasing after a younger man."

"I didn't think you were."

"Good, though I imagine that's what some people in town believe.

I reached out to Steve because I felt he needed me. He wasn't going to get any help from his boss—not with Corrigan in the ICU and facing serious charges. I knew there was a chance Steve killed Randy Plungas. As you were at pains to point out, he had a motive and the opportunity. But so did others."

Like Robert, Kathryn thought, but didn't say.

"I hadn't spoken to Steve since the night he tried to sic Solly on you," Charlotte continued. "I decided to call him and find out what his plans were. He said he was thinking of leaving the area. I told him that wouldn't be wise, considering he might be a murder suspect. We got into a heated argument and I hung up. Minutes later, he showed up at the house."

Kathryn gripped the arm of her chair. "Were you frightened?"

"Enough to get my grandfather's shotgun out of the closet," Charlotte said. "Fortunately, I didn't have to use it. Steve admitted he'd gone to Plungas's cabin that Friday before nightfall. Plungas wasn't there, but Steve heard him in the woods. He followed Plungas to the opposite end of the forest, near the Farley house. Plungas stopped and opened a metal jug.

"Steve confronted Plungas about shooting his dog, and Plungas taunted him. Said Steve had no business letting his dog run loose in Plungas's woods, but if Steve minded his manners, he'd give Steve a taste of the barbecue he was planning. Steve told him he was crazy. Plungas tossed liquid from the open jug at him and lit it with a kitchen torch.

"Steve lost it. He turned and ran. Plungas ran after him, laughing and yelling at him to come back. Steve kept running. Then he heard a whooshing sound. Plungas screamed. When Steve looked back, Plungas wasn't there any more, just a big fireball."

At some point in Charlotte's telling, Kathryn had stopped breathing. Now she gulped air. When the shock had worn off, she said, "Do you believe his story?"

"I do, and I think you would, too, if you'd heard Steve tell it. Still, I made sure he had a lawyer go with him when he went to the police. I also insisted he quit his job and move in here. He's better off with me and Solstice than alone in that trailer with a dog he hates. But don't worry, it's only a temporary arrangement until we see whether he'll be charged for Plungas's murder."

"Do you think he will be?"

"I hope not," Charlotte said.

And I hope Robert won't be either. Suzy's words came back to her: "One day Randy will go too far, and then I don't even want to think what might happen." Had he gone too far the night of the fire?

Kathryn finished her rum cooler and stood. "Thanks for telling me this."

"I wanted to clear the air," Charlotte said, as they walked to the door. "After all, I'll need your help convincing Corrigan to sell the Farley property to the land trust." Charlotte's gaze fell on a small wrapped package on a table near the door. She handed it to Kathryn. "I almost forgot. Here's a little something I think you'll enjoy."

Chapter 63

"Have you noticed how quiet it is without that damn dog barking almost non-stop?" Earl said, as he and Kathryn sat on the patio after dinner that evening.

"I certainly don't miss him. Or the trailer either. I just hope Charlotte's doing the right thing, taking in Reikart."

"Sounds like she is, from what you told me."

"What are the odds he'll be charged with murder?"

"At the moment, pretty slim, unless the police find evidence of foul play, which they haven't so far," Earl said.

"So, it looks like Randy died from a fire of his own making?"

"Yup. The owner of a hardware store down in Connecticut told the police he sold Randy two jugs of charcoal lighter for a big barbecue he was planning. Reikart also said Randy talked about a barbecue."

"How do you know all this?" Kathryn asked.

Earl slid her a sly, sidelong glance. "The Chief's my cousin. And sometimes he tells me things."

Kathryn gave him a playful swat on the arm. "Is there anyone in this town you're *not* related to?"

They settled into a companionable silence. But every once in a while, Earl appeared troubled. When Kathryn couldn't stand it any longer, she said, "What is it? I can tell from the look on your face something's bothering you."

"I'm just tired."

"No, something's going on. Out with it."

"All right, it's Em."

Kathryn tensed. "She's continuing to get better, isn't she?"

"That's what the doctor says, but you wouldn't necessarily know it from her behavior. She's agitated a lot. Keeps calling for Diana or you. I've tried to explain you were away for the time being, but that just seems to upset her more. I've been afraid to tell her Diana's dead for fear of really upsetting her."

"I better go see her tomorrow," Kathryn said, though she was worried how Emily would react.

"You don't have to. You can always wait until she's calmed down a bit."

"No, I'll go."

Chapter 64

Out of habit, Kathryn grabbed the cassette player as she left the house the next morning. She couldn't hide behind it, as she once had, but she took it anyway. At the hospital, a nurse drew her aside. "Don't be alarmed if Mrs. Goodale becomes distressed while you're here. It has nothing to do with you. It's simply a phase some coma patients go through on the road to recovery."

Kathryn thanked the nurse and continued. The door to Emily's room was partially open. The old woman sat up in bed. Her eyes were wide open, her gaze trained on the wall. It would be so easy to slip away without Emily even knowing she was there. Like Corrigan remaining in the reception area, day after day, while Gwen lay comatose. No, she would not be the person who hid in the wings, afraid to reveal herself. She would walk into the room and be recognized for who she was and what she had done.

Kathryn had no sooner stepped inside than Emily fixed her laser-sharp blue eyes on her. "You," she said. Her voice was hoarse from lack of use, but her tone was neutral without any of the rancor Kathryn had expected.

"Well, don't just stand there," Emily croaked. "Come here where I can get a better look at you."

Kathryn approached cautiously. "Where have you been?" Emily demanded. "I've been calling and calling for you, but they kept telling me you'd gone away some place."

"I had to go away, but now I'm back."

"I see that. But where's Diana? I've been calling for her, too, but they won't even tell me where she went. Do you know where she is?"

Kathryn hesitated, searching for the right words. "Diana had to go away," she said at last, "far, far away. So far, it's hard for her to come back. But she gave me this recording she made for you. When you listen to it, it'll be like having her here in the room with you."

"Sit down and play it." Emily patted a space beside her. Kathryn perched gingerly on the edge of the bed, inserted a tape and pressed "play."

At the sound of Diana's voice, Emily's face opened into a radiant smile. She listened for several minutes, then she said, "You don't know how happy this makes me. Right before Diana left, we quarreled. She was very angry at me. But now she's forgiven me and we're friends again. Thank you for bringing her back." Emily took Kathryn's hand and held it while tears came into her eyes.

In the days before Emily had her stroke, Kathryn had often wondered what to make of her behavior—whether she suffered from dementia or something else was going on. Maybe she was pushing her luck, but Kathryn couldn't resist asking, "Do you know who I am?"

Emily's grip tightened around Kathryn's fingers. Her eyes narrowed. "Of course, I do. You and Diana used to visit me often. While Diana and I chatted, you stayed quiet as a mouse. But you didn't fool me." Emily made a gurgling sound in her throat that could have been a chuckle. "I knew all along you were there... Kathryn."

Chapter 65

Kathryn grinned ridiculously as she drove home. How like Emily to reveal the joke had been on her, after all. True, Emily seemed to have confused the quarrel they'd had with one that might have happened between her and Diana. Still, in an odd way, Kathryn felt Emily had forgiven *her* and they were friends again—at least for the moment. She felt a peace she hadn't felt since before Emily's stroke.

In the living room of the Farley house, Kathryn noticed the small wrapped package Charlotte had given her on the coffee table. She tore off the wrapping. Inside was a slim hardcover volume about trees. She read a couple of chapters, deeply moved by their narrative of how trees nourished and protected each other. Now, maybe she wouldn't feel so sad looking at the burned trees. Comforted herself, she decided to reach out to someone else who needed comforting.

*****

No one answered at the Waite home, so Kathryn called the library. "New Nottingham Public Library, how can I help you?" Gwen said in her librarian voice.

"Hi, it's me," Kathryn said. "Is this a good time to stop by?"

"Sure."

*****

Except for a few people using the internet at the bank of computers to one side of the main desk, the library appeared empty. Gwen sat a low table in the children's section. A pile of picture books about fireflies lay open in front of her next to two completed fireflies made of construction paper, pipe cleaners, and tissue paper. She looked up when Kathryn approached and smiled wanly. At least Gwen wasn't so overwhelmed by the events of last weekend that she couldn't smile at all.

"I see you're back to making fireflies," Kathryn said.

"I have to. The children's summer reading program starts next week."

"How are you doing otherwise?" Kathryn asked.

"I've been better," Gwen said. "Let's go out back, where we can speak privately."

As they walked toward the rear of the building, Kathryn noticed Robert and, to her surprise, Pete sandwiched between two bookshelves. They spoke in low voices and fell silent when she and Gwen came close.

"I'm going outside for a bit," Gwen said to Robert, "so please keep an eye on the front desk. If anyone comes in wanting to use a computer, tell Mrs. Drummond her time expired two hours ago."

"Will do," Robert said, nodding a hello to Kathryn.

"Hey, Boston, how are things in the big city?" Pete said in the jokey way she'd found so appealing when they first met.

"It's still standing," she replied. "And in case you were wondering, I haven't been to any clubs yet."

"You'll get there," he said. "A folk-rock group I like is playing in Northampton next weekend. I could get you a ticket, if you're interested."

"Count me in," Kathryn said. She was pleased by the invite, which signaled to her that she and Pete were close to being back on their old, friendly footing.

When she and Gwen were outside, she said, "I didn't know Pete and Robert were friends, they're such different kids."

"They didn't used to hang together, but lately, after Pete reached out to Robert, they've bonded over the fact they've each lost a parent."

"I'm glad they can help one another," Kathryn said.

When they'd settled in the gazebo overlooking the stream that ran behind the library, Gwen said, "I want to thank you again for your help finding Scarlett. Without you and Earl, I'm not sure we would have figured out where she was, and gotten there when we did. I also really appreciate your tact in singling out Niall without letting Tim know I'd been seeing him. And, perhaps even more important, you didn't reveal that I was the Grant's Tomb Girl." She paused, staring out at the water with a regretful expression. "A fine role model I turned out to be."

Even though she knew what Gwen was talking about, Kathryn asked anyway, "What do you mean?"

"You must have realized a big reason Suzy Barker introduced us was to do a little backwoods matchmaking. I was supposed to be the model of a city girl who married a country boy and lived happily ever after. The irony is that while you were watching me and maybe wondering, 'how does she do it?' I was watching you and asking the same question."

"Wondering how I did what?" Kathryn asked, now truly puzzled.

"How you managed to stay with Earl after his ex-wife nearly killed you. If I'd been you, I would have gotten out of town as fast as I could and never come back. I fled the city because of the awful thing that happened to me there, and came here to make a fresh start. And for many years, that's what I did—until my past caught up with me. I should've known it would. But living quietly on Shuntoll Road, I thought I was home free.

"I knew I might be in trouble the minute Niall showed up. I was terrified he'd let it slip that I was the Grant's Tomb Girl. The first time I met him in private at the library, it was to get his assurance he'd keep my secret. But we went on meeting because we both wanted to."

"Why did you want to?"

"It felt good to be with someone who didn't judge me and who seemed to understand and even *like* the person I'd been. Tim disapproved so strongly of Scarlett's rebellious behavior that I worried he'd stop loving me if he knew what a wild girl I'd been."

Kathryn opened her mouth to comment, but Gwen said, "Hear me out. I admit I was flattered by Niall's attention. There I was, this middle-aged woman whom no one seemed to notice anymore, being courted by a rich and powerful man. I wanted to look attractive for Niall and I enjoyed flirting with him. But when I looked deep inside myself, I realized my heart still belonged to Tim, and I had to break off with Niall before I ruined my marriage.

"With hindsight, I wish I'd shared my secret with Tim a lot sooner. Then, maybe I wouldn't have gotten involved with Niall, and none of this would've happened. But if there's anything good to come out of this horrible mess, it's that I finally told Tim the truth about myself."

"That was brave. When did you do it?"

"Last night we were sitting by the jungle gym he built for the kids, talking about those days, and the words just spilled out. And you know what? It wasn't anywhere near as bad as I imagined."

It usually isn't, Kathryn thought, recalling her own experience of sharing her long-kept secret with Earl.

"Tim told me he loved me," Gwen continued. "And I shouldn't be ashamed of what had happened to me then. But he understood why I'd kept quiet, with Randy and just about everybody else in town except Grandma Waite opposed to our marriage."

"I'm glad for you," Kathryn said.

"Thank you. I haven't reached the point where I'm ready to tell Scarlett, but I'll get there."

"I'm sure you will." Kathryn gave Gwen's hand an encouraging squeeze. "What's happening with Grandma Waite?"

"We were able to get her out on bail, although it wasn't easy. We had to fork over a hefty amount, and assure the judge we'd be responsible for her. I think her age made a difference, since she's well into her eighties. Also, it looks like Niall will recover. So, instead of being charged with homicide, she can only be charged with aggravated assault—if she's charged at all."

"You think she might not be?"

"I don't know," Gwen said. "But if she is, Tim and I will both testify on her behalf. After all, she was the first to raise the alarm about Niall taking Scarlett. And before that, she sensed he was dangerous before anyone else, except maybe you. Difficult as Grandma Waite's often been, she's always wanted to protect Scarlett and me. I didn't fully appreciate that until she was gone for a few days. I realized then that I actually missed seeing the light in her window at night. It had become a beacon to me against the darkness that's haunted me ever since that night in the park."

Kathryn didn't know what to say. Her friend had obviously done a lot of soul searching both before and after the kidnapping. Gwen's words would linger in her mind a long time.

Chapter 66

Kathryn returned to the porch at the Farley house to do some soul searching of her own. Or rather, to continue the reflecting she'd done in Boston. She'd begun her most recent two-week stay in the Berkshires with questions: whether she and Earl could rebuild their relationship—and whether it was even worth trying. Almost immediately, she'd become distracted by the struggle to save the Farley property from being developed. Not only had she been distracted, but the battle had created a rift between Earl and her. With so much going on, she'd nearly lost sight of her original goal. But her heart and mind had been quietly working on it, almost without her being aware. And they had reached a conclusion that had become clear to her only after she'd left the area again.

There was magic in these hills. In the white stag that had appeared to her, not once, but three times. In the trees whose reflections beckoned to her across the water. In the peonies, flamboyant, fragile, but in the end, surprisingly durable. Earl was part of that magic. If he hadn't come into her life, she might never have experienced genuine passion. But it wasn't just passion that drew her to him. Even though they'd disagreed about the development, he'd been there for her when she needed him. When she was unhappy, he'd tried to cheer her up. And when she was tempted to do something rash, he'd helped her get back on track. They still needed to work out the details of what their life together would look like, but she'd be a fool to turn her back on this place and this man.

She felt connected to other people here as well, in a way that she, a loner by nature, had never felt connected to anyone anywhere else.

Not in California, where she'd grown up, or the Boston area, where she worked. Earl's family had become her family; his friends, her friends. What happened to them mattered to her. When they were in trouble, as Gwen, Suzy, and Robert had been, in different ways, she'd tried to help them. Just as she believed they'd reach out to her if she were having difficulties.

Like the trees, she wanted to put down roots in a particular spot. And what better place than here with a man she loved and people she cared about? She could try to explain this to Earl in so many words. Or she could find an action to convey her feelings. All of a sudden, she knew exactly what she'd do, and set about making the necessary preparations.

*****

"Looks like you've got a picnic planned," Earl said when he arrived that evening. He gestured toward the bulging basket, the cooler, and the bottle of champagne in a bucket of ice on the kitchen counter. "Where do you want to go?"

"A place where I've only been once before, but that I'd like to visit again."

"The lake in the state park?"

"No."

"Cameron Falls?"

"No." She smiled, enjoying keeping him in suspense.

Earl looked perplexed. "How about giving me a hint?"

"It's a place we haven't been in a while."

"The boat ramp on Lake Clyde?"

She shook her head.

"You don't mean the Barker family cemetery, or my trailer, do you?"

"No, but you're getting close."

His forehead knitted with concentration. "Only once before. Cemetery and trailer close," he muttered. For a moment, his eyes lit up as if he had the answer, but then they dulled with defeat. "I give up."

"Oh, c'mon," she teased. "You can do better than that. Would another hint help?"

"Shoot."

"It's a place where you go to be alone. Where you like to watch the mountains change color in the changing light."

"You want to have a picnic *there*?" His tone suggested he didn't quite believe her.

She nodded emphatically.

Earl's handsome face broke into a grin. "What're we waiting for? Let's go!"

Earl gathered up the picnic basket, cooler, and ice bucket. He and Kathryn left the house and piled into his truck. They headed up Rattlesnake Hill Road toward the hilltop property his father had given them months ago, in the hopes a bright future lay in store for them.

About the Author

An award-winning author of books about American history and biographies, Leslie Wheeler has written two mystery series. Her Berkshire Hilltown Mysteries launched with *Rattlesnake Hill*, and continue with this book, *Shuntoll Road*. Her Living History Mysteries, featuring amateur sleuth Miranda Lewis, debuted with *Murder at Plimoth Plantation*, recently re-released as a trade paperback by Encircle Publications, and continue with *Murder at Gettysburg* and *Murder at Spouters Point*. Her mystery short stories have appeared in numerous anthologies including *Mystery Most Geographical*; *Noir at the Salad Bar, Culinary Tales with a Bite*; *Day of the Dark, Stories of Eclipse*; and the Best New England Crime Stories anthologies, published by Level Best Books, where she was a co-editor for six years. Leslie is a member of Mystery Writers of America and Sisters in Crime, and a founding member of the New England Crime Bake Committee. She divides her time between Cambridge, Massachusetts, and the Berkshires, where she writes in a house overlooking a pond.

CPSIA information can be obtained
at www.ICGtesting.com
Printed in the USA
LVHW032335131021
700343LV00002B/206